SUMMER SWEAT

An Erotic Anthology

I0676924

SUMMER SWEAT

An Erotic Anthology

by

William Maltese

The Borgo Press
An Imprint of Wildside Press

MMVII

Copyright © 1999, 2007 by William Maltese

All rights reserved.
No part of this book may be reproduced in any form without
the expressed written consent of the author and publisher.
Printed in the United States of America

SECOND EDITION

► **summer sweat**

WILLIAM MALTESE

an erotic anthology

PROWLER BOOKS

Summer Sweat by William Maltese

Copyright © 1999 William Lambert
3 Broadbent Close London N6 5GG. All rights reserved.

No part of this book may be reproduced, stored in retrieval system, or transmitted in any form,
by any means, including mechanicals, electronic, photocopying, recording or otherwise, without prior written permission of the publishers.

First printing March 1999. Printed in Finland by Werner Soderstrom Oy.
Cover photography © 1999 Paul Stanley

British Library Cataloguing in Publication Data.
A catalogue record for this book is available from the British Library.

contents

FETISH?

"For what are we looking?" always asks the sidekick of just about every television or big-screen detective there ever was, his boss and he having just entered the apartment of a murder victim or the residence of some prime suspect.

"I'm not sure," always comes the reply, "but we'll know it when we see it."

Bullshit!

Some people haven't a clue. Not even when it jumps up and bites them on the ass, not once but time after time. I know from personal experience, albeit not as a detective, nor as the sidekick of some gumshoe investigating a crime. More of the "what" later.

For the moment, let's take a closer look at Marky and see how close he stands to an epiphany. My guess is about as far away as the North Pole stands from the North Star.

In short, Marky doesn't have even a hint. Actually, he's likely all the more confused, because he's such a little cutie and probably can't begin to fathom that none of this has anything whatsoever to do with looks. Because in the world in which Marky exists -- hustling -- looks play too much a part, too much of the time, for a kid like him to remove them entirely from any equation.

Would that looks were the key to what is going on here. How much easier that would make it for me. I've more than enough money to keep a steady stream of high-priced good-lookers entering and exiting my bed. I know at least three people who would even now be drooling all over their collective chin at having Marky so ready and willing to give them everything, or anything, they so desire.

Even I can't deny Marky is a genuinely nice-looking young man. I've always been a sucker for the aesthetics of delicate, fine-boned, hairless, young things. Young being above the age of consent, you understand. Anyone younger is really more bother than he's worth, and I've never been one who enjoys teaching anyone the ropes. Give the virgins to those who like that sort of stumbling around in the dark.

Marky has blond-blond barbered-short hair, the color of ripe-ripe corn silk. He has blue-blue eyes, with long-long lashes and well-defined brows. His lashes and brows aren't so light-in-shade that they make his face appear in any way washed out, as is the case with some blonds.

All around, he's blessedly tan. In that, while there's nothing I find more pleasant to look at than a well-browned blond, there's nothing quite as repugnant as someone downright ghostly and/or who goes absolutely lobster after a mere few minutes of exposure to sunshine.

Marky has two dimples, both hoarded by his right cheek. Actually, he has three dimples, total, if you want to count the cute little depression, dead-center his chin, that's neither deep enough nor well-defined enough to be termed a genuine cleft.

All in all, a nice bit of packaging -- if only, once again, packaging were what it was all about.

And, I do wish that he would quit trying to grope me at every opportunity, or persuade me to play touchy-feely with his rosebud-pink prick, or get me to fondle his firm young ass. Another disconcerting thing about him is his tendency to give come-on gropes of his own cock and ass at every to-him opportune moment.

Poor little (although five-foot-ten isn't exactly wee) lad just can't figure out what in the hell is going on. Anyone else who would have paid the cash, up front, for the privilege of Marky's company would, by now, likely have fucked and/or sucked the kid senseless. Or, been sucked and/or fucked senseless in return (too many people prejudiced in thinking that pretty young things are only good as bottom-men, when many can perform quite respectably in ride-positions, if just given the chance).

I suppose it might be fairer to try and explain it all to Marky, but how do I explain something that's not really all that crystal clear even to me? Because, like the TV detective and his loyal sidekick, I do know something important is to be found, somewhere. Unlike those guys, though, I'm not as well-scripted to search out the what, how, why, or when, to recognize it, even when it's stumbled across.

"Lovely!" says Marky, and he stretches his near nakedness in the adjacent chaise longue that's positioned within the near-tropical heat around my outside swimming pool. "I'm really glad you picked me."

Really, quite charming. Quite polite. Quite the little gentleman. If only it were only a matter of manners. The truth being, I've tricked with just as many uncouth thugs as I have with gentlemen in my none-too-many counted days of genuinely good sex.

In yet another indication that he hasn't forgotten why he figures he's here, he pets the garter snake bas-relief his cock makes in the crotch of the skimpy form-fitting briefs I've loaned him.

While Marky's cock isn't all that enormous, cock-size doesn't have anything to do with anything, either. I've never been able to figure out what the big deal sometimes is about a humongous whanger drooped from the base of some guy's midsection, as if he's sprouted an elephant trunk, or mutated his dick into the trunk of baobab tree. Doesn't exactly make for anatomical symmetry, does it? Ask the ancient Greeks who made it a point of providing their sculpture masterpieces with the wee-ist dicks imaginable. And, it would take more than a spoonful of sugar ever to make one of those monster cocks go down - - or go "up" if you're in mind of taking it up the ass.

So, Marky's cock, though on the average by way of size, is just fine. That he's mannerly is fine. That he's an all-around cutie-pie is fine. That he's obviously prepared to be obliging, in the sex department is fine. If only ....

I allow a few more minutes for the magical "click" that will put me into full sexual rut, or at least allow me a partial rut that'll provide me sexual performance capabilities. Sometimes, even with the right person, it takes a good deal of time in arriving. However, I've just about given up any hope whatsoever for Marky and me by the time my doorbell (rather, the doorbell of my house) rings.

I excuse myself and head for the front door. My home looking far larger than it is. Small enough, in fact, that I don't need any live-in servants for my needs, except for the cleaning lady who comes in twice a week, and the caterer I hire when I have more than a couple people in for eats or whatever. Although, I'd probably more seriously consider live-ins (lives-in?) if I could find someone, or someones, sufficiently discreet. In the meantime, I continue on, as I have for most of my life, pretty much taking care of myself.

"Jesus!" I mumble under my breath when I check the door's spyhole and discover Walter Linley on my doorstep with another one of his ... his ... his ... how else to put it but? ... one of his ... sleazy rough-trade male whores.

I haven't a clue where Walter manages to come up with so many teenage (this one probably eighteen or nineteen) varieties on the same shoddy theme. Or, maybe I do, in that he once told me he has them cruised off the street corners of Vancouver, British Columbia, and flown down to him special (Fed Ex? UPS? US Mail?) for his look-see, but I've never been all that interested enough to verify. None of them having ever proved of any sexual interest -- whatsoever -- to me, although Walter would have no problems sharing and, in fact, would likely enjoy it. He and I going back to our college days together -- a time much farther in either of our shared past than I usually care to remember or admit to.

Against my better judgment, I open the door.

"Hi," says Walter. "This is Zac." (Doesn't any of Walter's playthings ever ... ever, ever ... have a more than one-syllable name? It's always, "This is Zac ... or Jack ... or Jock ... or Brock ... or Butch ... or Hutch!")

This one grunts. No other word describes it.

"Zac," Walter rambles on, "this is my best friend, Howie."

Zac extends his ham-like paw with its beetle tattoo on its back. More tattoos have passed through my doors, on the bodies of Walter's tricks, than ever have graced the flesh of the whole Maori population of New Zealand.

"You said to bring Zac over for a swim and sunshine," says Walter.

Which I certainly had not. It's merely the ruse Walter always uses, ever since his pool drained automatically, on its own accord, when a crack appeared during an otherwise slight earth tremor in 1997. He insists the damaged basin will soon be repaired, but I suspect the pool men can't get around all that well with Walter forever down on his knees in front of them, their pants yanked down around their ankles.

Were Marky and I anywhere noticeably near the brink of a sexual "click", I would boot Walter and his Zac out on their collective tush. As it is, possibly Walter and Zac can provide adequate diversion (not bloody likely!) in the face of my -- yes, it's true -- disappointment with Marky.

"Pool is through there," I wave Zac on by. "If you need trunks ..."

"Never wear the things -- too binding -- unless you've neighbours likely to peek over the hedge," Zac calls back.

"Wouldn't wear them, even then," injects Walter. "Zac such a hopeless exhibitionist."

"My, my," say I and don't mean it as a compliment.

"Isn't he something else?" whispers Walter, proud as a peacock. "Wait until you see him naked."

"One giant tattoo, is he?" I venture. He wouldn't be the first.

"Just that marvellous beetle on the back of his hand, smart-ass," says Walter. "His Mum is against them. Beat him almost to virtual climax (his and hers) when she found he'd gone against her express wishes and gotten that one."

"Such a good time had by all, I'm surprised he didn't run on out and immediately get another."

"One-quarter Canadian Indian, too," Walter says.

Walter has this "thing" for Indians, part Indians, or for anyone who says -- no proof required -- that there was a red man somewhere in the family woodpile.

"Rather a long ride for him to have made on horseback," I say.

"My, are we in a snit," Walter says. "Your latest little trick-or-treat not doing all that much for you?"

I don't need to answer, so I don't.

"If this latest cute young thing of yours were a turn-on, you wouldn't likely have bothered opening the door, now, would you?" Walter answers for me. "Poor you, but lucky me, in that Zac has literally fucked me raw, and I'm looking to channel his non-stop horniness elsewhere. Someone might as well get some use from all the money you spread around to have such little cutie-pies be mere bits of your landscaping."

I shrug acceptance. Past experience leads me to suspect Walter will derive far more enjoyment from any show put on by Marky and Zac than I will, but so far I have no reason to suspect there's any better show in town.

Zac, by the looks, when we join him and Marky by the pool, has obviously been as anxious to get a rest from fucking Walter as Walter has been to get a rest from getting fucked by Zac.

Of us four, Marky seems the only one unaware of the change of plans. He looks downright guilty at his so obvious enjoyment of the naked and big-bonered Zac, on the edge of Marky's chaise longue, busily stroking Marky's Spandex-sheathed little pecker into a somewhat more substantial ridge than I'd likely ever have managed from it.

I smile reassurances in Marky's direction, by way of letting him know that just because I've bought and paid for him I'm not going to throw a fit when someone else comes along to get my money's worth.

Then, I turn some -- though not much -- of my attention to Walter who has taken a nearby chair, beneath the shade of the table umbrella. Mainly, I keep an eye on Zac and how, he having been detoured from the pool because of the more inviting prospects of getting "into" Marky, is beginning, hog-like, to sweat.

"It" has always had something to do with sweat, hasn't it?

Maybe something to do with, way back when, that lifeguard's naked body, and how all that studly flesh beaded jewel-like perspiration while he fucked me; I for the very first time experiencing the pain-pleasure of male prick thrust up my asshole. I actually tasted the salty drips from his face, muscled neck, and chest as I climaxed beneath him.

Maybe something to do with the sweat of my gymnastics' instructor, in that high-school locker room, after hours. A slick veneer of perspiration on his firm ass, on his naked back, on his broad shoulders, intensifying the sounds of my teenage belly slapping his buttocks with each inward ply of my teenage dick within his manly tight asshole.

More likely, though, it's to do with something else, undefined, never consciously recognized, during my formative years. My childhood filled with hot summer days, sunny beaches; super-heated locker rooms, filled with friendly semi-naked and naked jocks slapping each other's ass and copping feels. My father having played professional baseball for a well-known ball Florida team.

Something ... something ... something.

Is it the way certain beads of perspiration form geometrical designs, like the triangle of moisture suddenly materialized at the nape of Zac's neck? Is it the way other droplets slide Zac's body contours in an avalanche that cascade dampness through even more golden globes of perspiration that speckle the whole of his dark-skinned anatomical terrain? Is it the way, one or more rivers of his sweat converge along Zac's spine and drain to eventual disappearance within the crack of his ass?

My cock is hardening even before Marky lifts his slim young hips to allow Zac to pull the kid's orange trunks down the youth's lean flanks and off Marky's ankles and feet.

I figure Marky figures he finally has me figured out as a mere voyeur, plain and simple. A watcher who gets off seeing others get off. For

Marky, Zac's arrival makes the pieces fit. He feels better, now, more confident that he hasn't lost his touch. I haven't touched him, but it has had nothing to do, he thinks, with his expertise (or lack thereof) as a hustler; touching simply not my bag.

Wrong, Marky-boy!

More and more of my attention wanders to the lead-in perspiration Zac's body exudes prior to his fucking of Marky's young ass. Walter doesn't seem to care that I pay less and less attention to him, in that Walter is delighted to focus all of his attention on Zac and Marky. Walter a voyeur -- among other things -- for as long as I've known him. Without fanfare, my old college buddy unzips his pants, pulls out his cock, and begins languidly manhandling his impressive inches.

Marky, no longer encumbered by swum trunks, rolls to fuck his stiffly rosy-pink dick into the cushion of the chaise longue. He opens his legs, letting one thigh, knee, calf, and foot, drop to each side, making room for Zac to kneel in the available place between.

It's not Zac's ten-inch cock, slightly curved, and with its decided tendency to lean precariously to the left, before his belly, that has my attention. It's the sweaty stream of sweat suddenly turned loose to drain along that young man's left flank.

Dampness, too, fills Zac's jugular notch. Even as I watch, that sensuous pooling overflows its barriers, pours through Zac's pectoral cleavage, and spills a liquid delta across his washboard belly. Zac's knotted navel becomes an obstacle not flood-submerged by the deluge but surrounded by it.

I stand up, pretty much having altogether forgotten Walter.

"I do believe Zac, your new cutie-pie friend, you, and I aren't the only ones with boners around here," says Walter; I only vaguely hear him, but recognize his tone of surprise.

Walter knows a miracle when he sees one, having more than once, unsuccessfully, tried to supply me with the magical someone who could perform the transformation of my accordion dick into its presently to-be-admitted impressive dimensions.

Zac looks and acts prepared to ride Marky bareback, the head of Zac's dick already aimed and searching within the kid's asscrack for an accepting butthole. Even more frightening, Marky shows all indications of passively letting it happen. Of all the hair-brained ...!

In nothing flat, I'm on my knees beside their mutually shared chaise longue. I've fish between Zac's hairy legs, from the rear, and I've taken hold of both his hairy balls.

A drool of sweat trails his left buttocks.

"Hey, man!" he complains. He tries to roll toward me, but my arm, between his legs, and the lock I have on his nuts, keep him pretty much positioned where he is.

"We all practice safe sex, around here," I say. "Not that that means you'll be interrupted all that long. There being a copious supply of rubbers within the insulated box on the table, just right over there."

Walter already has the box in question open, a packet in hand. He throws the rubber to me, and I catch it with my free hand. I rip the packet open with my teeth.

"Now, I let go of your nads, and you come back to a kneeling position for as long as it takes to don this rubber, before you put it and your dick up this kid's tight ass, or you won't be doing any fucking, bare back, or otherwise, for a very long time -- if ever."

"Tough guy!" he says, but it doesn't come off all that threatening. I've dealt with his kind before, although usually not turned on by them.

I release his nuts.

"Public Health patrolman, are you?" he says but comes obligingly to his knees.   Actually, he smiles. A rather nice smile, if I do say so: full lips over surprisingly small teeth.

"Want to drape the old monkey, yourself, do you?" he asks.

I hand him the freed prophylactic to do the honors on his own. I'm more interested in the way some of his chest perspiration is somehow kept from his belly by the creases formed by the pronounced lower curvature of his pecs.

"Now, ready for short-arm inspection, sir!" he militarily announces, the job done.

Liquid appears at his left armpit and slithers its zigzag path along his flank. When he falls forward, one hand to either side of Marky's upper body, his cock again playing hot-dog to Marky's young assbuns, the sweaty trailing along his left side changes direction, as commanded by gravity.

The length of Zac's cock shifts along the entire length of Marky's asscrack, cocksweat and buttsweat combining in shiny runway. Pressed all the more tightly, by the increased weight of Zac's body, one-quarter-Indian cock burrows deeper ... deeper ... like a sea snake seeks disappearance in shifting subterranean dunes.

"Ready for one helluva big dick up asshole?" Zac asks.

Consummate performer, he's not just asking Marky but the rest of us, too.

"Yeah, plug the kid's tight butt," Walter says. His dick has gone beet red with his non-stop beating of it.

I don't provide verbal permission, but nor do I do anything to stop the progress.

I stand, more interested in the sweat pooled in the small of Zac's back as a result of his asscheeks clamped more and more tightly together as his cock more and more thoroughly inserts to his balls up Marky's rectum. The pool drains immediately when the tautness of Zac's buttocks relaxes as his cock drags back out of Marky's asshole to Zac's cockhead..

My fingertips trail the dampness from the nape of Zac's neck to his buttocks. On Zac's next near-complete withdrawal of his cock from Marky's asshole, I advantage Zac's widened asscrack to slide my fingers through the sweat of his hard-walled inner anal crease.

"Hey, man, I don't take it up the ass, if that's what you're thinking," he says, turning slightly in my direction and looking up, paused mid-fuck stroke.

"Too butch, are you?"

"Finger petting my winked pucker is one thing, but keep your cock clear. Got that?"

"No promises," I say. "There's something about your butt that I find thoroughly fascinating."

Actually, there's very little I find exciting about his butt, except for the way his curly butthair, lining the inward curve of each bun, grows a darker shade of sweat-dyed black as I watch it.

"Be forewarned," he says.

I move more to the bottom of the chaise. I straddle the longue and Zac's legs. I shuffle forward far enough to sit my ass across the back of Zac's calves.

He makes no move to interrupt his fuck-in-progress and deal with any assumed threat I present from his rear. Maybe he thinks I'm not rash enough to try anything, since I've been warned against it. More likely, he's just one more tough-talking butch boy who really wants fucked up his ass by someone with enough guts to carry it through. If there are femmes who ride ass like the butchest of studs, if but given the chance, then there are butch-boy studs who so enjoy their butts plugged by hard dick that they're reluctant to experience such pleasure too often for fear of completely succumbing to the pleasure derived and, somehow, surrendering some part of their pseudo manhood.

Gently, I place a hand to each of Zac's slowly bouncing asscheeks. Beads of his sweat collapse and spread beneath my fingers. His skin is sticky with his perspiration.

I hook his asscheeks with my thumbs. On each upward rise of his butt, I tug his buns wide. Each ensuing meeting of his asscheeks, on each downstroke, provides new sweat-designs inside his crack. A lick of my tongue changes the last sweaty pattern even more.

"Mmmmmm," says Zac and leaves his butt elevated a few extra heartbeats longer than usual, in order to let me lick his asscrack again.

I turn in Walter's direction. On cue, Walter's one hand still maintaining the constant pump of his almost-gone-to-purple dick, he tosses me a rubber. I drape my cock with it, in no time, then lubricate the resulting latex sheathe with the copious sweat both of my hands squeegee from midway on Zac's back to the sensuous bulge of his wet and glossy asscheeks.

On Zac's next downstroke, that drives his hard penis once again completely up Marky's tight ass, I fall forward over the two of them. The weight of my body presses them deeper into the support cushion, my hard cock lengthwise along the crease of Zac's butt. All fucking momentum comes to a stop.

"Hey, man!" Zac says, then echoes: "Hey, man!"

"Shhhhh," I hiss into his ear. My mouth is up close. I almost taste the way his sweat flavors his cheek. Beneath my chest, his back and butt are so slippery I can as easily slide them as a sled easily slides winter slopes.

"Heavy!" Marky weighs in, from the bottom of the pile.

I can care less about Marky's temporary discomfort. I wager he hs suffered far more for far less.

"No funny stuff, huh?!" Zac says.

I pay no attention to stud-boy's latest bit of bravura. I'm too fascinated by the way sweat curls each individual hair of his left sideburn. Intuitively, I know he'll take my cock up his butt when and if I decide to feed my dickinches to him. Real protest, by now, would have been more than verbal. I've had guys let me know they mean business by physical struggle and fisticuffs that leave no doubt whatsoever. All Zac does, by way of physical protest, is provide a half-ass jiggle so my cock nestles even deeper along the crease of his asscrack.

"Damn you, Zac," Walter says, likewise reading the signs, "you never once let me even near your precious asshole."

"That's because you're a pussy," Zac says, his head turned in Walter's direction.

"Shit-head!" Walter says and gives a good impression of being less than compensated, for his loss, by the way his hand continues its whip-strokes of his dick.

Sometimes, at a point as far along as this, I actually think I might come without any penetration by my cock up ass or mouth. That I always proceed into actual fucking, though, is because I've never had the willpower to take the time to prove true my suspicions of my ability to achieve a thoroughly fuckless orgasm. By putting my cock up ass, or mouth, I guarantee orgasmic results.

I'm hyped, my senses intensified by the ongoing experience. I see Zac's sweat in magnified perspective. I smell his sweat go funkier than ever. I lick, and thereby taste his sweat turn even more miraculously aphrodisiacal on my tongue.

How excitingly sensual the slide of my sweaty chest, belly, and face, against Zac's sweaty face, back, and butt!

To put my cock up Zac's butt, I don't need to use one or both of my hands, merely provide a skillful upward humping of my hips and butt, the top-heavy weight of my dick providing the downward angle that puts my cockhead on target. When my cock, once again, is more forcefully on the move, it progresses into and through Zac's anal pucker with the ease of knife penetrating if not warm butter than at least warm cheese.

"Ugh!" Zac says, maybe genuinely surprised by just how quickly and how easily my cock has converted from mere potential threat to fully-armed missile pushed nine inches up his targeted rectum.

No one able to convince me that this is the very first time either Zac or Marky fuck tandem. The complementary rhythm we so quickly establish is simply too smooth flowing -- my cock in and out of Zac's butt, Zac's cock in and out of Marky's behind -- to be the result of rank amateurs experiencing menage-a-trois sex for the very first time.

My cock is no sooner partially removed from Zac's butt, to the point where only my pulpy cockhead remains vised by his sphincter, than his ass rises to engulf my prick to my very balls, his hips elevating far enough, but no farther, to leave the head of his stiff dick securely lodged within Marky's clamping rectum. After which, Marky's ass elevates to reclaim Zac's cock. Marky's ass falls away, only to have Zac's cock go in quick pursuit. Zac's asshole disgorges my dick to my cockhead. At which point, I dive all my recently freed erectile inches back up Zac's swallowing asshole.

And, so it goes. Granted, a bit off, by way of coordination, in the very beginning, but so near-perfect, even then, that only a connoisseur would take notice.

Our combined sweat makes succulent sounds as our flesh connects, then parts, unites, then separates.

Each time I pull my cock almost completely free of Zac's ass, I look between my belly and his back and his ass to see punctuation marks left by my pinpointy nipples within the slick sheen of his perspiration.

My balls, once hung so low they almost flopped against Zac's scrotum, complete their ongoing shrinkage that pulls them tightly against the base of my dick to resemble the boosters of a rocket.

No way, now well into full-fuck status, do I have the sexual prowess to proceed into any kind of marathon pre-cum performance. It highly unlikely I will ever have the endurance and patience required to fuck someone to a merely ass-fuck stimulated ejaculation, even with Zac's sizable dick plying the depths of Marky's willing ass. Which is why, before I hopped on for my ride of this particular butt, I waited until Zac had been well started with his hump of Marky's young butt, in order to give Zac a better chance of joining me in explosion. Figuring, as I did, that if Zac is destined to put on a show of being ticked off, at completion, by my having supposedly taken unfair advantage, then he'll more likely be more pacified by my not having forgotten his needs entirely.

As for Marky's reward in holding up his end of the dog pile, it has already been sufficiently monetary so that even if he doesn't actually achieve orgasm, by cock-fucking the cushion pressed beneath his belly, or by Zac's one-quarter Indian pecker drilling his asshole, he'll have no reason to complain.

"Oh, man-cock. Oh, man, cock," Zac says, and I don't know whether he refers to my cock or to his. "Feeling oh, so, oh-so Jesus-damned good!"

Marky mumbles something guttural and completely indecipherable.

I notice a triad of sweaty rills trailing Zac's left shoulder blade, and I blast my wad into the rubber my cock, once again, securely shoves deep up Zac's butthole.

Zac's anal tunnel clamps inwardly along my exploding dick, in direct evidence of his own jellied spurts of cream basting the guts of the latex balloon his dick has so securely inserted within Marky's young ass.

I'm acutely aware of one glossy bead of perspiration that hangs, like an exotic earring, from the lobe of Zac's left ear.

I grind my erupting prick even more securely up Zac's behind. He grinds his exploding prick more deeply up Marky's trim behind.

"Jesus, fuck, yes!" Zac bellows. Or, maybe, it's Marky. I'm too taken by the sweaty tears formed on Zac's left cheek to tell the difference.

Suddenly, the wonderment of the moment is completely gone. Vanished like some magician's trick that sends it from center stage to undetected theater wings.

Zac's sweat, my sweat, Marky's sweat metamorphoses into nothing more sexy than sticky, slightly stinky body fluid, uncomfortably gluing my body to Zac, locking Zac's body to Marky, and binding Marky's body to the chaise-longue cushion beneath him. I'm acutely aware of summer-sun way too intense and scorching to be healthy.

I pull out my dick, step off and away from the remaining pile of asses, cocks, legs, and torsos. I reach for my recently discarded robe. I spot Walter's cum-splatter on the flagstones at my feet. When I look up, Walter's dick is stuffed back in his pants, and his face sports an asinine smile.

"Well, didn't you just put on some performance?" he says. "And here, I've been whispering for months that you've likely slipped into complete impotence."

"Oh, sweet shit!" says Zac, his dark dick still up Marky's butthole; I'm worried he'll leave it there until his cock shrinks into shedding its rubber and spilling Zac's potentially dangerously spent spunk up Marky's vulnerable butt.

When Zac's cock soon enough comes out, though, it's remarkably still hard.

"Maybe we can do that again," Zac says, having assumed a kneeling position between Marky's thighs in order to peel off used rubber, tie off its free end, and drop it, with a resounding accompanying "splat", to the patio. Not a mention by him, as of yet, as to how I'd sneaked up on him from behind and taken advantage of him and his asshole when he and it had been at their most vulnerable.

"Maybe we can," I say, although it's hardly likely. The magic never has struck twice for me with the same person.

"In the meantime, what say you give me a fresh rubber so I can give the kid here another go-round?" Zac puts in his request.

Walter throws him another contraceptive which Zac dons with long-practiced expertise and swiftness, his body having become disgustingly sweaty from summer sun and heated sex.

Immediately, Zac proceeds into a lusty screw of Marky's obviously still willing and receptive ass.

I watch for only a few short moments, excuse myself, tell everyone to be sure to close and lock the front door on their way out, and leave them.

I barricade myself in my den and write this all down. In that, sexual miracles, like the one just occurred, are for me exceedingly rare. I spend virtual hours scanning my written records of them, like a detective sifts the so-little evidence left behind by a clever serial killer. Desperately, I want insight into the commonality that will link one happening to another to another .... Desperately, I crave that one enlightening piece, or pieces, of still unrecognized "what" that will blessedly allow me never having to wait, ever again, for fickle sheer happenstance to provide me another sexual orgasm.

THE MUSIC, MAN

Thank God for the music, man!

Because, without it, were you to meet up with me on some dark street, I might very well beat the living shit out of you, just to relieve the stress of my frustrations.

My life full of stress and frustration these days. So much so that I don't even know where to begin..

How about with my fucking bitch of a wife, Rosalie. Left me, didn't she, and took pride-of-my-life Jamie with her? Won't even let me see him. Why? Just because she happened to come home early from one of her nights out with the girls and caught me, pants down, with my cock fucked into some guy's face. As if the bitch hadn't a clue I'd been doing the same before I met her, done the same on and off after we'd married. As if she truly believed her loose-as-a-goose cunt provided the workout a genuine A-grade love muscle the size of mine regularly needs and deserves.

Rosalie running home to daddy who's a mousy little turd of a bastard shit who I could handle, any day, if it were just a case of fisticuffs in some back alley. My luck (or lack thereof) being that Rodriguez Tolento, also, happens to be my employer of the moment. Mine and about a hundred other slave-labor types, like me, who keep Rodriguez's chain of pizzerias in the black.

While you may think what happened, AKA my dick in another guy's mouth, might see little-shit Rodriguez tossing me out on my ass, for all the trauma it supposedly caused his bitch of a daughter, it turns out he's no fool. Putting me out of work merely gives him a daughter and grandson to feed. Far better I keep working and funneling a large part of my paychecks to his daughter for child support.

Of course, Rodriguez is also a fucking sadist who suddenly saddles me with every shit-hole duty on the job. I'm back to cleaning toilets, which I haven't done since I first married his daughter and found myself working my way up from the bottom of the pizzeria business. From the bottom up supposedly how Rodriguez did it before me.

Well, wouldn't I like to tell Rodriguez to put his pizza empire where the sun don't shine? Except, he really has me by the balls, and genuinely enjoys (how queer is that?) putting on the squeeze. He came right on out and told me that if I ever made any attempts to find another job, he'd be on the phone in a second telling my perspective bosses what a cocksucker (literally and figuratively) I was.

I can take to selling my dick on the streets, being my own boss (fuck you Rodriguez!). Hustling something I've done a time or two, but only when I've needed a little extra cash. There's no real money to be made going that route, though, unless you're prepared to be versatile. No way I'm taking any guy's dick up my ass or mouth, no matter how much cash he waves in my face.

What I figure is to keep working the pizzeria until I've saved enough money to skip town with hopes Rodriguez's pizza-messy fingers can't reach any farther than his pizzeria empire extends (were only talking three states here). Except, I leave town, and my chances of ever seeing my kid again are completely nil. I don't' give a damn whether or not Rosalie or her father are suddenly swallowed up by a hole in the ground, but I do love to pieces my little Jamie-boy.

Grabbing up my kid and carrying him off, supporting the both of us by finding guys willing to pay for my dick up their assholes or mouths, at least until I can find better, isn't the kind of life-style to which I want to subject my kid.

So, I'm between the proverbial devil and a hard place, at least for the moment.

In the meantime, there's the music.

Hear it? Feel it? Never guess it's still a couple of blocks away, would you? That's the advantage to The Cavernos in this otherwise industrial part of town. Who's to complain of the noise? Warehouse night-watchmen who are supposed to be awake anyway?

I'm jauntier each step I take nearer that place. There's something so soothing about the musical vibrations oozing up through the sidewalk to make my steps lighter, even dance-like.

Except, I'm distracted by my reflection in a piece of dirty, broken glass window, aren't I? I move in closer, squinting at my imagine played back in the too-glare industrial lighting.

My fingers run my thick black hair. My hair my pride and joy. Not as much the pride and joy as my big Spanish-American dick, but damned close.

I'm starting to lose my hair, aren't I? The direct result of all the stress and strain. Oh, I'm not talking waking up mornings and finding fur-balls on the pillowcase. But, there's definitely more strands caught in the shower drain, these days, not to mention pulled free by the teeth of my comb.

Besides which, I figure, I'm getting an ulcer. Periodic pains in my gut.

I might, also, have prostate cancer, in that my streams of piss seem to be faltering, more and more, these days.

Also, I found blood in my stool, didn't I? Toilet water went pale pink. Doctor said it was haemorrhoids. Shit, how can I have haemorrhoids? I haven't sat on any cold surfaces -- can't even find a cool place to sit in all this summer heat. I haven't been pregnant with any babies. I haven't grunted and groaned to push constipated shit out of the old asshole -- at least not lately. The doctor simply doesn't know jack-shit; as soon as I can get the money, I'm getting a second opinion.

Discovered a mole, the other day, in the small of my back, where it went completely unnoticed until it started itching like crazy, didn't I? Might very well be skin cancer.

Goddamn, I do need the music tonight!

Hurry ... hurry ... hurry ... before I figure out the very good odds of my getting hepatitis from that fast-food place that served tainted meat a couple weeks back. I can't specifically remember eating there, during the time earmarked for primary exposure, but I might have forgotten a quick drive-through for a hamburger (God knows, I've grown sick-to-puking of pizza), some lunch hour. I've taken the first of the two vac-cine shots at Public Health, but it takes forever for those vaccines to kick in. So, are the whites of my eyes really turning yellow, or is that just some mustardly smear on the filthy glass into which I stare?

All of that not even the half of it; so, you have only a rough idea of just how fucked up my life is, my constantly feeling as if I'm being sucked down into a proverbial shit-hole.

It's only my weekends at The Cavernos, all its loud and all-consum-ing music flowing over and into me, that seem to soothe the raging beast inside me that's just waiting to get out.

I walk through the open outer door and push through the secondary swinging doors.

"Hey, handsome!" the bartender calls. "Your usual?"

"Catch you later," I say.

I beeline for the dance floor, not bothering with a dance partner. I'm at my best when I dance alone. Off to one side. Or, off in the corner, over there, where I'm now headed, where those two background mirrors meet up to provide just the right throwback of hypnotizing light spun off the spinning crystal ball that hangs center-ceiling above the dance floor.

Oh, it doesn't take me long to get sucked in by the rhythm. I weave. I sway. I experience tension draining, draining, thank-God draining, until I actually feel halfway human again.

It's easy to lose all sense of time and place and reality on The Cavernos dance floor. Even during the short breaks that sometimes happen between songs, echoes of the last-played melody keep sounding in my ears, and I keep right on dancing to those, until something new blasts through the amplifiers.

My body moving ... moving ... always moving. Sometimes with my eyes closed, although I'm not banging into anyone or into the walls, because I've the inner radar of a bat.

Good ... so good. So fucking ... fucking ... fucking ... good!

I open my eyes to see someone join me. Blond kid. Blue eyes obvious when and where the sparkling light-show plays across them. Kid looking only fourteen; but the place has stringent ID checks, so he's at least eighteen.

I'm twenty and beginning to look twenty-five. A balding twenty-five? A cancerous, ulcerous, haemorrhoidal, twenty-five?

Where's all the superb muscle tone I had less than a year ago? Rosalie said she married me because I had the sexiest body she'd ever seen.

Can't think about bitch Rosalie now, though, can I? Don't want to spoil the welcoming calm that's finally settling in.

I shut my eyes again. When I open them seconds? minutes? hours? later, the blond kid is replaced by twins (like in that TV show Ally McBeal, only better-looking), who twist and turn, swirl and twirl, like duplicate pieces of space flotsam caught in the eddy of a black hole.

I've seen the twins lots of times. Red-heads. Pale-pale skin. A flouring of pale-pale freckles just about everywhere on them. Pink-pink nipples seen because all during the summer, like now, they have their shirts off. Nice pecs. Nice abdominals. I would let either or both suck my cock and balls, and I'd even made the offer, but ...

"Taking home your big cock and balls is one thing, Manuel," Dan (or, maybe, it was Stan, said). "But neither Stan..." Or, maybe, it was Dan. "...nor I want anything to do with all the other personal baggage you're toting around these days."

The word is out: Manuel Guillermo is one fucked-up motherfucking bastard dude!

I shut my eyes and will the pink-pink twins to dematerialize ("Beam 'em up, Scotty!"); and, they do. Leaving me to dance, dance, dance, by my lonesome, in a room jam-packed with nearly naked men. More and more guys stripping off various and sundry pieces of clothing as more and more of the outside summer heat seeps inside and joins body heat to produce gallons and more gallons of sweet summer sweat.

I pull off my T-shirt which has gone yellowy (hepatitis yellowy?) beneath its armpits. There's a dark wet stain on the material where perspiration drained along the center of my muscled chest. I drop the balled material into the mirrored corner.

I dance until my body oozes sweat like a sponge oozes water when vigorously squeezed.

"Sexy, sexy man," says someone nearby. I don't know to whom he refers. Could be to anyone. I like to think he refers to me.

My arm muscles still in damned good shape: nice biceps and correspondingly nice triceps. My pecs firmly rectangular: my nipples curving right along with my lower pectoral folds. Quarter-size nipples with nubs that are pin-pricks even when I'm not sexually aroused. Flat-flat belly etched with square-to-rectangle designs. A navel only slightly indented at its upper end. A sexy line of black hair from my belly button to disappearance at my trouser waistband.

God, but anyone who thinks I'm sexy now should have seen me a year ago -- before all of this shit in my life hit the fan. But, I don't want to think that.

I dance all the faster until, finally tired and dripping sweat like I've flash-danced beneath an open shower spigot, I head for the back room, this room's music moving with me like an isolating and comforting cocoon.

I push through a tinkling of beaded curtains. I push through two sets of heavy black drapery.

The music becomes muted but not disappeared. The distant drumbeat matches exactly the beat of my heart.

I ignore the exploratory brushes of hands against my face, belly, chest, crotch, legs, and ass; it's as if I walk through spiderwebs in a Halloween-darkened haunted house. By the time I reach the long wooden partition, my eyes have adjusted sufficiently to maneuver every obstacle without being able to identify all of them.

The partition is high and long, like a miniature wall. It's perforated with holes, some of which are blocked from my view by men standing in front of them. Mainly the men are positioned face-to-the-wall, although one readily noticeable stud faces outward toward the room; he's naked from the waist down, bent over at his mid-section, his ass jammed tightly against one hole in the wall, his dick jammed tightly into his fist.

I know the partition's hole pattern intimately and know which of the perforations are best positioned for my height and for my anatomy. I head toward one of those.

The hole I select is crotch-level. It's big enough to swallow my cock and my balls, and I immediately prepare to feed just that sexual triad to it ... by unfastening all the buttons of my jeans; the swell of my ass able to keep the denim from falling.

I don't wear underwear; I prefer the chafe of Levi's to the softer caress of cotton. My cock and balls spill out as soon as the front flap of my pants comes open.

No one ever having said Manuel Guillermo has anything less than a magnificent cock and pair of cajones.

"Fucked up," they may and do say about me. "Mental case." "Mind-fucked." "More problems than the Titanic after it struck iceberg." "Do-do, do-do," sung to the tune of a popular horror-show series of TV reruns. "Squirrelly as a chipmunk."

Never, though: "Pencil dick." "Pea-balled." "Ugly, ugly schlong." "Pitifully pitiful prunes."

More than one guy, back in the days before my present personal problems branded me social pariah, said I have the perfect cock and balls.

"Uncut perfection personified," I was told. "God had a very good day, indeed, when he ended up having made your cock and balls. You had a very good day, Manuel, when God decided to bless you with these."

My cock is thick at its base, tapering only slightly to its thick head.

Enough vein striation to make it convincingly the real thing and not someone's bland idealization of what a perfect cock might be. A fore-skin that, when my cock is flaccid, doesn't quite close over my cocktip; the deft slit of my cockmouth always visible and making it easier for me to piss in a straight line. My prepuce slides my cockshaft, during cock elongation to erection, and turtlenecks just beneath my coronal flare. Nine inches of penile length: not too big, not too small. Impressively able to stand tall, despite its bulk, and never-ever, when primed for a fuck, merely a downed-drawbridge poked straight outward from my belly.

Purposely, I push my dick to an uncustomary parallel-to-the-floor, and I dip-stick it through the hole in the wall.

Apricot-size balls contained within my scrotum which comes off as custom-designed for its contents. Two distinct scrotal compartments, hung side by side, neither hanging its contained nut any higher or lower than its companion. My scrotal sac sufficiently bagged to provide ade-quate pillow for my dick, when flaccid, all of the way to the tip of my cockhead.

Purposely, I hoist my balls up and over the lip of the hole and water-fall them to the other side.

I assume a well-balanced stance before the cock-and-balls-plugged wall. My palms go to the wall, slightly above and to each side of my head. My body leans my sweaty cheek, sweaty chest, and sweaty belly, to paint wet designs to the graffiti-covered woodwork.

I don't have to bait long to get results. My seemingly disembodied dick and balls invite far more quickly and enticingly than if the rest of me were presented along with them.

Cocksuckers, especially connoisseurs of male sexual equipment, intuitively know a good thing when they see it and, if not otherwise put-off, will automatically be drawn to the perfect dick and pair of nuts. Even rank amateurs, kids who've never sucked cock before, want to be initiated by the likes of what I've put on display for them this evening.

The lucky guy I get, this time, comes with a juicy hello-lick that ele-vates both of my testicles on his upturned tonguetip, then releases as he washes a spitty line up the belly of my dick from my cockbase to my pulpy cockhead.

There's music resonating within the wood pressed tightly against my cheek, chest, and belly. I hum along with it.

Ovaled mouth caps the tip of my dick, and a tongue washes clean whatever sweaty residue remains from my dickhead's partial sheathing in prepuce earlier that evening.

My initial opinion of what kind of cocksucker I've ended up with, this luck of the draw? One disadvantage of this catch-as-catch-can method of getting my phallus serviced is my inability to pre-pick whomever ends up hanging on the other end of my dick. It's not like I spot Joe, know Joe sucks cock like crazy, and I let him have a go at it. It's not like I spot Karl, know Karl can't keep his teeth sheathed while giving head, and I take care to keep my cock away from him.

This cocksucker's lead-in, his lick from my balls to my cockhead was a nice touch. His lingering over my cocktip, now, as if savoring it a bit before swallowing my whole-meal dick, let's me think I have myself a real winner.

So does the way he slowly begins to consume my erection.

With just the right amount of suction, his cheeks collapse into a snug compartment for all my entering inches, as my cockhead progresses to the opening of his throat and slides right on in. So good is this guy that I attempt to feed him the few fractions of an inch of my dick made unavailable by the ply of the partition that separates him from me.

His deep-throating has been accomplished in one long and smooth ride. Not a hint of gagging; I would have felt the spasms along the shaft of my cock. No hint of impending choke-reflex; his head stays calmly put, no efforts to rear up for air.

"Yessssssssss!" I hiss and press my ear even tighter into the wood-work.

I shut my eyes, and let myself be thoroughly washed by the sheer wonder of it all.

He knows the benefits to be had from not neglecting my balls. You'd be surprised by how many amateur dicksuckers become so consumed by the mechanics of eating stiff prick that they forget a good accompanying roll of a guy's gonads, nice and easy collisions of testicle against testicle, moves cocksucking into a completely higher plane. This guy's hand, palm toward him, inserts between the partition on his side and my nuts cascaded on through. His fingers, one at a time, fold forward against the back-drape of my scrotum, his thumb, in finale, joining in from the side. His thumb and fingers unfold, and he repeats the process. It's a sensuous strumming that keeps my balls shifting this way and that, as well as has them gently bouncing off one another.

When his mouth begins its slide upward, my balls are still being played to perfection. It's a seemingly reluctant disgorge. The amount of suction he exerts strives to keep my dick stationary while the upward drag of his head works in opposition. As a result, all loose outer skin on my dick is begrudgingly ferried upward, along the shaft of my cock, until my foreskin is forced into a well-defined tight snout that it never achieves on its own. At which time, suction is completely withdrawn. While I'm caught up in the sensuous cascade of my cock's loose outer skin back along the neck of my dick, Mr. Cocksucker opens his mouth genuinely wide and, without even touching my cock, dives all of the way to the bottom, only then clamping down and beginning yet another drag to cowl my cockhead with my foreskin.

This man is what cocksucking is all about. My cock worked over by a pro. My body alive with the pleasures of his suck and of the accompanying music. He and the music can make me forget my problems. He and the music can make me forget the stress. He and the music can make me disregard fanciful imaginings of my impending death from hepatitis, skin cancer, haemorrhoids, and/or abdominal ulcerations.

Another instrumental begins playing in the other room. It's something I recognize as Teen-Rock Bolero. I guess it's a takeoff on some classical piece that's supposed to be a musical representation of sexual intercourse.

The guy who hangs from my dick head-bounces over my cock in direct tempo to the music. Slow at first -- so slow I wish he'd speed it up just a bit.

Oh, man, but this is marvellous, especially when the beat of the music picks up, and the cocksucker's head manages up and down slides in faster and faster intervals.

Just when I figure it isn't going to get any better, it does.

I try to remember how close the musical piece is to completion. No doubt in my mind that this cocksucker can keep dancing with my dick until musical finale, but can I hold off ejaculation until that last dissonant riff of screeching electric guitar?

It'll take a real expert, on the receiving end, as well as on the delivery end, of this suck, to get my jism spewed at one and the same time the music reaches its crescendo. If anyone is that expert, though, I am. Rosalie once told me she never knew a man could be so long in coming as I was. It was a compliment at the time. Later, of course, she insinuated my endurance with her was only disinterest; any normal man unlikely to have held out nearly as long.

But, I don't want to think of Rosalie. This is my time, and even thoughts of her have no right to be here. Especially since the pleasure I derive from my cock getting sucked by this unknown gobbler is far greater than anything I ever experienced while plugging Rosalie's loose-by-comparison pussy.

"You're good, cocksucker," I compliment through the wood, through the music, through the vibrations of the wood, through the cacophony of sexual moans and groans that fill the room. The his-face-to-the-room pants-dropped-to-his-ankles dude, off to my right, climaxes into his pumping fingers; his naked ass pulls away from a sweat-horse-shoed gloryhole to reveal a rubberized lengthy dick still poked through from the other side.

I hold out for a long while longer without actively participating in the ongoing suck of my dick but, in the end, I've little conscious control over my reflex fuck motions that suddenly begin. Spontaneously, my lower body draws back every time the cocksucker surrenders most of my dick. Just as spontaneously, I buck forward every time he drops for a complete swallow. My movements would be even more pronounced if he didn't take such a firm handhold of my nuts, on the other side, and refuse to let even a portion of my scrotum be tugged on back to my side.

I become one with the swelling music, identifying myself with its final guitar riff that would spoil the whole musical composition by occurring anywhere but at its assigned spot at the ending.

Patience ... patience ... only a little ... more ... patience. Except, patience is harder and harder to come by as the sheer upsurges of pleasure inside of me increase to the point where they, and what they lead up to, are what becomes of predominant importance in my quickly narrowing world.

Actually, I think I'm going to come, then and there, my expectations for greater endurance shot all to holy hell. It's only a well-timed squeezing of my testicles, with just the right amount of pain to skim off just enough pleasure, that keeps me from falling over the brink of sexual oblivion.

"You are good ... good ... more than good," I whisper to my cock's sucker by way of endearment, although it's doubtful he hears me above all the other racket.

A guy, down the line, fucks gloryhole with such force and tenacity that the wall actually concaves each time his lower belly batters against it.

Oh ... oh ... oh-nly a little longer ... little ... little ... longer.

God, but I'm sweating up a storm. Perspiration runs my scalp to cascade my face and the nape of my neck. It burns my eyes. It salts my tongue. It sensuously tickles my summer-tanned skin, pouring over my pecs, over my abdominals, over my ass, and running in a steady stream down the crack of my ass. Even my balls sweat within the handhold maintained by the sucker sucked so securely to my quickly priming erection.

My sex-hyped body dances against the wood partition with greater abandonment than I displayed on the dance floor in the other room. My body sways and paints the graffiti-stained wall with more streaks of dark sweat.

"Ohhhhhhh," I moan, totally off-key to the dissonant clash of music in my ears.

When I come, it's not because I realize the final guitar riff of the music has not only begun but reached its final crescendo. I come because I have to come. There's no other alternative for me. I either release, through my prick, the deluge straining to all limits the storage capacity of my testicles, or I die of massively ruptured blue-balls.

"Take it! Take it! Take it!" I bellow to the wall pressed so hard beneath my cheek and torso that I think I've actually merged with the wood. "Eat my creamy ... creamy ... stud-heavy ... ahhhh ... agghrrrhu-uuuh .... AAAAGUNGGGNGH!"

Not that anyone as experienced at cocksucking as the guy hanging onto my dick for dear life would ever actually spill even a precious drop. He claims the squirts with which I feed him and does so with such all-consuming suction that I fear he's popping my dick right off my belly and sending it spear-like down his gullet.

It's only when I've fed him my very last globule of spermal goo, his handhold having released my cum-depleted balls, his mouth rising for its exit off the top of my prick, that I realize Teen-Rock Bolero has ended and been replaced by another song.

I remove my cock and my balls from the gloryhole. I look down my body, between my belly and the wall. My cock has pretty much lost its previous stiffness and is in its rarely seen half-droop stance.

I cup my balls, weigh them, wonder if I've merely imagined the left nut hanging slightly lower than the right.

And, what about the filigree of veins along my cockshaft? Hadn't it once been less old-man-like noticeable? Less vibrantly old-man-like blue?

I stuff my cock and balls into my pant and button up. I backtrack and exit the room ... through double curtains and beaded drape. I skirt the dance floor and retrieve my crushed T-shirt from its mirrored corner. I head for the front door, hoping that what I've managed tonight will keep me sane until next weekend.

"Hey, Manuel, about that drink?" the bartender calls. "This is a bar, after all."

"Sure," I say and make a place for myself where he deposits a full schooner, and I deposit the cash, plus his tip -- the latter all he's really been interested in all along.

I'm hot, and the beer is deliciously cold and good.

I'm looking good, too. I can tell by my reflection in the mirror behind the line-up bottles of hard booze.

Looking good, but no one here is going to pick me up and take me home. Because I have personal problems. I have I'm-not-really-gay and won't take cock up my mouth or ass problems.

I finish my beer, head for the door, stop short when I hear a song begin that's a particular favorite of mine.

What, after all, do I have waiting for me at home? Home is the pits!

I about-face and head for the dance floor.

Thank God for the music, man!

GUESS WHO?

a.m., Day One:

I disembark the airplane at LAX, and there's no mistaking the intense blast-furnace heat of an LA summer in full-swing. LA summer heat is different from summer heat elsewhere. Don't ask me why. That's just the way it is. Certainly, it's different from the heat I just left in Alaska. Maybe, it has something to do with the way LA summer day-heat lingers, usually all through each night, to become cumulative with the heat of the next day, and the next day, and the next day. In Alaska, hot as any day may get, no matter how deeply into summer it may be, the heat usually dissipates after sundown and forces you to don a sweater.

Gainer Wynden meets me.

"Dig your tan!" he says and takes my carry-on. "The result of the sun reflecting off all those icebergs?"

Gainer is one of several wanabee porno stars with Bigg Gunn Shoots who willingly plays go-fer for Kendall Prollic while waiting for, hoping for, his big "fucking" break.

There are two ways to describe Gainer. The first is how he appears as he walks the maze of corridors at the airport. Namely, he has blond hair that looks like, and has, come out of a bottle; although, not even Gainer seems to remember its original color, swearing it, once upon a time, was only a slightly different shade blond than it is now; although, the mousy-brown of his pubic bush probably gives a more convincing clue. He has nondescript blue eyes set a tad too far apart across a rather too broad and too flat nose. His lips, in a town where people pay big bucks to get the bee-stung look, are actually too thick; his mouth too wide, his chin too weak ... even his dimple too much dimple in that it actually slices his whole right cheek, with a Grand Canyon groove, whenever he smiles. He has an okay body, albeit too hirsute for my particular taste, but it has nice muscle definition underneath all its hair. His cock is so enormous that his avid willingness to fuck and suck, not even to mention get fucked and get sucked, on screen, should have seen him showcased in one or more porno flick a long time before now, in that -- let's face it -- success in this business counts a helluva lot more upon what's between your legs, and your versatility in bed, than it does on what's perched atop your neck, or can be found between your ears.

Gainer's lack of success in porno is entirely to do with the second way to describe him. Namely, as someone a camera -- motion-picture, still, video, digital -- loathes with a passion. I know, because I've seen outtakes from the several times Kendall made the attempt to put Gainer before the cameras, hoping to capitalize on the potential offered by Gainer's obvious lack of inhibitions and the big schlong between his hairy thighs. Swear to God, each and every time, something happened during film processing -- whether to the color, or to the clarity, or to the whatever -- that made the end results unusable. One time, everything else in perfect color, and in perfect focus, Gainer's stiff dick came out not only hopelessly fuzzy but actually pea-green. There are still people, having seen that outtake, who whisper, "Here comes the Jolly-Green," every time they see Gainer headed in their direction.

Bigg Gunn Shoots actually just the latest stop on Gainer's ongoing quest for porno fame.

The rumor has it, although Gainer denies it, that his parents, members of some kind of ultra-right-wing religious cult, and fearing their gay runaway son destined to end up just where he's trying to end up, had gathered in a prayer circle with others of their group and had summoned up some kind of celestial interference. Probably pure bullshit, but I know people actively trying to wheedle out of Gainer, on an almost daily basis, the name of the cult so they can take precautions against offending any member or members of it.

"Kendall is going to be one happy dude that the delay in your flight doesn't have you checking in looking like shit," Gainer says.

"Funny, but I certainly feel like shit," I say, not lying. Damned plane was two hours out of Juneau when it had to turn back. It was another two hours after that return landing before we were able to re-board and start over. Something to do with a red light that kept going on, then off, in the cockpit, purely -- or, so they said -- because of a minor glitch in the electrical system.

"You always look good," says Gainer. If he's brown-nosing in hopes that I'll put in another good word with Kendall, regarding yet another chance for him in front of the cameras, he better not hold his breath. Word is out that even if some good footage ever did come in, the end result would likely be a jinxed production; so, Gainer's chances for a career in porno are, by now, pretty much completely dead in the water.

"No other baggage but the carry-on," I say when he tries to steer me toward the baggage carousels. Immediately, he veers for short-term parking.

We don't say much of anything else, at least of merit, until we're in the car, the airport behind us, although we're still pretty much bogged down in airport traffic.

The car is Kendall's red-Jag convertible. Its top down, its air-conditioner isn't on. The heat of the day begins to make me sweat. Gainer has been sweating from the get-go.

"Kendall says that I should mention a little something before you check in for this morning's shoot," he says.

Talk about red flags of warning!

"Oh?" I venture cautiously.

"Powers Dick has been replaced," says Gainer, looking nervous.

That the case, it's Kendall who should be worried. I've been around long enough, been successful enough in the business, so that I don't fuck or suck, get fucked or sucked by, anyone, in front of any camera, without having given prior go-ahead. Kendall thinks he can pull the very-last-minute switcheroo of a pre-approved cast member for someone else, for the presently scheduled shooting of "Dangling", and he has another think coming.

"Although, Kendall doesn't figure you'll have any problems with the substitute," says Gainer.

"Oh?" I learned a long time ago that if you want to give someone enough rope to hang themselves just keep quiet and let them have at it. That Gainer hasn't immediately given me the new guy's name has set off alarm bells to accompany all of those initial red-flag warnings.

"It's not as if you haven't fucked and sucked around with this guy before," says Gainer.

Which, in reality, says nothing about my giving my okay, at this stage of my career, in that I've fucked and sucked a lot of people, in my life, some of whom I hope never to fuck, suck, or even see again.

"This guy have a name?" I want Gainer to know that I've noticed just how reluctant he seems to pass on that key bit of information.

"Just don't get your tail in a kink, right off, okay?"

"Get my tail in a kink? Right off? Saying what about Kendall's notion that I'm supposedly not going to have any problems with this substitution?"

"Come on, King," he says, "I'm just the messenger, aren't I?"

I still have trouble realizing that when people talk to me, they often preface, or suffix, with "King". Though the screen name King Richard never seems to hinder my success in porno, I've always thought, and still think, the moniker, assigned me by Kendall (while I admit, yes, "Richard" can be abbreviated to "Dick", King Dick thereby correctly describing a certain part of my anatomy), is a bit too far a reach to expect from the majority of my hard-core viewing audience.

"Christ, Gainer, spit it out!" The Juneau-to-Seattle-to-LA flight, what with all of its delays, has left me irritable. I'd prefer twenty-four hours of sleep, about now, instead of the scheduled eight-hour LA-summer fucking-and-sucking before-the-cameras marathon that suddenly includes someone I suspect I don't even like.

"Boy Young," he says.

His follow-up pause tells me he thinks he's just told me something. Wrong!

"And, man, old," I remind. "And baby, very young. But what's any of that to do with the price of tea in China?"

"Boy Young is Tanner Wilson's screen name," says Gainer.

And, finally, we get somewhere; although, it's nowhere I've expected, or anywhere I particularly want, to be.

"Jesus H. Christ!" I say.

Tanner and I used to be lovers in Pilboiken, Nebraska. Went to the same high school. Screwed around underneath the bleachers, on the football field, in the shower room, in the boiler room, on the roof, in a broom closet, in the bushes. Actually, truth be known, we screwed around anywhere, any time, any way, we could. Rutted like rabbits. I, a senior; he, a junior. I graduated, came to LA, took to fucking and sucking for a living, first on the streets, then in front of a camera. Tanner, still back in Pilboiken, felt deprived when suddenly unable to overdose on sex with me on a regular basis. So, the very day he became legal, he chucked Pilboiken, as well as his mom and dad, and headed off to me in LA. Where we fucked and sucked for five months before it finally struck him as to how I didn't have quite as much energy, after my fuck-and-suck workdays, as I'd managed for, and with, him in our high-school days.

At one and the same time, Tanner started getting all sorts of invites from my business associates to become an active part in the porno business, where my star was fast rising. As surely as B follows A, Tanner having been tempted. After all, I, his chief example at the time, was getting plenty of sex, aside from what he gave me, was getting paid good money for it, and, more and more often than not, was heading off to exotic shoots (i.e. Juneau, Alaska), while Tanner was frustrated as hell in being unable to get a run-of-the-mill job with a decent wage.

I did as much as I could to discourage him from the porno life-style. Not because I wasn't completely satisfied with my lot in life, my mother dead and my father with Alzheimer's. Show my dear daddy a movie of me getting fourteen-inch cock up my butt, and he'll only smile and drool a little. Show Tanner's middle-class mom and/or dad a peek of that same fourteen-inch pecker buried to its hairy balls up their son's behind, and .... Well, you get the picture. My having quite fond memories of his parents, although Tanner complained, from the get-go, never to stop, that the two are forever "locked somewhere in the morally uptight Dark Ages".

Last I'd heard, Tanner hadn't "gone porno", but probably not because of anything I said or did by way of dissuasion. Leo Renoir came into the picture, and I have no qualms whatsoever in giving him full credit for Tanner's career sights veering elsewhere. Leo had managed a few bit parts in a couple legit, albeit B, movies, and he convinced Tanner that the same avenue to a legitimate "Big Time" was open to him. By way of farther persuasion, Leo, Tanner's age and quickly to become Tanner's lover, provided my ex the kind of heated sex that was possessed of all the vitality and scope of fucking and sucking that Tanner had shared with me back in Pilboiken before I'd taken to channeling most of my sexuality toward satisfying, and being satisfied by, other porno stars, before cameras.

I've since been pleased to see Tanner in a couple of movie and TV walk-ons, his once even having spoken a line, as a dying victim of a gruesome murder on Chris Carter's TV "Millennium". More recently, I heard Tanner auditioned for a key part in an upcoming blockbuster from the legit powerhouse FantasyWorld Productions. So, how, I wonder, does any of that have Kendall suddenly changing Tanner's name to Boy Young and substituting him for Powers Dick in the thoroughly porno flick, "Dangling"?

"I thought Tanner was doing legit stuff with Leo What's-his-name," I say.

Gainer shrugs. He knows very little about legitimate films, porno having been his one and only goal for as long as anyone, probably even he, can remember.

"Christ!" I say and settle back into my seat, saying very little else until we pull through the gates of the Beverly Hills mansion Kendall rents for today's shoot.

Whoever is on the gate's intercom (Peter Giles, I think), must forewarn Kendall I'm on the way in, because Kendall is out the mansion door and down the front steps before I'm completely out the car.

Kendall is all smiles. As well he should be -- at least on one count. He has wanted Tanner into porno, since way back when, not having been more persistent at the outset only because I, already a proven money-maker at the time, had threatened to jump ship if Kendall went too far against my own plans for Tanner's well-being in Hollywood. On the more important count, my continuing notion of what remains best for Tanner isn't necessarily what Kendall, or even Tanner, may think best at the present time.

"You're looking great!" says Kendall. "I mean, you are looking really, really great! Nothing like a Caribbean tan to highlight all of your scrumptious body parts, yes?"

I don't bother to remind him that Alaska is far removed from the Caribbean. I've been on loan to Big Projectors Films, despite Kendall having tried to renege on the deal which had seen him borrow Big Projectors' big-at-the-time, in more ways than one, Ridum Gettyup for a flick that had genuinely bombed (go guess!) at the box office.

"What's this bullshit about Tanner?" is what I cut-to-the-chase say.

"How about we head around this way?" he says and, without being too pushy, directs me around the side of the house, through a small garden, toward the back.

"You gave me cast approval on this one," I say, and it's not a question.

"You telling me you can't get it up for an old lover?" he says and sounds disbelieving. "Come on, King, you're the guy who once managed an erection for the hole of a doughnut."

We're just about to break through the shrubbery on to the grey-slate patio around the pool in back when Kendall comes to a complete stop, his hand on my arm persuading me to do the same.

"Shit!" he says.

It's Tanner headed in our direction.

Seeing most of Tanner's pale-as-a-ghost-skin exposed, except for its glossing of sweat and his swim suit, I can't figure, as usual, what it is that has Kendall's sixth sense telling him the kid "is a natural for succeeding in this business". I suspect Tanner's success, if and when, will have an awfully lot to do with the way porno audiences are becoming more and more youth-oriented. Tanner, despite being only a couple of years younger than I am, looks amazingly pretty much the same as he did when -- he, a junior ; I, a senior -- the two of us diddled our brains out regularly in high school. Back in those days, Tanner's willowy, almost girlish slimness, pale skin, and strawberry-blond hair, had had definite appeal -- no denying it. However since I've added a bit of muscle and bulk to my own physique, my tastes have evolved more toward guys with pretty much the same build as mine; although, I'm still admittedly partial to strawberry-blonds.

Can I still get stiff at the prospect of fucking Tanner's tight ass? The immediate stirring of my cock pretty much answers that question. Or, does it? As Kendall has so kindly just reminded, I once got an erection for nothing more stimulating than the hole of a doughnut -- un-sugared at that.

"Goddamn, buddy, do you look good enough to eat!" says Tanner, stopping in front of us and giving me a once-over reminiscent of client-to-hustler, or vice versa.

"Tanner, I do distinctly ..." begins Kendall.

"Don't you mean, 'Boy Young', you 'do distinctly ...' etceteras?" Tanner interrupts. Then before Kendall, who isn't all that used to being interrupted, can get his wits about him, Tanner continues right along. "However, Boy Young knows for a fact that no one is more likely, than he is, to convince King Richard about my determination to be part of the shooting cast of 'Dangling'."

"Kendall, why don't you do us all a favor and leave Tanner and me alone for a few minutes?" I say and can't help wondering whether Tanner has intercepted us by design, everything having been choreographed and directed, from the get-go, by Kendall who, I figure, should be far more upset by Tanner having supposedly taken the reins to run with them.

"No bruises, kiddies, please," Kendall says. "This, after all, isn't a b&d flick." After which, he proceeds to poolside where he pours, from an awaiting pitcher, a drink likely far more alcoholic than lemonade.

"I thought you were up for some big role in some big movie?" I say.

The movie is "Lusitania", and there is good buzz about its chances for major success, a la "Titanic". at next year's Oscars.

"They didn't me call back, did they?" Tanner says. "A lot of people never called me back, including you. Truth is, I just got tired of waiting. Leo, too. Did Kendall or Gainer tell you that Leo just signed with Jack N. Off Films?"

"I thought you got two call-backs on your 'Lusitania' read," I say. I'm more aware of what he's been up to than he probably realizes.

"I'm talking no final call-back," he says. "As for the other call-backs, about ten-thousand other hopefuls got those, too, didn't they? The movie, I might add, already into shooting."

"Although, they've still not cast the part of Johnny," I remind. "I hear they're shooting around the character until they can make that final casting decision."

"Yeah, and I hear a young actor, you might very well masturbate over while watching his last FantasyWorld picture, just got the part sewed up."

"So, you're next career move is to get cock shoved up your ass, so your mom and dad can check out the results at their local XXX-rated video store?"

"Not likely any chance they'll be going into any XXX-rated video store, local or otherwise, is there?"

"How about one of their more daring friends giving them the news?"

"Anyone they know any more likely, than mom and dad, to go into one of those places? Get real!"

"They'll find out about you taking, or giving, cock up the ass, believe me. Good-intentioned people will be falling all over themselves to give them the news."

"Oh, well, it's about time I finally came completely out of my closet."

"I always liked your mom and dad."

"They always liked you. But, then, they never had you figured for a queer, did they? They figured the only gay, in that whole damned town, was yours truly. I'll merely be confirming their suspicions."

"Their suspicions and their finding out for sure aren't one and the same."

"This chance in 'Dangling' is something I want, King." Jesus, even Tanner now calls me by my stage name. "I intend to get it."

"Except, it's not a case of you getting it because you, or even because Kendall, wants it, is it? Or, hasn't Kendall mentioned that I have full cast approval on this particular production?"

"I kind of want my porno debut to be with you, but .... If you won't let it happen, I've an offer from Jack N. Off. Would have gone there, right off, with Leo, but Kendall always seemed to do right by you. If I'm going to make the plunge, figuratively and literally, I'd like it to be around people I can trust on both sides of the camera."

"Big mistake not waiting for FantasyWorld at least to make a final decision on that part of Johnny in 'Lusitania'!" I play Cassandra. "Your agent may be trying to get you, even as we speak, to tell you that you've the coveted part locked up."

"Look King, I've decided that porno is something I'm going to do, with or without you. Because I'm sure as hell not about to head on back to mommy and daddy. Nor am I prepared to continue mere sustenance-level survival, here, in money-conscious Tinsel Town."

"You really should stick with legit," I say; I'm a poet, I don't know it, my cock shows it -- Longfellow! "I've seen the work you've done so far, and I'm genuinely surprised by just how naturally good you are at it."

"This town is full of good actors, natural and/or otherwise, mostly waiting on tables and surviving on little more than hope. I don't want to wait on tables. I don't want just hope. I do want what you have, and what Kendall promises, and I can have just that, here and now. You think you're big in this business, wait until you see what I do in it, both on the receiving and giving end of big cock. Or, are you afraid of the competition?"

"Get me a bowl of water, and I'll do my Pontius Pilate bit," I say, knowing full-well he'll get the Biblical reference because his parents used to make him read scriptures on a regular basis. "That's how worried I am about competition -- from you, or otherwise."

"Why call for a bowl when you've a mansion's swimming pool just a few steps away?" he says and smiles widely.

William Maltese

p.m., Day Seven:

(ACTION!)
(CAMERA!)

Boy Young has never seen alluvial gold, wet and glistening in stony riverbeds, but King Richard's hair and body are just that golden, just that wondrously wet in the shower.

Even before Boy slides the shower curtain to one side, his naked skin is almost as wet as King's. Boy's wetness, though, is purely the result of summer heat and anticipatory excitement.

When King turns, at the slide of the opaque plastic, it's merely a glance over his muscled left shoulder.

A smile dimples both of King's cheeks. His full lips are moist and inviting over his oh-so-white teeth. His thick blond lashes are beaded with water.

He provides a farther exotic torque of his neck and massive shoulders, his back halved by a sensuous spinal indent that extends all of the way from the base of his powerful neck to the veed beginning of his asscrack. So matched are the twin globes of his buttocks that the edge of a putty knife would be as hard-pressed to breach their shared seam as to breach the juncture of some much-boasted example of fine-wrought Incan masonry. The lower curvatures of his buttocks form a well-defined "W" hung above the backs of his firm thighs, triangular calves, well-formed ankles, and big feet. The toes of the latter are parenthesized by the swirl of slowly draining shower.

He reveals more left bicep, then his well-delineated left pectoral to its golden-brown nipple. His stomach appears on the landscape of his increasingly helixed torso. His abdominals are ridged as any scallop shell.

His cock is presented before any proof of his equally impressive balls, because King's cock extends from his lower stomach, from compact bush of blond pubic hair, in a lengthy forward thrust of cockmeat that parallels the floor for only as long as it takes additional penile convulsions to heft the massive drawbridge more completely to vertical.

Within seconds, King's up-jutted and vein-striated cockshaft presents the full length of its broad and curved underbelly. His cascaded blond-hair scrotum shifts with the increased weight of constant cum-filling. His cockhead, stripped of all turtlenecking foreskin, is rocket-like. His cock's deeply cleaved meatus exudes an "Hello-there!" bead of pre-seminal fluid, like a jewelry setting presenting some rare and translucent crystal. The back of his cockglans rests upon the small bump of his pillowing navel.

"Just in case you have any doubts as to the final outcome of all of this," Boy says and hands King a waterproof packet that contains an extra-large condom.

Boy's own extra-large cock is hard, too, as it's stepped into the shower.

King's suddenly spread arms are an open invitation, and Boy eagerly enters the welcoming embrace.

Boy's face rests against the curvature of King's neck, and both of his hands mold the contours of King's muscled back even as King's massive hands flatten across Boy's spine. Boy's thumb-tack nipples indent the silky hardness of King's impressive chest. King's nipples, just as hard, poke the frontal creaminess of Boy's far thinner and far more boyish torso.

King's drawbridge dick is completely vertical, thickened, hardened, and pulsing, and it nestles more firmly beside Boy's cock, within the narrow space provided between their mated bellies. King's scrotum, gone more thick-skinned in his excitement, still hangs low enough, and possesses enough swing, to slap sexily against Boy's low-hanging balls, as the two wet figures commence their slow and sensuous grind.

"Oh, boy, Boy," King whispers. His lips butterfly-kiss the length of Boy's neck to one shoulder. He presses his mouth to the pulse spot at the base of Boy's neck, and he sucks at the pale wet skin.

His hands slide Boy's back, along and over the swell of Boy's ass, to cup Boy's buttcheeks. His fingertips meet within the upper tightness of Boy's anal crack. He takes hold of, and presses open, those dual mounds of Boy's butt, along their shared juncture. His fingers delve for another meeting, this time atop the hair-parenthesized pucker of Boy's rectum.

King's superb back provides the barricade that deflects shower-head spray into the wet background nimbus that leaves King's front, and all of Boy, pretty much free of deluge.

King turns slowly, with Boy, though, to put Boy's back toward the spray. In turn, King's ass is freed from the wash although left glossy.

Boy drops to his knees, uncaring how hard the water-slicked bathroom tiles. He's spellbound by the hypnotic hardness and metronome dance of King's erect penis so near his face. The cock, a monster from a distance, is genuinely gargantuan close-up, especially as another reflexive constriction of King's groin muscles slaps the hard dick back against King's belly button, with an accompanying splatter of preseminal goo that's soon washed away in the spray Boy's kneeling allows to splash the front of King's torso.

Boy kisses the burgeoned head of King's erection. Then, he looks upward, over King's washboard belly, beyond the overhang of King's chiseled pectorals, to the handsome face and passion-dilated eyes above and beyond.

"Soap, please," Boy says.

King obliges with a slick bar retrieved from a shower-wall niche, just off to one side.

Boy threads his right arm between King's legs, his other arm around King's flank. He successfully lathers all of his fingers. He cups his soapy right hand upward between King's legs. His thumb divides King's one nut from the other, his soapy fuck-finger sliding all of the way back and up onto the entrance of King's asshole.

"Finger-poke my asshole!" King commands.

Boy has every intention of doing just that, his suds-soaked finger quickly through King's camera-lens anal opening. Simultaneously, Boy's pursed lips return to the head of King's cock and exert the suction necessary to lever King's supporting cockshaft slightly away from muscled belly. Boy opens his mouth wider and successfully entraps entire penile corona and a good inch of cockshaft. The swallowed glans immediately provides additional pre-cum liquid, then gushes all the more when Boy's poking finger unceremoniously jabs King's prostate deep up finger-fucked rectum.

"Eat me!" King says, his voice guttural. His command, though, is superfluous, in that Boy is doing just that, feeling the bulged filigree of King's cockshaft veins, against hugging lips, as Boy's nose pushes all of the way to blond pubic bush.

Boy's chin punches King's contracting, thumb-separated, scrotum.

Boy wishes King's crotch less shower-clean. How he would relish stronger, even more manly, summer-heat groin smells, made exceedingly sexy in their raw and undiluted state.

King's hands go to Boy's head, fingers claw-like among water-soaked strawberry-blond strands. A helpless bucking of hips drives King's erection its final fraction of an inch into feeding face.

King's cock balloons even large and threatens Boy's air passage. The cock's heartbeat proclaims a life all of its own as King takes mercy and pulls Boy's face back along the length of mouth-sucked erection.

If Boy thinks King will push head right back on down, once lips again hug the grooved under-flare of cockcorona, he's wrong. King has other plans, as regards where he wants to blast his first hearty splashings of cum. He pulls Boy completely free of cock with an audible "Pop!" that's quickly followed by the resounding "Whack!" of King's freed penis rebounding to slap hard belly.

"My turn," King says and waits patiently for Boy, in no great hurry, to remove finger from rectum. The final exit of Boy's digit causes King's cock to leak more goo, and King to purr in accompaniment.

Boy comes to his feet, and King's mouth and tongue lick from the base of Boy's neck to the strawberry-blond-furred vee at the apex of Boy's trembling thighs. King's hands lag behind to reconnoiter the tack-like nubs of rosy Boy boy-nipples and massage, then pinch, each nipple to greater hardness.

When King licks back up Boy's stomach as far as the kid's belly button, he pauses to fill that slight navel indentation with spit, then to siphon the spit off, then to fill the cupping with spit again.

Boy's cock leaks wetness that drools all of the way into the strawberry-blond hair of the kid's balls.

King's mouth hovers over Boy's swollen erection.

Carefully, slowly, King's lips touch down and his mouth swallows each and every inch of Boy's stiffness, without pause. Then, he commences a series of long and lengthy bounces that spits the kid's cock out to its crown, then siphons the total right back down to the strawberry-blond hair that clusters Boy's thick cockroots.

For King, the familiar contours of Boy's erection in no way make his mouthful any the less sensuous. Quite to the contrary, it's reassuringly pleasurable for King to renew his acquaintance with a dick so well-suited to the spit-drenched terrain within which King presently locks it.

It's been a long time since King has indulged in sucking off any such pale-pale cock, having convinced himself he far prefers the more brown, darker, even pitch-black dicks of Mediterranean-type and/or

African porno stars. Now, though, there's no denying that Boy's more Scandinavian prick, all creamy white, accompanied by strawberry-blond bush, is as exotic as it is erotic.

"Mmmmmm," King hums over the cock once again slid so far into his face that his nose is tickled by the strawberry-blond hair on Boy's belly, King's chin tickled by the strawberry-blond strands that fuzz Boy's nuts.

"Eat my big dick, cocksucker!" Boy says, drops the soap with a bounce that dulls the bar's leading edge, and he buries both hands into the silky gone-wet strands of King's blond hair. His grip exerts the additional pressure that, had there only been more cock to swallow, would have socked King's face with whatever the remaining fraction of an inch.

When King sucks, swallows, then sucks, then swallows again, the juices he retrieves from the length of Boy's cock are like liquid siphoned through an impressive length of hose.

"Oh, sweet Jesus!" Boy says and moans.

King again swallows and sends his throat muscles into a rubber-glove compression that vibrates around the entire length of Boy's submerged dick.

Boy throws back his head, his Adam's-apple suddenly thrust into bas-relief.   Boy's lower body provides the sensuous grind that chafes strawberry-blond hair against King's nose, cheeks, and chin.

King knows what sucking techniques Boy likes best. That knowledge not having been in the least dimmed, nor forgotten, in spite of long neglect. So, he twists his face, and pulls his lips tightly up Boy's cock to cockhead, despite the pressure of Boy's fingers that deceptively seem determined to make King's head stay put.

King runs his hands upward into the water-cascaded crack of Boy's ass and, although King's fingers and Boy's asscheeks have long been washed free of all trace of whatever natural body fluids that might be used as lubricant, King fucks his right fuck-finger deeply into Boy's rectum.

"Christ!" Boy says and low-moans. His pelvis fucks forward in a reflex designed to put Boy's cock back, all of the way, into King's face, and to allow Boy's asshole escape from any additional sticking by King's fuck-finger.

King's free hand finds Boy's nuts, takes hold, and gives a squeeze.

"Goddamn! Goddamn!" says Boy, suddenly molested, one and the same time, on three different fronts: at cock, at ass, and at balls.

Shower water splatters Boy's back, runs his spine and flushes the crack of his ass. Whirlpools of liquid eddy the base of King's stuck fuck-finger and, from there, proceed downward along King's arm to waterfall into the ankle-deep flooding on the floor.

As if there has never been a lengthy break in his schedule of regularly sucking this particular penis, or of his finger-fucking this particular asshole, King's coordinated attacks ream Boy's asshole, orally maul the kid's stiff cock, and vise the young man's tender gonads.

Boy reacts like a puppet on strings that, though played by a master, gives jerky movements in indication of a puppeteer temporarily out of control. Boy's dancing fucks his cock in King's face, fucks his butt over King's probing finger, collides his nuts all the more within King's massaging fingers.

"Oh, shit ... oh, shit!" says Boy and gives a flip of his head that's supposed to move his wet-heavy hair out of his eyes but doesn't. His expression is halfway between angel's smile and victim's grimace, but that's only because he can't decide whether King's assaults are pleasurably painful or vice versa.

King's expertise is what makes his at-sex action such desirable viewing for voyeurs who get off on watching. He doesn't gag, not even once, where Boy's dick is certainly big enough to choke any novice. He never once screws up the rhythmic cadence of his head's down-and-up, up-and-down, bounces. He never once screws his finger too hard, or too deeply, up Boy's butt. He never once squeezes Boy's nuts too hard.

Boy's cock is never made unacceptably limp for the cameras, by any too-far crossings-over of pain thresholds.

Boy flies higher than he ever thought possible, at this early stage of the game. If he remembers just how good King was, in the past, at sucking dick -- and he does -- he's not forgotten, either, that King regularly does this sort of thing for a living. King has a whole new repertoire of sexual tricks, upon which to call, that wasn't at his disposal when last he swallowed and sucked Boy's hard and steely erection.

"Easy! Easy!" Boy is forced into chanting, because he's genuinely embarrassed by how quickly King teeters him on the edge of bona-fide orgasm. "Easy, or ... easy, or ... Jesus, or ... you, bastard ... bastard ... Oh, Jesus, bastard ... I'll ... I'll ... I'll ... I'll ..."

King's finger twists up Boy's ass, and King simultaneously sucks the kid's dick to burgeoned cockroots. King crooks his butt-submerged finger and torques it hard and fast against the tender nub of Boy's prostate. King helixes his face around the total length and circumference of Boy's cock until Boy fears his dick is being screwed loose.

"Cum! Cum! I'll ... fucking ... come!" screams Boy.

Knowing he shouldn't, but unable to control himself, Boy tries his damnedest to keep King's face anchored all of the way down as sucked dick pulses in final prelude to actual release of cannon-fodder goo.

King, though, has had some of the cleverest and strongest gays in the porno business reflexively try everything in the book to deprive, albeit usually inadvertently, the camera of its all-important cum-shot. Therefore, King gets his way, and the film-maker gets his way, by King popping his head completely free of Boy's dick.

(CUM-SHOT!)
(JESUS, GET THE FUCKING CUM-SHOT!)

Boy's freed dick whips right and left, up and down: a fire hose out of control, spewing great gushes of cum to King's hair, forehead, cheeks, nose, chin, neck, and chest. Boy's cock gyrates so frantically that even Boy's initial attempts to grab it miss their mark. When he finally does capture his dick, Boy trembles as he holds so tightly to his prize that he seems determined to strangle off any additional helter-skelter spewing of his life-force.

Taking advantage, King's tongue, long, large, and wet, laps at the sticky head of Boy's cum-depleted erection, much as a little kid licks the rosy-red head of a saliva-wet cherry lolly.

By the time King gets to his feet, Boy hopes to proceed with a better show of self-control. He extends his right arm, seemingly to shake hands. Instead, he rolls his extended hand palm-up and curls his fingers slightly. His thumb leads to hook between the up-jutting stiffness of King's cock and the well-defined scallops of King's abdominals. He tugs King's erection to a firm lie-down within Boy's extended palm, and seemingly threatens to snap the claimed dick off at its turgid base.

When he's succeeded in putting the extended cock parallel to the floor, Boy's fist slides toward King, as far as possible, along the cock-shaft until the "O" of Boy's thumb and forefinger burrows King's blond pubic hair.

Boy's fist closes all the tighter on around King's dick and tugs to milk King's huge sexual pap until the heel of Boy's fist extends beyond the tip of King's penis and claims the last sticky drool from King's cocktip.

With a forward push, Boy's fist torques back along cockshaft and smears the powerful sexual truncheon with its own juices.

"Jesus! Sweet Jesus!" King says with an accompanying groan of appreciation. His large hands anchor on the smooth curve of Boy's shoulders. With a forward buck, he thrusts his penis through Boy's hand as soon as the young man's fist returns for another pause over King's cockhead.

King's lower body commences a back-and-forth swing that works his cock's stiffness within Boy's hand, much as King's cock might fuck Boy's asshole. He's fascinated by the appearance and disappearance of his cockhead through Boy's hugging fingers, each and every time his cock smears with more and more leakage.

"While it'll be easy enough to shoot off in your hand, what say I give my dick a bit of fun and games up the tight hole of your funky pale-pale ass?" King says.

"You're talking to the guy who stepped into this shower with a rubber, just in case, remember? Although, let me get the soap to make sure that giant dick of yours has every chance for a successful slide up my butthole."

Boy figures he has all the time in the world -- "fill-space" -- while King rubberizes fat dick for fucking. Most of the time, film footage taken of actors putting on rubbers ends up on the cutting-room floor, because many movie-goers find the whole interruption-of-flow a disconcerting turn-off. However, because more and more film-makers are succumbing to outside political and moral pressure to portray safe sex, minor inconveniences and all, King knows how to don a condom in record time -- just in case the footage is included in the final cut.

Therefore, not only does King have the condom out of its packet and raincoating his dick, while Boy still attempts to retrieve an exceptionally slippery bar of soap from a corner of the stall, but he has his newly rubberized dick rammed up Boy's ass as well. Not just an inch of his dick inserted, either, but all of it, to the point where King's hard belly slams Boy's upturned ass with a momentum that would propel Boy into the wall opposite, except King's hands clamps hard to the strawberry-blond's hips and provides badly needed balance.

Boy has been completely caught off-guard. No doubt about it. His eyes go impressively large. His mouth opens and shuts -- opens and shuts -- like a fish out of water, producing a watery-like gargle, by way of guppy sound effects. As if on automatic pilot, though he feels he's experiencing a tree trunk thrust up his rectum, Boy keeps his hands on their continued sweep for the soap, his right hand finally palming the recalcitrant bar, even though the lubricant it offers is suddenly super-fluous.

"Jesus, tight ass!" says King and lets go his handholds on Boy only long enough to slap the kid's upturned, and thoroughly-fucked butt, and set assflesh into earthquake tremors as he takes hold again.

In retrospect, his surprised ass actually having fond remembrances of King's cock, which allows the asshole faster adjustment to its present stuffing, than would otherwise have been the case, Boy should have anticipated this turn of events. Kendall having warned him to expect improvisation which comes off far more natural, on screen, than any-thing originally scripted.

Why else a lubricated rubber given Boy as a prop to carry into the shower, if not to assist the possibility of King's cock up Boy's asshole, without need for any as-written-in-the-script soapy accompaniment?

Boy lets the soap go, gliding it across water-soaked floor and out of the way. King or Boy slipping on the bar isn't the kind of improvisation appreciated by discerning viewers, by film-maker, by participants, or by anyone else.

As far as acceptable improvisation, Boy has some ideas of his own. He has no intentions of coming off as virgin butt taken off guard by King's expert maneuvering, no matter how appealing some viewers might find that scenario. Boy has had his fair share of sexual adven-tures, and maybe -- just maybe -- he has a few tricks of his own for the audience that not even super porno star King Richard, what with all the bastard's sexual know-how, can easily match.

(GODDMAN, YOU TWO, GIVE US WITH A BETTER CAMERA ANGLE!)

Boy stays bent at his waist but continually shifts his stance, ever so slightly. Finally, Boy merely lets King's power-fucking move them both slowly forward, one inch at a time, until Boy's head is bowed far enough into one shower corner to put one of his shoulders to each of the veed walls. He lets the next series of King's belly-to-butt thumps wedge him into the corner all the more tightly, Boy's upper body going into a deeper and deeper curl.

Boy takes hold of his cock, which is still significantly softened by its previous blast-off, and he stretches its length to where his mouth can get at it.

(DAMN, GET A SHOT OF THE KID SUCKING HIS OWN JOINT!)
(JERRY, GET YOUR CAMERA OVER WHERE YOU CAN COME IN CLOSE ON BOY'S SUCKING!)

Boy's cock still isn't into full resurrection, but it won't take all that long to achieve that desired status. Not long at all, what with the increased momentum of King's cock fucking Boy's butt, combined with the been-here-before sucking Boy delivers the head of his own prick.

Within a very few seconds, Boy's cock, like a cable muscled into tautness between two points, distinctly loses its central sag and visibly stiffens its bridge between Boy's fucking face and the kid's strawberry-blond furred crotch.

Boy's left hand takes hold of his left calf, pulling tenaciously to increase the arc of the kid's spine. Boy's right hand travels beneath his strawberry-blond hair balls and up behind his ass into the breach filled by the swing of King's steadily compacting scrotum.

Boy grabs King's nuts and compresses his fingers to make the blond stud's nuts collide within the resulting squeeze.

"Jeeesus!" King says, and his fuck progresses into even higher gear.

(GET A SHOT OF BOY FONDLING KING'S NUTS!)
(GET MORE OF BOY'S SELF-SUCKING!)
(SHOW ME A GOOD FINALE CUM-SHOT, KING, OR YOU'RE NOT THE STAR WE KNOW YOU ARE!)

Boy feels very much in his element. It's now confirmed that King has been saving all of the vim and vigor of their high-school years for his performances before the camera, and Boy is delighted to experience, again, all of the teenage intensity he'd once known beneath King's skewering erections. King's ongoing enthusiasm spurs Boy into wanting even more of the same.

The kid revolves his pale butt, drops his face deeper over the length of his pale pole, and squeezes King's blond nuts all the more.

Boy has always known he'd be a natural at this fucking-and-sucking stuff in front of the camera. Hell, he was born to be a porno star. He is destined to be even better at it than King. Boy feels that with a certainty that prevails within his each and every bone, including within the phallic bone he so vigorously sucks between his legs.

Boy is a fool for ever having allowed himself to be waylaid from this, his one true calling as porno-star extraordinaire. No wonder he never made it in the legit end of the film business, having never had the enthusiasm for all of that need-to-take-classes "acting" shit that he has for what's taking place, here and now, cock up his ass, his mouth laving his own dick like sixty. Boy is a virtual fuck and self-suck machine!

Boy swallows more of his cock. He can tell, from old times, that King's balls, still contained securely within Boy's hand, are priming for discharge. Boy hopes that he'll be able to time his suck-off blast-off to coincide with King's upcoming orgasm. It will be interesting to see which explosion ends up receiving more film-time in final editing.

(MAKE THE FUCK LAST, KING!)

Boy doubts King will allow the butt-screw to progress much farther. No way, no matter what King says about not being worried about the competition, is the veteran porno star going to want his rip-roaring orgasm sharing screen time with any simultaneous explosion of newcomer Boy's cock into newcomer Boy's feasting face.

"Get ready!" King says.

(COME ON, KING, YOU CAN MAKE IT LAST, SO DO IT!)
(ENDURANCE IS WHAT YOU GET PAID THE BIG BUCKS FOR, FOR CHRIST'S SAKE!)

"Fuck you!" says King.

His scrotum is a glove of tough and hirsute skin pulled almost as tightly around his balls as Boy's fingers are squeezed around the whole.

Boy figures to prolong the exercise at least a few seconds more by exerting even more of a vise to King's cum-ballooned gonads. Boy figures all it will take will be a touch of additional pain to keep King from ...

"I'm going to come!" defies King.

Nonetheless, Boy squeezes the bastard's balls all the harder.

"I'm going to come!" persists King, despite all of Boy's efforts to hold off the inevitable conclusion for just one ... more ... moment ... longer.

The tug of King's cock from Boy's asshole is so powerfully achieved that the blond stud's scrotum is dangerously stretched by Boy's continuing handhold on it. Once free of the asshole, King's cock immediately inserts into King's whipping fist long enough for King expertly to unroll and discard the rubber.

Then, unhanded, King's naked cock slides its belly, like a streamline sled preparing for a fast and furious run down a slippery luge run, back and forth, back and forth, along the vee formed by the upper juncture of Boy's asscheeks.

The first comet-like blasts of King's spunk hit the corner of the shower and stick like spider-webbing. The next hearty spermal blasts provide parabolas that dead-end, like coagulating paraffin, within Boy's strawberry-blond hair. The final, less powerfully blasted bullets, speckle the nape of the kid's pale neck and the length of the kid's pale back.

In a final reclaiming of his cock, by his right hand, King's fingers expertly milk his penis for the very last drop of its tardy sperm. Coaxed from his now-strangled cockneck, a cascading of goo drools the crease of Boy's ass, like icing cascades a fissure in the rim of a pale-white cake.

(DAMN IT, KING, YOU SHOULD HAVE WAITED UNTIL THE KID'S COCK LET GO!)

"So, who says I'm finished?" King says and gives Boy's asscheeks a loud whack, an open palm heartily laid hard to each wet and sweaty buttcheek. "Or did I just use the last condom budgeted for this cheap movie?"

(GET HIM A FRESH RUBBER AND KEEP ON FILMING, YOU MORONS!)

King rubberizes his cock even faster than it took him to shed the condom that preceded it. His cock is so quickly back up Boy's ass, so quickly fucking away, all stiff and steely hard, that Boy isn't sure there's even been a pause in the proceedings.

"You want a mutual climax, we'll see what we can do," says King.

(GODDAMN, I DO LOVE A STUD WITH SUPERHUMAN ENDURANCE!)
(BOY, TIME TO SHOW US WHAT YOU CAN DO, TOO!)

King's cock back up Boy's butt, Boy's cock up its owner's mouth and throat, Boy is fully aware of two alternatives. One, he can proceed posthaste to get his rocks off and make King come off guilty of ill-timing in not having held out for a mutual blow the last time his cock fucked Boy's ass. Two, Boy can bide his time, take it slow and easy, advantage his familiarity with his own dick and his skills at auto-fellatio to parcel out his self-pleasure until King catches up. Boy and King proceeding in tandem from there. It not likely to take King all that long, which Boy very well knows. Even when King isn't at his best, he has always shown, at least in Boy's presence, superlative ability at recovering sexual prowess for multiple repeats.

Boy's conviction that he is destined for starring roles in porno films, and has been so destined from Day One, is bolstered by how easily he decides to choose alternative two. Mutual orgasm what the director wants and hopes for. Mutual orgasm what the audience wants and hopes for. Therefore, mutual orgasm what any full-fledged porno pro should strive to achieve. No matter what personal satisfaction Boy might derive from making King come off less the professional he's supposed, and is rumored, to be.

After all, Boy still likes King. Their history has been loving, friendly, amiable. Boy's split with King, in favor of Leo, had been free of stress and recriminations. Boy can even forgive King's efforts to keep Boy out of the porno business, even though Boy hopes King now sees, as well as does Boy, how wrong King has been in having done so. King has been merely anxious for Boy to consider his options, which Boy has done. King sweet to the end, in insinuating that Boy ever had a genuine chance in the legitimate mainline cinema. Boy, now, convinced that whatever genuine talent he has is best highlighted by the makers of this porno flick, and by the countless other porno flicks, starring Boy, that the kid expects to come after.

"Mmmmmm!" Boy hums around his own cock. Since, by now, he has the total impressive inches of his erection pressed on through his receiving lips, the vibrations from his sounds tickle the entire length of his priming pecker.

"Fuck ... fuck ... fuck," King says, keeping verbal cadence to each and every in-and-out of his cock within Boy's tight asshole.

Boy judges where King is on the road to sexual recovery. A butt fucked for its first time might be hard-pressed to distinguish between the hardness of King's cock, now, and the same cock's hardness just awhile back, but Boy's ass isn't first-time, by way of getting plugged by King's dick. The present stiffness up Boy's asshole requires a bit more workout to get to its optimum steeliness. Then, it needs a bit more friction, up Boy's butt, before it's fully capable of squirting any new pulsations of thick and creamy cum.

Boy self-sucks in accordance with how he figures both King and he build toward climax. He allows the constant slapping of his ass by King's pelvis, on each forward swing, and the equally quick withdrawal of King's fat penis to its head, provide the majority of movement of Boy's cock in Boy's face. He puts on a really good show -- a lot of wet and drooling sounds -- to make it seem he provides his dick a far greater workout than is really the case.

Boy's scrotum, usually pretty much pulled flush to the base of his cock, during orgasm, still has enough slack for definite swing momentum, and Boy watches that back-and-forth, especially when, in close-up, his nose nudges the spot where the belly of his dick connects to his balls.

King, in order to provide the cameras with as much uninterrupted shooting as possible, as regards what his cock does to Boy's butt, puts both of his hands behind his back, his right hand locking his left wrist. His legs slightly flex at their knees, and his hips provide the back-and-forth rhythm sufficient to yank his cock out to its head and put it back to his balls.

King can tell Boy bides his time. That the kid waits for King's renewed sexual prowess tells King that Boy already knows what acting in porno movies is all about. No doubt, the kid is a natural. No doubt, Boy will prove as popular to film-goers as Kendall has always predicted.

William Maltese

Nonetheless, King remains saddened that someone with Boy's acting talents, above and beyond the sexual, are likely to vanish under the
focus of productions that care less about character, and about character development, than about a guy's big dick, or willing asshole, and
what's being done to or with them.

No rewards to be had in crying over spilled milk, however, is how
King figures, as his so-recently spent passions arise anew within him.
No doubt, Boy's asshole is successfully resurrecting King's desires as
well as the solidness of King's dick, and it will probably do the same for
most other porno stars in the business. Good thing, because, what with
the cameras rolling, Boy is pretty much committed to the choice he's
made. While King can name a couple porno stars, one male, one
female, who went on to moderate success in mainline movies, neither
of those had appeared in gay porno. Boy, appearing in gay XXX-sex,
can wave any chance of success in legit film bye-bye for good. A
shame, except that, as King fucks and fucks away, there's no denying
that Boy has no problems whatsoever in adapting to each and every
nuisance his chosen career is more than likely ready to demand of him.

King slides his hands around and down to his crotch, so that his
thumbs hook the back of his butt-fucking dick, his fingers angling downward to parenthesize his cock and balls. By pressing both hands
inward at his lower belly, he makes his pumping dick all the longer and
stiffer.

Boy's nuts elevate the extra fraction of an inch that allows the kid full
viewing beneath them, all of the way up the crack of his ass to where
he can actually see King's cock going in and coming out of Boy's rose-
bud asshole. Boy's nose burrows so deeply between his legs that, his
cock completely lost inside his mouth and throat, he would smell his
own asshole if it wasn't so sanitized by shower water.

"Okay, kid," King says, by way of alerting his partner to the fact that
passions, once waned, have waxed full once again. He suspects Boy
still a good judge of where King is, by way of onward to orgasm. Past
practice has made Boy acutely aware of telltale signs, like King's elevated scrotum, King's faster fuck-strokes, King's sudden all-over blush,
King's breathless little grunts, but it has been a long time, prior to this
filming of "Dangling", that the two last fucked. Under the best of circumstances, mutual orgasm is difficult to achieve. It happens more in
books than in real life. If it seems to appear more often than not in fuck

films that's only because ingenious editing inserts cum-shots that never really happened at one and the same time.

Holding tight to both of his calves, Boy pulls himself into a more complete bend. Boy's nose presses hard into the cord that runs from the base of his dick to his asshole. Later playback will show his head all of the way between his legs, certainly far enough to see and recognize the compact state of King's balls and react accordingly.

Boy increases the compression of his lips around his cock. While King's continued fucking of the kid's butt continues to provide much of the impetus that works Boy's dick inside Boy's sucking face, the kid now supplements by surrendering more of his cock inches on each withdrawal motion of King's cock from Boy's asshole.

Likewise, Boy's tongue goes to work, concentrating on that one spot, on his cockbelly, where his cockhead flares from his cockshaft, that is particularly sensitive and push-button as far as increasing the level of Boy's spiraling enjoyment.

Boy increases the suction provided by his suck. Not only do his cheeks concave along the full face-fucking length of his self-fellatioed dick, but his whole throat collapses to strangle the kid's cockmeat.

"Riding high," says King. Frankly, he's surprised by how quickly he approaches orgasm. No denying, though, that he finds fucking Boy's ass, pretty much with the vim and vigor that he'd mustered in their high-school days, a genuine turn-on. Despite all of the indications he's had that he's graduated to a preference for more muscled, studly bodies, with tan-to-dark complexions, he genuinely is excited by once again putting his stiff meat to Boy's pale-but-tight asshole whose opening is haloed by strawberry-blond hair that mingles with King's blond pubic strands on each forward swat of King's belly into Boy's buttocks.

(CUM SHOTS, BASTARDS!)
(DEAR GOD, GIVE ME THOSE MONEY-IN-THE-BANK DUAL COMES!)

Since Boy's ability to speak is pretty much impeded, except for the slurping sounds he manages around his face-sticking dick, he counts upon King to provide whatever verbal guidelines to tell Boy where King is, en route to orgasm, so Boy hopefully can coordinate to join him.

"On a scale of one to ten, I'm up to eight, kid," King doesn't disappoint.

– 51 –

Boy is pleased that his butt brings King's cock so far so fast. No doubt, the two have always been good together, but high-school times had always been better -- at least until now.

Boy sucks his dick in greater earnestness, freeing one hand to caress his balls.

"Now at nine, on a scale of nine to ten," says King. He's still in control of the feed and withdrawal of his erection, in and out of Boy's asshole, but that control is about to slip into that mode completely monitored by more primitive centers than his conscious brain.

Maybe, thinks King, his build-up turns out to be too fast for Boy's expectations. Hell, not even King dreamt he'd be where he is now after having so shortly before seen his balls seemingly emptied of their full-capacity load of creamy cum.

King tries to slow his fucking momentum. He anchors his hands firmly to Boy's hips with every intention of using his handholds to aid in slowing the speedy bang of his cock into, and the hearty sliding of cock out of, Boy's upturned ass. All King achieves is an increased fucking rhythm.

If he questioned before, King knows for certain, now, that the fuck has pretty much achieved a life of its own. From this point on, it will be all King can do to provide himself with the concentration and willpower necessary to deprive his hyped senses of the final luxurious flooding of his cum up Boy's sucking butt, in order to provide the voyeuristic viewers of "Dangling" with the all-important cum-shot that can only be filmed with King's cock pulled completely free of Boy's thoroughly fucked asshole and skillfully disrobed of its rubber.

"Ten for ten!" King says.

Like most of the dialogue during shooting, this has a fifty-fifty chance of appearing in the final cut, even though it's not scripted. Whatever dialogue, on and off camera, that occurs but isn't suited to the story format (King once heard a well-know, well-hung, porno-star complain, albeit not of King or King's butt: "Fucking this guy's asshole is like fucking an empty barn!"), is deleted by voice-overs, and/or by a soundtrack of simple grunts and groans, and/or by building-to-crescendo musical accompaniment.

Boy only hopes that when King said "Ready" that he meant just that, because Boy reaches a state of excitement that requires superhuman capabilities to abort, and Boy -- at the moment -- isn't feeling particularly superhuman. Cum fills his nuts to capacity, his balls a weighty burden, even though his scrotum, once again, provides the powerful compaction of thickened skin that almost completely disappears Boy's gonads into his lower belly at the base of his face-fucked dick.

"Incoming cum, kid!" warns King. "Oh ... Jesus ... Jesus ... incoming ... cum ... cum ... Jesus ... cum!"

His cock pops free of its anal slot, its belly thrusting forward along the slideway of Boy's back.

No need for King to manhandle his primed prick beyond simple removal of its rubber. The whole length and circumference of his erection has been stroked to grand finale by Boy's asshole. TNT would be less likely, than King's dick, to explode.

"Christ!" says King, his fingers claw-like on Boy's hips.

Boy's face pulls forward and off his dick. His cock squirts, even as King's cock lets go in a spray of molten spermal magma that rains droplets of hot goo along the entire curvature of Boy's back.

(CHRIST, YES, YES, YES!)
(SLOW-MO THOSE SEEDY GALLONS!)

Boy's cum splatters his face and neck. He licks a particularly viscous glob of the stuff as it clings precariously to his lower lip. When he swallows, he tastes the saltiness of his cum as it slides all of the way down to his belly.

Even at regular film speed, the mutual climaxes go impressively on ... and on ... and on. Even the very last of the cum to find its way out the tunnels of long dicks does so with an impressive squirt and not with a mere snot-like drool.

(CUT!)
(PRINT!)
(WRAP!)
(FUCKING GREAT!)
(IS THERE A BONERLESS GENT IN THE HOUSE?!)

William Maltese

p.m., Day Fourteen:

"Go ahead, it's your ten dollars."

"Tanner? Where in the bloody hell have you been?"

"Out. On vacation. Attending a jerk-off marathon. By the way, to whom am I speaking, please?"

"Don't fuck with me, kid! I've been trying to get hold of you for the past three days."

"Well, Monty, believe it or not, I do have a life without you. When I think of all the wasted hours I've sat right here, by the phone, waiting for you to call, well ...." "Why the hell wasn't your answering machine on?"

"Well, Monty, it goes something like this: a couple of weeks ago, the damned machine went belly-up, and I've been waiting, since then, to buy another one with the money I earn from all the acting jobs you, my agent, gets me. The way I have it figured, had I counted upon you, I may -- just may -- have had enough cash for that replacement somewhere around the year three-thousand-and-three."

"Yeah, well ...."

"Although things may suddenly be looking up for me, Monty, old pal, old agent, old ...."

"Who the hell told you?"

"I don't need anyone to tell me shit, do I? Can think for myself, can't I? No help from my -- quote -- agent -- unquote?"

"I'm talking the call-back. What in the hell are you talking?"

"What call-back?"

"They want you for another read."

"Who?"

"FantasyWorld, for Christ's sake! Who the hell else? Get your fucking head out of your ass and listen to what I'm saying here!"

"You expect me to get excited by another call-back from FantasyWorld when I'm, once again, one among thousands?"

"One among two, you asshole! Two! Two! Got that? It's down to you and you-know-who. If the powers-that-be decide on a big-name, then you-know-who gets it. If they decide to risk on an unknown, the part is yours."

"You're pulling my leg, aren't you Monty?"

"Don't fuck this up, kid. Don't you dare fuck this up! This could be the beginning of big things for both of us in this town."

"There's not a chance of a snowball in hell I'll get that part, no matter how many times I read for it, is there, Monty?"

"Maybe not. Then again, miracles happen, don't they? Even if this isn't 'the' miracle, you down to the last one-on-one cut causes a lot of people to sit up and take notice."

"Jesus! Jesus! Jesus!"

"Tanner?"

"Yeah, Monty?"

"Tell me that was excitement I heard."

"Yeah, excitement."

"Because, you should be excited, kid. I know, I sure as hell am."

"It was excitement you heard, Monty. It is excitement you hear."

"Get a piece of paper and a pencil and write this down, kid. You haven't forgotten how to write over the last few days, have you?"

p.m., Day Four-hundred-fifteen:

"I have been instructed by my client, Tanner Wilson, to issue the following statement on his behalf, and on behalf of my firm Jenner, Jenner, Payne-Sampson, and Scott.

"Our having filed for an injunction against Bigg Gunn Shoots, as regards any and all use, and/or showing, and/or distribution of its erotic film 'Dangling', as well as a cease-and-desist as regards any and all future utilization of my client's name, and/or likeness, and/or insinuation thereof, by that company, as pertains to that film in question. Substantial damages being asked, on behalf of my client, as a result of the defamation, and the severe mental stress, having occurred because of the utilization, by Bigg Gunn Shoots, of a body-double, and/or -doubles, via electronically, and/or other means, to give the appearance and/or impression that my client was and/or is a participant in said movie and in its promotions.

"It a sad reflection on our society, and on our times, when a company on the very farthest fringes, like Bigg Gunn Shoots, feels free to ride the coattails of good publicity generated by the much-ballyhooed late-

William Maltese

in-the-game selection of my client, from a field of virtually thousands of young actors, for the key role of Johnny, in the soon-to-be-released FantasyWorld Production blockbuster 'Lusitania'. That Bigg Gunn Shoots has so unabashedly accessed modern computer technology to morph my client's head on some porno star's body, the porno star in question performing sexual acts that can only be described as lewd, lascivious, and abhorrent to the majority of society, only makes what has been done all the more demanding of substantial legal redress, surely to be ordered by our judicial system, to be paid by Bigg Gunn Shoots, to my client. Only by putting society's collective foot down now, can we save ourselves, and save our children, and save our children's children, from what shows all indications of becoming a runaway train of technological abuses, and invasions of individual privacy, within the ongoing computer age.

"Thank-you."

COP OUT

Nothing brings out weirdoes like a hot-hot summer night and a full moon.

In case you haven't noticed (meaning being of zilch IQ), this is a hot-hot summer night, as evidenced by the way my purposely baggy shirt still manages to stick to parts of my sweat-soaked upper torso.

If you say you can't see any full moon, that's only because all the city lights run interference; any good almanac will tell you the moon, full as can be, is up there somewhere.

As for the weirdoes, the chances are more than likely there's yet another headed, even now, in my direction in that car that slowing draws up to the curb.

Except, I recognize the driver. His coal-black hair, cut short without sidewalls. Square jawline. Cleft chin. Full lips. Excellent physique.

Blue eyes, although my remembrance of that isn't confirmed until I hurriedly open his car door, and the immediately triggered dome light better illuminates his nervous stare at me.

His smile is nice, albeit tentative; more than a little antsy, as well it should be.

"Get the car moving and be quick about it," I say, "unless you want to become part of the police's latest arrest-a-queer project. Cops are all over here this evening."

He looks as if he may order me out, but he doesn't. Instead, he puts the car in gear.

"A quick right here," I say when we reach the designated corner, "followed by a fast left into the first alley."

He obliges. Probably not all that concerned that I may be leading him off to a mugging, because he knows he has the physical advantage. Were I to have associates waiting in the shadows, I have no doubt my driver has a gun under the seat that could take care of them, too.

"A bit faster, please," I say and put my foot on his gas-pedal foot, in order to send his car into greater speed, through three empty -- thank

God! -- crossroads. "Next left," I say and return to him all control of the gas so he can make the requested tight turn at a speed that won't have us careening off buildings.

After which, I count off two more alleys and direct him into the third.

"Park in the alcove behind those three Dumpsters," I say and leave him to it.

With the sensory perception of a bat, he wedges the car into the available slot. He cuts the motor.

"You're a cop," I say into the silence that follows the motor sounds that, now dead, had, despite our sometimes high speeds, been incredibly low-and-smooth.

"I look like a cop?" he says.

What he looks like is one all-butch stud, from the word go!

"That wasn't a question, guy," I say. "It was a statement. I used to live in Brentridge Hills, and you were called to my building on a domestic."

"Jesus!" he says.

"You part of this latest ongoing catch-a-queer operation?" I ask.

"Hardly," he says.

"What, then?"

"I liked your looks."

"Right. And, you've a bridge you'd like to sell me in San Francisco."

"I just separated from my wife," he says, "because I was having more and more trouble getting my cock up for what she has between her legs; rather, what she doesn't have between her legs."

Sure! Studs, like he, fall into my lap, every day of the year. Not!

"You're gay?" I say and make it a question.

"Used to figure myself bi, but marriage cured me of that illusion."

"You out for a little action?"

"As I said, I liked (like) your looks."

"And, you have no objections to my patting you down to assure myself you're not wearing a wire?"

"Be my guest."

I shift to my left to better get at him, and I take my time, starting at his head (as if he may actually have wiring braided into his short hair, or hanging from his ears, or draped along his muscle-corded neck). It's sexy as hell running my fingers along his arms, down his back to its small, along the clothed contours of his muscled pectorals (square), his ridged abdominals (scalloped), his sexy navel (innie).

Momentarily, I bypass his obviously impressive crotch-bulge to fondle both of his legs, finding not an iota of fat on either of them, nor having found any anywhere else on his well-sculptured body.

Finally, I slide my right hand, fingers up and leading, along the car seat and into his veed crotch. My fingers nuzzle between the seat and his ass, cupping his balls. The side of my little finger rubs his stiff dick that's anchored downward along his right thigh.

"You happy to see me, or is that some kind of phallic broadcasting device in your pants?"

He doesn't answer. His eyes are shut. His head is fallen slightly back on his powerful neck, his Adam's apple a sensuous punctuation mark.

"You okay?" I ask. He looks more than okay. He looks good enough to eat.

"You know the last time a guy fondled my crotch?" His eyes are still shut, his head still hung slightly back. He licks his lips and makes their fullness sexually glossy with spit. He swallows, and his Adam's apple moves up, then down.

My hand shifts to better pet his presented evidence of big cock. Beneath the material of his pants leg, his outer layer of cockskin shifts sensuously beneath my exerted pressure, gliding one way along the hardness of his cockcore, then back again.

"When was the last time you had a guy fondle your crotch?" I answer his question with a question. "As sexy as you look, it was probably only an hour ago."

Does he know there was a period of weeks in which I, every night, fantasized fondling his crotch -- and not all that long ago? Does he know that I always figured my odds of latching onto the real thing were about a billion-to-one?

"The last time was in high school," he says. "In fucking high school."

"How do I know there's not a cadre of your fellow police officers out there, right now, one of those sound-detection units aimed in our direction and recording all of this bullshit?" I ask.

"Associates hearing me say just how much I'd like to suck your cock, you mean?" he says.

His suddenly open eyes readily portray his get-real attitude. He has bedroom-sexy eyes, by the way: blue-made-black by the shadows, dilated centers even blacker. His eyebrows are thick but not too thick, the space between them having just enough fine, stray, hair to appear "naturally vacant" and not "purposely plucked". His eyelashes are, by far, the thickest I've seen, on male or female, bar none.

"Your lawyer would have you out of the slammer in seconds, right-fully claiming entrapment," he says.

He covers my buried-at-his-crotch hand with his right hand and increases the friction my palm exerts against and along his erection.

"We may not have much time," I say. "The cops are swarming, this evening, like ants over sugar. Might have been safer for you to have checked for vice activity, in the area, before you showed up."

"I'm not from this precinct," he says. "I would have had trouble explaining my need-to-know."

"I'm not saying we don't have enough time," I say. Having been pre-sented this stroke of good luck, I intend to take whatever the danger-fraught time to advantage it fully. "I mean if you've not had your rocks off with another guy since high school .... Not, mind you, that you look all that far removed from the high-school classroom."

"Speaking of classrooms, how old are you?"

"A little late for that, isn't it?" I say.

"Tell me you're underage, and you'll see how quickly all of this stops, here and now."

"I'm flattered," I say, "but I've been legal for far longer than I care to admit."

"If you're legal, it's only barely, and don't try to tell me otherwise."

"So, having gotten that hopefully final obstacle out of our way, what do you have in mind for this evening?"

Hell, he can ask for the moon, and I'd likely try to produce it for him. Being with him makes me just that hot and horny. And, it's not as if I haven't had my opportunities to suck and fuck some thoroughly hand-some dudes. All self-flattery aside, I'm not all that hard to look at; although, I'm far too skinny and boyish for my own tastes. I've the looks that people, who claim to know, describe as "farm-boy naive", possibly because of my perpetually tousled blond hair that gives the false impression I'm fresh from a romp in the hay. Or, maybe it's because I'm so well tanned for a blond, thereby giving the false impression that I work mainly out-of-doors.

"Officer Pringle!" I say. His name just popped into mind. "Like the potato chips, only singular"

"And, why don't I remember you?" he says. "And, don't say I wouldn't have noticed you at the time."

"Kind of hard to notice bystanders when you're wrestling a knife-wielding bitch to the ground, her rabid and gut-bleeding boyfriend trying to get at her, too."

"So," he says with a quick exhalation of breath, "what now?"

"Depends upon what you'd like to happen, remember?"

"What I'd like to happen, having gotten this far, is anything and everything."

"Maybe, we should just get your rocks off and save anything/everything for some less cop-saturated evening?"

"I can see you again, then?"

"You might not even want to see me again when you find out what a bum-fuck I turn out to be."

"I very much doubt that'll be the case -- bum-fuck or otherwise."

"Flattery, getting you ...?" I leave his options open. My cock pulses to extra hardness from my having admitted I'm his for the taking.

"Jesus, I really would like to suck your dick," he says.

"Which does what, exactly, for this?" I ask and give his hard cock another caress that provides additional proof that I remain well aware of his continuing stiffness.

"I feel like a candy-starved kid suddenly turned loose in a candy store."

"What say we get your dick out of your pants, for starters?" I suggest.

"Could you pull out yours, too?"

"Sure can, if the old dick of mine isn't already too stiff to pry out."

"I know mine is definitely too steely for any easy poke through my open fly," he says. He unfastens his belt buckle, in preparation for an unveiling via another route.

His belt released, he unfastens the top button of his pants. He releases the locked zipper-tab at his crotch, and he pulls down to separate metal zipper-teeth.

Obviously, he comes prepared for his night on the prowl, in that he's left his undershorts, if he ever wears them, at home. His breached fly opens over a swath of tanned muscled lower belly that's covered with dark hair soon erupted into the thicker growth of his veed pubic bush. Just the base of his thick dick is unveiled, what with his dick aimed downward along the inside of his right pants leg.

I follow his lead and open my pants over my belly to reveal the thick roots of my dick which, by the way, is just as unburdened by underwear as his is, and just as secured along a thigh; although, it's my left thigh. I scoop beneath the lower neck of my stiff dick and give a pull, simultaneously lifting my ass slightly off the car seat. The result is a painful bow of my cockneck that resembles the handle of a beaker. Lest my poor cock snap under the exerted pressure, I give another tug and yank my cockhead, and whatever attending cockneck, completely free of my containing pants leg. As if a giant spring, bent over on itself, is suddenly released, my dick leaps into full and total erection.

"Christ, seems I've netted a blond King Kong," he says, "complete with gorilla dick that has me wonder if it can be real."

"Want to pat it down for life signs?"

He doesn't have to be asked twice. His right hand is on my dick in a flash, even before his prick is brought as fully into view as mine.

I lift my ass to push my stiff cock up and through the fist he uses to frame it. His handhold is just firm enough to catch and hold my outer cockskin, my more-solid cockcore sliding on through.

"Cockflesh like steely velvet," he says.

"You're not about to be bashful, as regards your own dick, I hope?" I cajole.

My request to see his prick isn't merely to flatter him. I genuinely want to see it. I want to know if it's as big and as impressive as it looks, as it presently forms the ridge in his pants leg, only his cockroots visible through the breach of his open fly, all my other measurements having been made via the Braille method.

"My cock is just too stiff to pull out without breaking," he says.

"Maybe if you just slip off your pants to your knees," I say.

He makes the attempt, and I give a helping hand. I tug on his particularly recalcitrant right pants leg that seems intent upon getting hung up on the impediment his thick dick provides against an easy slide.

"Christ, I don't remember my dick ever getting this hard, not even in those long-ago days of first hormonal rush," he says.

About that time, his pants realize their losing battle, in the face of our combined determination, and another lift of his sexy ass sees the material pulled free as far as his thighs. His dick, no longer trapped within his pants leg, extends noticeably upward and outward, kept from complete vertical by his cockhead having been caught and contained by a part of his trouser waistband.

Yet another jerk on his trousers pulls his pants all the way over his knees, and his cock finally bounds to become its full and impressive phallic totem.

My left hand touches his cock, fists it, draws its bulky outer layer upward so his foreskin, apparently pulled free of his cockhead in erection, cowls his cockcorona and forms a small steam-vent-like spout at the apex. Against the palm of my hand, the latticework of his cockshaft veins provides sensual contrast to the otherwise silky surface of his erection.

His cock grows thickest where it connects to his belly and balls. The only exception to its uniformly slight taper, from cockroots to cockhead, is where his mushroomed cockcorona blossoms in its impressive flare. As I use my handful of loose outer cockskin to caress his harder cockcore, I feel that slight coronal irregularity. It's a sexy anomaly made more sexy by my imagining it sexily bumping along the tight passageway of my asshole.

"Jesus!" he says, and his fingers wrap my fingers and stop all masturbatory movements I'm making over his dick. "I'm already hot enough to cream, here and now, and I'd like this to last just a bit longer."

There's probably a better case argued for the-faster-the-better, what with all the cops-out-for-queers patrolling the neighborhood. While I've provided us a spot pretty much out of the immediate areas where hustlers troll for customers, and vice versa, nothing says the vice squad isn't, even now, enlarging their original sting parameters. In fact, the chances are more than likely that's exactly what's happening.

Nonetheless, I no more want this moment to end than does Officer Pringle. I've not, in a long time, lucked out on anyone so thoroughly sexy as this guy, a cop to boot, and there's no denying, while recognizing the probable foolishness of it all, that the risk is an added turn-on.

"Let me watch you jack-off, while I whip my dick," he says. "My dick more familiar with my hand, and more jaded to it, maybe we can coordinate something that won't see me cream prematurely."

I'd like to see him cream, prematurely or otherwise. I can jack-off my own dick, any time, can't I? Likewise, he can flog his hog, any time, in the privacy of his own room. Then again, any such jacks-off, if performed solo and elsewhere, wouldn't likely include the voyeuristic turn-on of each of us watching the other maul his own stiff pecker, or include the very good chance that one or more of the city's finest could, at any minute, zoom on in and reward our faggoty behavior with our lock-up behind bars. Officer Pringle's career not likely to survive any such discovery. As for my job, and my long-range career plans ...

He releases his handhold on my hand, so I can release his dick. Only reluctantly do I part with his boner and bring my fingers, still warm from the heat of his erection, into a fisting around my stiff meat. It's my left hand, but I've long since learned to be ambidextrous, at least as far as things sexual.

"So, we'll both whip our dicks," I say and proceed to provide the long slide of velvety skin up the full length of my pecker. "You let me know when you get near blast-off, and I'll see if I can coordinate. You have a hanky or something to contain your mess?"

It's just luck that I've come prepared, intuitively -- I guess -- having long ago learned that spermal goo can leave inconvenient evidence. Try explaining cum-splattered shirt and/or trousers to ...

"Jesus, you make me so fucking horny," he says and, for not the first time, interrupts my train of thought. "As many times as I've strangled my monkey, I'm genuinely afraid just taking hold of my dick, here and now, is going to see it squirt my load from here to Kingdom-come."

He fishes a wad of tissue from his pants pocket, and I wonder whether his "Kingdom-come" has been a purposeful play on words.

No doubt, my view of his hard pecker, standing tall between his legs, his black-fur balls pooled on the car seat between his open thighs, gives me more pleasure than would just my mere manipulations of my cock with my left hand. If I've come to figure circle-jerks, since high-school days, as having pretty much lost their ability to excite, Officer Pringle proves that variations on an old theme can still resurrect fun and turn-on enjoyment.

The fist he provides his cock is tentative, as if his cock is genuinely a hot poker prepared to burn his enfolding fingers. While his first cock-stroke slides his curled fingers a respectable distance up, then down, not much of his outer cockskin actually moves. When he unfists, I figure he's decided his cock still too primed toward automatic firing to mess with. As it turns out, much to my delight, on more than one count, I'm wrong.

"What say I jack us both?" he says. Familiar enough with how such a situation is supposed to work, he doesn't wait for my okay but switches left hand for his right, along the neck of his dick, after first having dropped his wad of tissue to the seat between his open lap. He takes a firm grip of my dick with his right hand as soon as my fingers come free and allow him access.

His manhandling of my boner is a far greater turn-on for me than my own self-serving masturbation. Granted, a stranger's hand is never as familiar with the phallic terrain of my dick as my hand is, but whatever the degree of pleasure possibly lost by lack of know-how, it's more than compensated by the pure novelty of unfamiliar fingers wrapped snugly in place. No man's hand ever holds my cock in quite the same way as another. But, there's something about Officer Pringle's fist, the pressure it exerts on my stiff dick, the ease with which it pumps up, then down, coordinating with his left hand that performs mirror-image movements along the length of his dick, that spirals my pleasure like sixty.

"Praise be the Lord for ambidexterity!" I say, sensuously fascinated by his hands simultaneously jerking my meat and his.

"My only question: Why have I denied myself so long?" he says.

"Can't be easy being gay and a cop," I say.

He doesn't disagree.

"Pussy never turning me on like your cock does," he says.

I scoot deeper in the seat, open my thighs wider. Even while he pumps, I fish the open fly of my pants and cascade my nuts in a waterfall of hairy flesh. Meanwhile, his balls roll sensuously within his hair-fur scrotum. Even as I watch his battling nuts, the flesh of their containing sac toughens farther, in little tic-like jerks, the resulting tautness forming a container distinctly compact and circular. A thickened ridge vertically halves his scrotum like a welder's seam halves opposing half-spheres of a metal globe.

He rests his head back against the seat and turns in my direction so he has a good shot of what he's doing to the length of my uplifted prick.

"You keep me posted as to how close you get to blasting," he says. "Even going this route, something tells me I'm going to beat you to cum-time."

"Don't know about that," I say. "You're sexy as hell, and I'm only human, after all."

Hopefully, I won't ever get so jaded that I'm not easily turned on by another stud's hand whipping my dick. Especially when that other stud so readily provides the additional viewing pleasure of his other fist riding his own horse-size boner."

"Love it when you talk dirty," he says and licks his lips.

His dark hair has become mussed, a sexy flop banging his sweaty forehead and sticking damp but still-feathery tips within his thick eyelashes.

"Love fucking your hand," I say. "Really ... really ... really do ... love fucking ... it!"

"I've been so horny for so long," he says, "although I'm sure my soon-to-be-ex wife will tell you otherwise. Can't really blame her, though, can I? She has between her legs what any red-blooded heterosexual man ever dreams of. Can she help it if the guy she married needs cock instead?"

"Her loss, my gain," I say, and I'm not just whistling 'Dixie'.

The more Officer Pringle does his thing with my thing and his thing, the hotter things get.

I wish I had a better view out the car windows, by way of detecting possibly incoming cops. It's not the widows, themselves, that contribute to my lack of a good view, as much as it is the niche within which I've had Officer Pringle park his car. The same aspects of our parking spot that keep us concealed allow a whole patrol of law-enforcement officers the ability to creep up unaware.

By this time of the game, however, worry about discovery by cops, or by whomever, takes second place to my building need to cream my load not only for my benefit but for the sexual and viewing pleasure of the policeman who pumps my dick and his own.

"Bet that cock of yours would feel damned good rammed to your hairy balls up my tight ass," I say. "If you think you've fucked tight ass before, wait until you've pumped your dick into my cherry-like asshole."

"Oh, baby," he says, shuts his eyes momentarily, then opens them. Likewise, he interrupts his masturbations, but only for a brief, almost imperceptible, pause in his jacking.

"If you've really been without another guy's cock since high school, you must have been doing a helluva lot of practicing on your own boners," I say, "because I've never had anyone manhandle my pecker with quite the expertise your fist manages over and along my erection."

"I'm going to seem a rank amateur when I cream my nuts, you not even close to orgasm," he says. "It's just so damned hard, having waited so long, to hold so much pleasure in for very much longer."

"I'm close, too," I say, actually surprised that I'm not merely flattering his ego. Truth is, I'm not really as jaded to this kind of scene as my persona is designed to insinuate. It's not as if, hustler-stud that I appear, that I actually ...

"Oh, sweet ... sweeeeeeet Jesus!" he says, his handholds going into even faster masturbatory cadence.

I'm so close to popping my load that I'm suddenly fearful that I'm going to go first, despite all of Officer Pringle's predictions to the contrary. Hoping to at least hold off long enough to join him, if he's really as near ejaculation as he claims, I grab my balls, handkerchief still in hand, and give a hearty squeeze of my entrapped gonads.

The resulting pain, conjured by my effort to curb the spiraling rise of pleasure inside of me, turns out to do the exact opposite of what I'd hoped. I might as well have injected an aphrodisiac directly into a vein, what with the pain-enhanced pleasure that suddenly catches fire in my groin and threatens complete and fiery consumption of my total being.

"Good God!" I say and bounce my ass on the car seat.

I'm so far gone that I no longer allow him total control of my dick but take hold of his hand with my right hand and physically increase his flogging momentum over my well-primed stiffy.

"I'm going to fucking blow!" he says.

I might just as well have made that statement, because if I've ever known the when and where of a personal creaming, it's here and now.

God only knows how I maintain enough forethought to realize Officer Pringle isn't able to tissue-claim his cum while both his hands are occupied climax-jerking his dick and mine. More than likely, it's innate reflex that allows me to unhand his hand, at work over my pecker, his fingers still around my cock and beating like sixty, while I claim the wad of tissue he's discarded onto the seat between his spread thighs.

His scrotum and mine are spherical containers of thick flesh so tightly hugged to the base of our respective hard-pounded pricks that they appear burls grown at the bases of phallic trees.

I cap his dick with his tissue, and I lid my dick with my hanky.

"Aaaghhhrrr!" he says, and his ass lifts from the seat, the head of his dick so forcefully fed through his fingers that I feel his cockhead compress all the tissue and butt the palm of my hand.

My gonads explode creamy oceans so thick that they're not easily absorbed by hanky linen and, as a result, flow back, over my cockhead, eventually to drool the neck of my erection. There to be snatched away by Officer Pringle's pumping ... pumping ... fingers and smeared along the shaft of my cum-shooting cockshaft.

"Shit! Shit! ... oh, shit!" I say, in response to my orgasm, to his orgasm, and to the flash of light in the alley that runs beside our car. The light, more likely than not, a patrol car's spotlight illuminating the alley from one of the bracketing streets.

If the cops are on their way, however, I'm beyond doing anything beyond noting that possibility. No way I exit the cataclysm, in which I've become so completely and helplessly locked, until the very ... last ... iota ... of my creamy sex cream ... is pulsed ... pulsed ... Jesus, pulsed ... juicily from my balls ... along the length of my beaten-to-creamy climax dick ... and jettisoned through the pouted mouth of my friction-hardened erection.

I'm panting when I finish.

"Did you see the spotlight?" he asks breathlessly. "Jesus ... did .. you ... see ... the ... spot?"

"Yes," I say and find immense consolation in how, now that my over-powering ejaculation, to the detriment of all else, is over and done, the light is gone. Whomever drenched the area with momentary illumination has either gone, or ...

"Do you think they're gone?" he asks.

I only hope that's the case, my dick still not sufficiently softened from its ordeal to be easily stuffed back into the safety of my trousers.

His hands free his cock and mine. He takes the pass-off of cum-wadded tissue that I've used, somehow, to contain his exploded mess.

"I saw the spot," he says, "and, besides being scared shitless, I thought my whole insides were suddenly dropped to my balls and out-gushing the pulsing mouth of my erection."

"Tell me about it," I say and try my best to get my still-too-stiff dick positioned back in my trousers to be made seemingly innocent behind a lifted and locked zipper. Officer Pringle tosses his cum-nutty tissue to the dashboard, lifts his sexy ass, and hoists his trousers. His balls catch on the leading edge of his pants . Nonetheless, he successfully crams his cock and balls into the crotch of his pants, like a snake charmer re-bagging a recalcitrant python. His zipper doesn't want to zip. When it does and finally places his cock and balls out of sight (if not out of mind), his zipper tab doesn't want to lock-down.

"I'm all fucking thumbs!" he says.

Minutes later, both of us look fairly presentable. His cum-soaked tissue is in the glove compartment. My folded and refolded hanky is back in my pants pocket. Simultaneously, we indulge in a quick moment of silence in which we listen for any telltale signs that we're not alone in the alley.

Our laughs are collective and spontaneous thank-you-God, the result of shared realization that, whatever the potential for disaster, emphasized by the spotlight having almost caught us in flagrante delicto, we seem to have passed through unscathed.

"Talk about living dangerously," he says. "Scary!"

My heart still beats, none too gently.

"Best cum I ever had," I say, not lying. I only hope the experience doesn't leave me addicted to sex under equally precarious and danger-ridden circumstances. Luck, like we've just experienced, isn't likely to be long-running, let alone too often duplicated.

"I want more sex with you," he says. "Not here, though. Another close call, like the one we just had, and I'll be dead and gone before the accusing cops even get the car door open. Let's meet up somewhere safer and take off where we've left off."

"I'll give you my number," I say, "if you've a pencil, pen, or pad."

"Call me a Boy Scout, always prepared," he says and stretches across me to unlock the glove compartment. There's a sudden wafting of cum-smells, concentrated, until now, within the small space into which he's socked, for temporary storage, the wipe-up from his spermal explosion.

I write down my first name and the phone number of a friend who acts as middleman when I luck on to someone I really want to see again.

"If I'm not there, leave your name, your number, where and when you'd like a meet, and/or any combination thereof," I say.

I hand him the piece of paper with my scribble on it.

"I'll just exit here," I say. "I'll hightail it on back to my street corner on foot. You take this alley straight ahead, cross two side streets, then turn right. That'll have you pretty much in the clear, as far as any still-patrolling vice is concerned."

I open the car door.

"Jesus, we never talked money!" he says.

I'm tempted to tell him it's all on the house, but what kind of hustler gives out freebies? Hell, what kind of hustler forgets to discuss price and forgets to collect his fee up-front?

"A twenty will do it," I say.

He finds his wallet and removes two twenty-dollar bills from it.

I take both of them when he offers, and I exit the car.

I'm out of the alley, on a side street, when I hear, sense, and/or get the ESP vibes of the grey-panel truck rounding a bend to access the street behind me. When the truck comes abreast, its side door, on my side, slides open, and I'm saved the bother of stepping inside by being manhandled into the interior. The door slams behind me. The truck is off in a burn of rubber that should attract ticketing from any convenient traffic officer within miles.

"Where in the hell have you been?" grills Sergeant Sandy Driver.

He's stereotypical older cop: good-looking, in a definitely butch, square-jaw, kind of way, but with a heart of gold. He has a son my age, and he has kind of taken me under his protective wing for the short time I've been on loan to vice. I knew, all along, he'd be worried shitless, but
...

"You were specifically instructed not to get into any car until we were positioned for eyeball surveillance!" he accuses.

"Come on, Sarge," I say. "You knew from the microphone feed that the guy was legit."

"Your microphone went dead, you shit!" he says, as if it's my fault. Which, actually, God help me if he ever finds out, it is.

"Fucking inferior garbage!" I condemn the inanimate electronics and, by inference, the jerks-off, whomever they are, who ever provided inferior equipment for a cop-in-the-field.

I unbutton my shirt and show him, sure enough, how one of the wires is loose that connects the microphone, taped to my sweaty chest, to the power pack and transmitter I wear in the small of my back. I give the loose wire a jiggle, and the resulting feedback to the pick-up monitor, in the panel truck with us, is ear-splitting.

"Jesus, fuck!" exclaims the Sarge, one hand to an ear, the other hand waving in the direction of Corporal Peter Rhys who sits at monitor controls.

The high-pitch wail fades.

"What in the hell do you mean, 'the guy was legit'?" Sarge asks.

"He's a father flashing a photo of his runaway daughter. Actually, I saw the kid, over a couple of blocks, just last night. I let the guy drive me to the spot for a look-see. He's likely still there, passing around her picture and asking questions."

"You had specific instructions," he repeats.

"Come on, Sarge," I argue. "What if your kid ran away, you not having a clue where the hell he'd gone. You wouldn't want someone, a cop, for Christ's sake (even if I don't presently look like one), giving you a chance to see where your kid was possibly spotted only twenty-four hours before?"

"We're out here to catch queers," he says, "not play Good Samaritans."

Maybe so, but I can tell his lingering anger has more to do with his having imagined I'd met with foul play, from one of the many weirdoes drawn out by the hot-hot night and the full summer's moon, than it has to do with his genuinely being ticked that I'd supposedly given a distraught father a helping hand.

DOUBTING THOMAS

I nailed his young body to the bed: he, belly-down, his arms extended; I, his cross to bear, laid on his back, my arms along his arms, my belly atop his ass. The only nail I used, though, was the steely spike jutted from my crotch with which I hammered -- deep, deep -- the pitch-clinging depths of his tight rear end.

"I love you," he said. Paolo: his name.

I wished he hadn't said it. At least not so soon. Who but some homeless little Brazilian street urchin, which he was, who figured my cock his ticket to the US, which he did, would come up with such a cockamamie bit of sentimentality, our very first fuck?

"I love you, too," I lied. I never said it first, but if someone wanted to play love-you games, I could play with the best of them; although, I preferred more business-like relationships.

I was especially ticked at Paolo's game-playing, because I genuinely liked the little fucker, and I had even liked him before I'd poked my dick up his butt that first time. Something about his mop of unruly, albeit poorly cut, black hair ... his black eyes ... his thick eyelashes ... his slightly off-center nose ... his pouty mouth. I'd even been attracted to the boyishness of his body; boyishness, up until then, usually not all that much of a turn-on for me.

If there are guys, and I know there are, who come to places like steamy Brazil to advantage the going-for-cheap underage cock and ass, I was never one of them. Even in a country where it didn't much matter what you did to a kid found homeless on the streets, up to and including killing him, I went out of my way to assure Paolo was of an age legal for fucking in the States. Granted, in Brazil, I wasn't likely to have been caught or punished for putting my dick to some street kid who didn't even have pubic hair, but I liked to think myself with none of the predatory characteristics of a pederast in heat. In that, even having gotten several separate assurances, from sources I figured I could trust, I remained so doubtful of Paolo being over the age of US consent, that I hadn't immediately taken the kid home. No matter that poverty conditions in and around the luxury living of Rio make some guys in their twenties look as if they are still in their bulimic teens.

It was Tory, definitely underage and blatantly propositioning me to take him home for a fuck, who convinced me I wouldn't violate my standards by taking Paolo home. "What do you want with an old pecker like his, when you can have a young one, like mine," Tory said. "Paolo's dick has twenty years on it if it has a day." I doubted the twenty-years bit, still do; but, I decided to compromise and assume Paolo at least eighteen.

I bent my fingers so they laced Paolo's and squeezed. I pulled my cock almost out of his rectum before inserting it right back into place.

"Love you, love you," he said and provided accompanying grunts into the sheet beneath his face.

How many Third-World kids, selling their cocks and their asses to rich-by-their-standards US oilmen, like I, speak those very words? Certainly every one of them I've ever fucked and/or sucked. The smarter ones, though, wait a few weeks, even a few months, as if to insinuate that what begins purely as business somehow, quite unexpectedly, blossoms into more.

Take Abdul, for instance. North African, that one. Black as the ace of spades. Cute as a bug's ear, allowing for the bug having been pursued by predators its whole natural life. He waited six weeks to tell me. Called it a miracle comparable to Moses and the burning bush. Which had me trying to remember if Moses was part of Islamic theology, or purely Judeo-Christian. Trouble was, Abdul, unbeknownst to me, at the time, was likewise professing his undying miracle-of-the-burning-bush love for my best friend, Gary Feldson. Abdul figured, I guess, that if he were smart, and covered all his bases, he would sooner or later end up crossing home plate (AKA, into the good old US of A).

Up to and including my time spent with Paolo in Brazil, Gary and I often found ourselves stuck in the same exotic locales. He likes to play Pied Piper to street kids, as well as fuck them silly. He spends more than need-be amounts of the local currencies to see they have a slightly better lot in life for having known him.

Gary's problem being his tendency to believe -- as gospel -- each and every waif who ever whispers, "I love you," in his ear. Whether during sex or otherwise. Whether at the beginning, middle, or end of a relationship. Gary's salvation is his marriage to a pretty little girl back home, with whom he's fathered three pretty little daughters. Gary's father-in-law has enough connections in the oil business, not to mention enough fingers in other corporate pies, to make it a living hell for Gary were Gary ever actually to bring out of poverty, let alone bring to the US, any of the urchins whose butts Gary so loves to fuck.

"Love you, love you," butt-plugged Paolo continued saying to me. Which really was overkill. Right then and there, I decided Paolo would be one of the kids Gary and I shared. All of his I-love-you shit having made me less inclined to hold to my original plan of keeping the kid for myself, despite Gary's blatant hints that this was one time he'd really like to share. Gary having tried to cock-crash Paolo's ass for the entire two months prior to my arrival. I figure Gary's lack of success was because someone told Paolo the well-known fact that Gary gets all the more horny, and all the more monetarily generous, in direct proportion to how long a kid can keep him waiting.

"Fuck me, fuck me," Paolo said, and I did my best. Glad he had, at least for the moment, dropped his I-love-you mantra. I would have been less critical of something more general, like, love your cock, love this fuck, love the way your belly slaps against my ass. But, love me - - "me" being Thomas Laurent -- after I'd been just a few minutes in the saddle? Give me a fucking break!

All of that aside, the kid, as I expected, was a pretty good screw. I was thoroughly impressed by the tightness of his asshole, so form-fitting around my pumping cock as to seem rubber glove on a hand. A genuinely tight asshole, for a kid nearly out of his teens, considering what he probably had to do, and go through, just to keep alive, day to day, was a welcome rarity indeed.

I particularly liked the way Paolo's sun-tanned dark-from-the-get-go complexion complemented my tanned Mediterranean. The more than one Italian lurking in my family's proverbial woodpile, in my humble opinion, as a connoisseur of good looks, has done wonders to improve the original French stock on my father's side of the family, as well as the original Scandinavian stock on my mother's side.

Paolo's striking good looks, of course, resulted from the hodgepodge gene pool that's Brazil, where generations of Portuguese, English, Italian, Spanish, native American, and whatever, constantly mixed and stirred their sperm, with some truly marvellous results. Gary can't be persuaded there's any such animal as an ugly Brazilian, at least by way of male of that species. What's more, during my time with Paolo, Gary seemed out to fuck every last Brazilian man. On the other hand, I was far more picky. Where Gary literally could number in the hundreds the kids he'd fucked in Rio alone, I was in Brazil two whole months before I got around to bedding "nice-ass Paolo" (as Gary liked to call him).

Gary quite right in regard to Paolo's nice ass. Nothing I enjoy less than some buttless wonder; although, I didn't exactly beat down the available doors to access some of the really large black ass found on just about every Brazilian street corner. For me, Paolo's rump was just big enough. It offered excellent possibilities for spoon-cuddling, during a fuck, and/or after.

Anyone interested in street urchin with a nice cock and balls wouldn't have been left wanting by Paolo, either. Although, I suppose, somewhere, somehow, there's a size queen who would turn up his nose at Paolo's ten solid inches. I was quite content with what I found between his legs, thank-you very much, even appreciative of his uncut foreskin which kept the kid's cockhead partially covered even when Paolo's dick was in full erection.

That Paolo's cock and balls fucked the bed, between his belly and the top sheet, that first time I fucked him, didn't mean I'd forgotten their existence. I can be pretty damned reciprocative, sexually, when I want to be. Up until then, even with Paolo's disconcerting love-you shit, the kid kept me interested in his each and every appendage and/or orifice.

My dick, surgically deprived of foreskin bulkiness by a doctor's scalpel, quickly got fired up within the furnace-hot wrapping provided by Paolo's oh-so-tight butt. There was a distinct sizzling sensation quickly arisen from the base of my dick all of the way to my cockhead as my dick proceeded, yet again, to a full-depth penetration of Paolo's rectum. It was heat far different from the blood-boiling Brazilian heat experienced out-of-doors.

I initiated the little grind that punched my belly tighter against Paolo's buttcheeks and allowed my cock even deeper settling within the kid's widened asscrack. His sphincter very much like several rubber bands, looped and doubled back, to wrap the spot where my dick anchored to my lower belly.

It had been some time since I'd actually fucked ass. Time protracted by how, even after I'd found Paolo's ass, it had taken me so much time to decide whether or not Paolo (and all of his anal charms) fell within my personal parameters for a legal fuck. All of which meant I wasn't exactly at my best, that first time, as regards control of my cock, especially once it was in and fucking about. At optimum performance, I can pretty much prolong most any screw far beyond the limits most people most often think likely. All to do with muscle control and focusing my concentration elsewhere than on any fuck in progress.

There on that bed with Paolo, though, I was well aware that my pleasure had jumped, fast and furious, into high gear. Not that Paolo probably cared if I prematurely let go, without having had my dick shoved up his asshole hardly at all. Professional street kids in Brazil, usually to a boy, early realize, if nothing else, that the most important thing in any fuck is that the paying customer gets his rocks off. Whether or not the kid does is of no consequence whatsoever.

Except, I've never been one of those selfish guys who figure it my due to take, take, take, without providing a bit of something in return. Possibly because I've never limited my sexual adventures to available-for-pennies Third-World kids. Whenever I head back to the States, I like a bit of my sucking and fucking with non-hustler types who are ready, willing, and able, to label anyone a poor fuck who doesn't hold up his end of any sexual liaison.

So, I vaguely contemplated fishing for Paolo's cock and balls but, simultaneous orgasms not easily achieved, under the very best of circumstances, I was simply too horny, too turned on, too sweaty, too ready for blast-off, to exert myself by way of playing sexual Good Samaritan.

"Yes, yes, yes," I said and rammed into an even hardier fuck-gear. I nuzzled my face tightly against his perspiration-damp cheek and gently bit the lobe of his left ear.

"Fuck me with your cum," he said and gave his sexy ass a roll that twisted my dick up his butt even as I continued to fuck. "Drown me ... drown me ... drown me!"

The kid's near-perfect English, as far as his voicing of what any American guy wanted to hear, as the moment of truth rushed upon me, merely confirmed for me that the kid had been butt-fucked plenty of times before I got to him.

My belly made sloppy slapping sounds each time it collided with his sweaty ass. My rubberized cock made wet, soupy sounds each time it popped full-length up his butt and pulled out to its cockhead. My nipples got tack-like against his back.

"Okay, kid, here it comes!" I predicted, right on cue.

My cum splashed -- hot and heavy. My hips force-fed my cock to my balls, up his asshole, one final time. My hips ground to skewer the kid all the farther.

"Love it, kid!" I said. Notice I said love "it" not love "you".

Paolo, of course, heard what he wanted to hear.

"Love you, too," he said.

I didn't realize he'd orgasmed, right along with me, until he rolled over. His belly and a large part of the sheet, both of which had been beneath him, were covered with gobs of his discharged teenage goo.

I was impressed, in that I know very few guys, professional or otherwise, young or old, who cream with only cock-up-butt. I've known even fewer who can summon orgasm, apparently on cue.

I moved the kid permanently into my apartment, because, frankly, sex with him was a helluva lot better than sex with my hand. As for his incessant fantasizing of our life destined to be lived out together, I turned a deaf ear. His daydreams progressed from our merely playing house to our frequently visiting Disneyland. Disneyland, for Christ's sake! I was there once and hated the place.

Aside from his wild flights of imagination, the kid was otherwise a real pro. He sucked and fucked with the best of them, and more than once provided evidence of his uncanny ability to get off his rocks at one and the same time I did.

When my transfer to Australia came through three months earlier than expected, due to a troubleshooting problem for which I seemed particularly well-suited, I was genuinely sorry to be on the verge of vacating the convenience and enjoyment of my Paolo-filled bed.

I lied to the kid and said I had to visit a company site in deep-jungle. Not at all far-fetched, in that Gary was doing the very same thing, at the time.

I left Gary instructions that Paolo could stay on at my apartment, rent-free, until my lease officially ended. Also, whatever stuff I left, aside from the few pieces of furniture, from the company warehouse, were Paolo's to sell. Also, I left the kid some cash to hold him over until his next paying john came along. Not likely to be all that far in the future, if the kid didn't scare him away with bullshit talk of love, marriage, and playing house, albeit sans baby carriage, in America.

Once Gary got back from Amazon 6, I heard from him. I was in Sidney at the time. He was surprisingly upset by "how shabbily" he thought I'd treated Paolo.

"The kid fucking loves you, you uncaring shit!" was how Gary put it. "How could you pull up and walk out on him, without even an official good-bye?"

I figured Gary's ravings were mostly an act, maybe because Paolo was somewhere within hearing, on Gary's end of the line. I certainly didn't figure Gary would remain permanently upset, not after he finally managed to get Paolo all for himself, on the rebound. Undeniably, though, Gary and I suddenly stopped running into each other as often as we once had; so, after awhile, I genuinely suspected Gary purposely was out to avoid me.

I managed to get back to Gary, by phone, some time later, when he was in New Guinea and I took some rest and recuperation on Bali.

"You shit!" That's what he said to me, by way of hello. "Paolo never did get over you."

I still can't believe Gary raved on about all that water under the bridge.

"I'll bet Paolo's not getting over me didn't stop you from enjoying sloppy seconds," I said.

"I loved him, you bastard!" he said and hung up.

I've been cut off by hinky Indonesian phone connections before, but I have this sixth sense they weren't the cause that time.

All Paolo's talk about love for me, then Gary's confession of it for Paolo, remained a complete mystery to me and continued to remain just that for the next three years.

Then, one hot summer night ... in a super-heated San Diego bar ... where I'd hauled my sweaty ass for a cold drink ... having similarly done so on countless other occasions ....

Well, let's just say, I'm still embarrassed by how vehemently I always used to pooh-pooh love at first sight. Because, there in that summer-heated bar, I glanced up, made eye contact with Jimmy, across the crowded room, and I got literally weak in the knees, started to ooze even more sweat and, honest to God, felt my heart literally skip a beat.

Jimmy is simply the most handsome, most sexy, most exceptional teenage package I can conceive God ever having put together. In fact, it seems too much goodness, in one person, for even God to have managed.

Utter, pure, unadulterated physical perfection. Blond-almost-white hair, worn short but long enough to exhibit its natural curl. Blue-blue eyes. Eyebrows and eyelashes, the latter the thickest I'd ever seen and enough of a deep blond so that his handsome face doesn't have a trace of that bleached-out look with which some blond-blonds are saddled. A button nose. Full and sensuous lips. A body slim and trim enough to come across downright boyish, but without any baby-fat. Enough muscle definition for me to identify, right off, even through the skimpy covering offered by his sweat-damp T-shirt, his barely etched square pectorals and his pretty-much-flat-to-concave abdominals.

The continuing miracle: he came right on over, weaved through the obviously worshipping multitudes and said hello -- to me, for Christ's sake! -- just like that. Which left me pretty much speechless, although he didn't seem to notice.

It was, Jimmy said, one of his "rare nights on the town". They were becoming less and less frequent, those days, because of "an ever-growing workload and an ever more gung-ho boss". I asked what kind of business he was in, and he said "personal services", but he preferred we skip all talk of anything except whether or not I was going to invite him up to my place for a cold beer and/or ...?

I figured I was dreaming, right?! No way does Thomas Laurent get bowled over by some teenage Mr. Studly on the make; especially, not by someone with Jimmy's exceptionally good looks. Miracles like that just don't happen.

Can't be happening, I told myself as we checked in at my place, drank cold beers that didn't seem to quench the ever-increasing heat, and walked into my bedroom where Jimmy immediately started taking off his clothes.

I thought I would shoot my wad, right then and there, even before he totally shed even his T-shirt. When his shirt did come off, and revealed, in all its superb nakedness, the tanned, slightly damp, and completely hairless, contours of his chest and belly, of his shoulders, of his arms and back, my cock gushed such a sudden mess of preseminal goo into my undershorts that I thought I'd actually squirted cum.

"Please tell me you're not one of those bashful types who insist upon fucking with your clothes on," he said and unbuckled his pants. At least, not in this hot-as-hell summer weather.

Although I couldn't manage words, I managed a denying shake of my head.

"Good," he said, "because I could tell right off that you've just the kind of body I like. I see far too many office types, complete with sagging asses and round bellies, to waste any of my free time on them. You, now ..."

He dropped his pants. He didn't wear undershorts. His big cock and sweaty balls, his firmly muscled ass, his perfect legs, were just suddenly there, in full view. A boner-producing wonder to behold, let me tell you, except I'd carried around my boner since I first spotted him in the bar.

He plopped on the bed, propped slightly by pillows behind him. His hands folded behind his head.

"I'm versatile in the sack," he said.

I tried to guess his age, had been trying all the while. Eighteen ... maybe nineteen. Legal ... but only-just. Still a boy-man, rather than a man-boy.

"You, on the other hand, look all top-man," he said. "What do you think?"

His knees bent, he hiked his heels up against his ass and filleted his legs. He lifted his ass ever so slightly so I had a bird's-eye view of his sexily sweat-damp brown pucker.

"Want to stick that big cock of yours home?" he said. "Anyway, I'm assuming it's big. It does look big, stuffed so insufficiently into your pants. Hoping to get out. My hoping to see it succeed in getting out."

I was still pretty much glued to the spot. I was all sweaty except for my mouth which was dry as a bone.

"Except, if it's not as big as it looks, not to worry," he said, probably by way of trying to rationalize why I seemed reluctant to unveil and join him on the bed.

I'll bet his usual gamut of lucky partners beat him into the bed; they so hot to trot.

"I like all sizes and shapes of cock," he said. "Big, medium, small. Fat, thin. Cut, uncut. Bent, curved, straight, corkscrewed. Uplifted-to-belly-button or merely drawbridge hard. Heavy-to-drooping. Rocket-like. Mushroom corona, or heart-shaped dickcap."

I was on automatic pilot when I began unbuttoning my shirt. Some primitive center, quite aside from my still-numb brain, kicked in and took advantage of the wondrous moment.

"I like a man who knows the advantages of a slow and languid strip," he said. "You in the business, too?"

That's exactly what he said, whenever I now replay that scene. He didn't say, as I assumed at the time, "You're in business, too?"

"Oil," I said, although I should have known from his curious look that I'd gotten something wrong. He shook his head slightly, then ...

"Oil?" he queried. "You mean, lubricants, like on rubbers?"

"Off-shore rigs," I clarified. "Desert outposts. Jungle hell-holes."

"Oh! Right! Hot, horny, and muscular men, ever on the ready. How I envy you that, in that you should see the gone-to-seed, haven't-exercised-in-decades, types who are constantly in and out of my bed."

He provided all the hints, but I just didn't pick up on them. Probably because there was no mention of money. How had he put it?: His "free night on the town"? Even if there had been a mention of money, though, it wouldn't have made a scintilla of difference. The kid had hooked me from the very start. No need to reel me in. Were I a fish, he a fisherman, I would have swum right on up to his boat and jumped aboard.

I wore undershorts but, once my belt and trousers were undone, I hooked the waistband of my underpants, along with everything else, and dropped the whole kit and sweat-damp caboodle.

"A naturally bulged pants crotch seldom lies," he said. "No way a tiny dick could have masqueraded as that heavy basket you're sporting."

My dick had risen to put its head into the cupping of my navel. My cockcorona and cockshaft were bathed in preseminal goo. Another puddle of the stuff, beaded within the mouth of my cock, overflowed as I stood there.

"Natural lubricant, from and for a monster like yours, almost makes me want to take your dick rubberless up my butt," he said. "'Almost' the key word here."

"One thing I'm not short on, it's rubbers," I said and walked my boner to a nearby dresser for the condom I quickly slipped on, having scrunched up my doffed undershorts, en route, and used the result to mop up the sticky glossing on my pecker.

"Another thing you're not short on is dick inches," he said. "Nor, on bull-like balls. Nor, on hunky-hunky stud-muffin body. Nor, on well-muscled ass. Nor, on legs and arms, and torso, that look carved from one-hundred percent alabaster."

He grabbed his asscheeks, a hand to each one, and gave opposing yanks that widened the crack of his buttocks and provided me with an even better view of his puckered asshole. His butthole became the biggest magnet in the physical universe, black holes included. My dick became a heavy hunk of iron, or metal hunk of space flotsam, helplessly drawn to the target area, the rest of my body merely following along.

I felt a kid again, about to fuck for the very first time. Except, I had enough know-how, this time around, to realize all the signs of premature ejaculation, and I used every trick in the book to keep it from happening. I didn't want to come off a rank amateur by popping my nuts before my dick even made first contact. I wanted the sex to go on and on and on, although I simultaneously knew that, what with my already high state of excitement, I was going to be hard-pressed to provide Jimmy with more than, by his definition, a mediocre fuck.

"Stick me hard and ram me fast, stud," he said, my cockhead finally on target. "I want to hear, as well as feel, the hearty slap of your balls against my sweet-sweaty ass."

Did he know that my doing what he asked risked my eruption of cum, right then and there? More likely, he assumed I was in better control. Shit, with anyone else, I would have been in better control. Only with Jimmy was I suddenly a rank amateur.

Nonetheless, what Jimmy wanted, I was compelled to give him. It was as mysteriously simple as that.

So, without farther pause, I drove my admittedly big dick all of the way inside Jimmy's willingly accepting asshole. The way my perspiring balls obligingly whacked Jimmy's slick butt, as requested, was what produced the decidedly painful pleasure that allowed me to keep myself from spilling into helpless orgasm.

"It doesn't get any better than this," he said, raised his legs into a more defined parenthesis of my body and locked his ankles over the top curve of my ass.

For him, his words might have been mere bullshit. For me, though, no truer words had ever been spoken. There had never been a better moment for me. It was inconceivable there would ever be better, except possibly for whatever moments, between Jimmy and me, were yet to come.

What makes Jimmy's rectum so exquisite, I haven't a clue. There are tighter assholes, many of which I've screwed. There are buttocks more solidly muscled, and anal puckers more firmly pursed, and anal walls more snug-sleeve tight.

It's impossible to put into words, without sounding like a complete ass, the how and why of his asshole so quickly, so much, and so thoroughly, becoming the absolute center of my universe.

Pure and simple, I transported to a higher plane. All my senses became more acute. My dick swelled harder and bigger than I can ever remember it managing. My testicles produced far more cum than even they must have thought possible, having become weighty pendulums that stretched my scrotum to limits never before achieved. My whole body possessed this all-consuming sensual ache, sautèed in womb-like heat, bearable only in that it was as much pleasurable as it was painful.

"My lucky night!" Jimmy said in echo of my own more-silent self-congratulations.

I fucked him longer and harder than I've ever fucked anyone. Even though, each and every push of my dick up his ass, each and every slide that popped my cockhead outward to the very doorway of his gumming anus, saw me teetered so near the brink of orgasm that I couldn't believe there was anything left for me but the glorious fall into oblivion.

Somehow, from somewhere, I summoned that something that metamorphosed me, for those few remaining moments of heated fucking, into a veritable superman, a yogi with perfect timing, coordination, and control.

Even when my hips helplessly humped into an even faster gear, I maintained the tenuous hold on reality that kept me from the ultimate plunge into climax.

My penis turned all the more fiery from the constant friction caused by its ever-more-frantic movements up Jimmy's butt. My balls were suddenly so cum-laden that they hardly could be carried during each additional ride of my cock within Jimmy's teenage butt.

"Yes ... oh, yes ... fucking shit, yes!" Jimmy said and rocked and rolled beneath me. His ass lunged to meet my each and every stroke, and he flopped against the bed in direct sync with my every movement.

I groaned. He groaned.

I sighed. He sighed.

I anchored my lips firmly to his lips and drank his spit and fed him mine.

Once our kiss was broken, I slobbered his chin and the long arch of his neck as his head pushed harder back into the pillow.

Even then, I could wonder if my playbacks of those moments -- any more than playbacks by witnesses to the first A-bomb explosion -- would ever do justice to what I felt when all of my body's atoms coalesced for that one mighty and powerful ignition that heat-vaporized my insides.

"I love you!" I bellowed. No denying it. No helping it.

Even in the turmoil of my cum-bursting guts that gushed my creamy streamers up and out the length of my butt-submerged dick, I knew what I said. Nothing about loving the screw of his butt, the tightness of his ass, the way he moaned and groaned beneath me, the way I moaned and groaned atop him. I'd been specific. On target. Having pinpointed my love -- of him.

"Oh, Jesus, fuck, I love you ... love you ... love you," I chanted, having found the words and finding it impossible to stop my voicing of them.

Then, my spasms finally done, his cockjuices likewise miraculously splattered -- to my chest, to his chest, to my neck, to his neck -- I repeated in sheer wonderment ...

"I really do love you."

"Me, too," he said. His generic response leaving me to wonder whether he loved himself or offered me a return of affection.

"I mean, truly love you ... thoroughly ... completely," I said.

"Me, too," he said. "So much do I love you that I'd like you to sheathe that big dick of yours with another rubber and make for some quick seconds. You're not going to tell me, I hope, that you're one of those one-shot wonders, are you?"

"I could fuck you all bloody night," I said.

"Well, maybe not all bloody night," he said, "but we might manage fucking and sucking away most of it."

Which was the prelude for our sucking and fucking into sheer, utter, thorough, sweet-sweaty exhaustion. My final ejaculation, his cock up my butt, actually painful in my attempts to expel cum which simply was no longer there, my ability to produce sperm, at least for the moment, having gone into complete shutdown.

My mind was blurry and hazy from pleasure. I was surely in as complete a stupor as any of those fabled Lotus-eaters of myth and legend.

It was such pure, unadulterated, complete contentment to feel his
dick pull free, feel the length of his sexually sticky body roll closely in
beside my sweat-run flank, feel his head on my perspiration-glossed
chest, feel one of his legs throw sexily over one of mine, feel one of his
hands open and lie lightly upon my belly.

"Tell me you love me," I said and fought the sleep that threatened to
engulf me. I knew sleep would soon come, any attempt to resist it as
futile as it was for me to resist those new wondrous emotions turned
loose inside me.

"Sure enough, stud," he said, and his breath stirred the damp hair on
my chest. "I love you."

And with his sweet words floating, like stardust, in my head, I drifted
into blissful never-never land, my body eagerly seeking rejuvenation for
more and more -- endlessly more -- exhausting sex with this young man
of my dreams.

Except, when I languidly regained consciousness, like a scuba diver
slowly maneuvering sea levels in his long climb toward the surface, I
reached for Jimmy, and the kid wasn't there.

Had he, then, been a dream? Had he, then, been a fantasy! My
immediate reaction: yes, he'd certainly been too perfect to have been
real!

The mess only partially dry on the sheets, however, couldn't possibly have been the product of just one man's sweaty wet dream, no matter how horny, no matter how impressive my capabilities for perspiring
and spewing nutty cum.

No phantom, either, had left the indent in, or the note on, the pillow
beside mine.

"Tom... Thanks! Much fun! ...Jimmy," the note read.

I couldn't believe he was gone. It were as if a piece of me had gone
with him.

I felt it difficult to breathe. I found it difficult to walk. I found it difficult
to shave. I found it difficult to shower. I found it difficult to talk.

Thoroughly, I searched the apartment, sure Jimmy played some trick
on me, in that surely ... surely ... surely ... he couldn't be gone.

His having left was as inconceivable as the moon not revolving
around the earth, as the earth not revolving around the sun. If Jimmy

had experienced only a small portion of the wonderment I had, as regarded our shared sex, he couldn't have left without first discussing with me the miracle in detail and, trying, like I, to get to the bottom of it.

I was distraught to find myself alone. I was inconsolable. I was -- yes, I admit it -- heartbroken.

I spent three whole days, two-and-a-half whole nights, looking for him. In and out of every summer sweat-baste bar, in the city. Asking bartenders and complete strangers if they'd recently seen the most wonderful boy-man in the world. Some of whom said, yes; Jimmy always having been somewhere other than where I was or had been. Some of whom said, no; it completely inconceivable to me that anyone could be so clueless as to whom I referred. As if, even in a city known for its good-lookers, Jimmy wasn't a star who outshone all stars!

I got drunk, more than once. Then, I sobered up by walking the muggy streets and staring into every available window on the off chance I'd spot him.

I couldn't believe I didn't know his last name. I couldn't believe I didn't have his address, or his phone number. I couldn't believe I'd figured myself with days, weeks, months, even years, to get to know each and every little thing about him. When, in painful reality, all I'd had was one night whose intensity made me fearful that, if I didn't find him again, all sex that came after would be pitifully insufficient and unsatisfactory in comparison.

I randomly paged through the phone book but came up with nothing. I took to examining bathroom walls, looking for his name and his number, my dick so hard I couldn't actually piss, no matter how badly my bladder cajoled.

Finally -- thank-you, dear God (or, maybe not)!, I found him. It was yet another super-hot night ... in exactly the same bar where we'd originally met. He sat at a table, across from a sweaty guy big enough to be a professional wrestler.

I spilled part of three beers in my hurry to get to him, although only one of the beers was mine. Luckily none of the other badly shaken brews belonged to anyone butch enough to take me on for my obviously clumsy and rude behavior.

Jimmy looked up as soon as I got there.

"Hi," he said, without missing a beat. "How you been?"

How had I been! Jesus, how did he think I'd been?

"We have to talk," I said. Arrangements had to be made so that we didn't get so thoroughly separated again.

"You going to introduce us, or what?" asked the wrestler.

"This is Tom, Filbert. You remember, I mentioned him."

How in the hell could anyone who looks like that guy looks be called Filbert? Unless, he gotten so muscle-bound by having defended himself against guys who made fun of the name -- "Filbert's a nut! Filbert's a nut!" -- with which his dim-shitted parents had labeled him.

"Right!" said Filbert. "Tom Freeby."

"Actually, Tom Laurent," I said, having missed his point entirely.

"Definitely your type," said the wrestler.

I assumed he spoke to Jimmy, although I might have looked as moonstruck as I felt, being wondrously back in Jimmy's presence.

"We have to talk," I repeated. No doubt about to whom I spoke.

"Sure," said Jimmy. "Sit and have a beer."

"I'd prefer that we talk over there," I said and motioned toward a comparatively quieter section of the bar.

Jimmy looked to Filbert for what looked like -- and turned out to be -- permission. Filbert shrugged consent.

I waited for Jimmy to lead the way, afraid he'd once again slip away if I turned my back on him for a second.

"Lucky you caught me," Jimmy said and checked his watch which was one of those advertised on television as being "museum pieces". "I have to be at a party with Filbert in a couple of hours, but that gives me those couple of hours to spare. Luckily for you, my man, the gathering in question doesn't require I be 'up for' anything but networking. Filbert says there's someone going to be there who can arrange for me to spend some time in exotic locales, if I only smile and chat him up nicely."

Then he entirely shifted gears and said: "You feeling all right?"

It had taken him that long to realize I looked like shit.

"I thought I'd never find you," I accused.

"Well," he said, "whatever we're going to do this evening, we'd better get to it. You realizing, I hope, that it's going to cost you, this time. Filbert lets me off the leash every now and again (all work and no play makes Jimmy a dull boy), but tonight isn't one of those nights."

Filbert?

"What in the hell does Filbert have to do or say about any of this?" I said in a voice loud enough, I'm sure, for Filbert to hear across the room.

"Well, in the vernacular of my world -- he's my pimp," said Jimmy, calm as you please. "Although, admittedly, Filbert likes me to refer to him as my manager."

No loud, aghast, "You're a hustler?!" from me. I was definitely surprised by it but, by that point, it didn't make any difference to me what Jimmy or Filbert did for a living. I'd slept around more than my share, too, and hadn't expected Jimmy, despite his younger age, to have been any less active.

"I love you," I said. Like all the other time with him, it helplessly just slipped out.

"And, I'm prepared to give you some mighty good loving, over the next hour or so," he said. "Let's go on over to Filbert and get the business part of this over and done with."

He turned toward Filbert who looked none too friendly. I caught Jimmy by the arm and literally spun him back toward me.

"Didn't you hear what I fucking said?" I literally screamed and brought people on the dance floor to a complete stop. "I love you, for Christ's sake! Love you!"

He laughed. In retrospect, I figure he couldn't have come up with any other response. I must have looked damned silly doing my flap-armed love-you performance for everyone in the super-heated bar to hear and see.

"You hardly know me, Tom," Jimmy said, not laughing since I'd refused to join in. "We've hooked up a grand total of one night."

"That one night was enough -- for me," I said.

"Look," he said and, for the first time, looked nervous. "Maybe we'd better put off any rematch for when I've a bit more time. Maybe when I'm back from those exotic locales I soon hope to get to, and you have all of this in better perspective."

"But, I love you!" I said.

"Jesus, Tom ... get real!"

Which hurt me far more, in the long run, than Filbert's arrival and sucker punch to my jaw.

In the short run, of course, Filbert did the most physical damage, in that I ended up an assumed mugging victim, in an alley two blocks from the bar. I was in the hospital two days, much of the time just making sure I only suffered a broken jaw.

After which, I searched for Jimmy. No success this time, except for three people who told me they thought Jimmy and his manager were "out of the country". One thought to Miami (proving how well our school system had done by him), one thought to Mexico, one thought to the French Riviera.

To this very day, I'm still looking for Jimmy.

In fact, I'm at my apartment, one more time, for only as long as it'll take me for a quick shower and a fresh change of clothing, before I take up the search again in all those bars filled with all those sweaty half-naked old and young men, when the phone rings. I think it's Jimmy, and I trip over my own feet to answer. It turns out to be yet another job offer. From which I, yet again, try to beg off, only to be threatened, this time, with "... never work again, in this business, if you don't come through for me on this one, this one time, Tom!" The tough guy on the other end has a helluva lot more clout in the oil business than my old oil-business buddy Gary Feldson's father-in-law ever had.

It having been ages, since I've thought of Gary.

The night before I'm scheduled to leave for the oil-drilling operation in Argentina, all my hopes of ever finding Jimmy pretty much gone, I try to track down Gary for old time's sake.

Two calls later, I'm told by a mutual acquaintance in Hong Kong that Gary was killed in a freak drilling-rig accident on Sumatra, over six months before.

On the plane to Buenos Aires, I dream of Paolo -- first time ever. He whispers, "I love you," but it's my sobbing those very same words that brings me awake in a sweat and brings the stewardess over to ask if I'm okay.

EATING CROW

Sing a song of six pence,
A pocket full of rye.
Four-and-twenty blackbirds
Baked in a pie.
  -- old nursery rhyme

FILLING:
1/3 cup butter
1/3 cup flour
1 tablespoon sauteed onions
1 tablespoon chicken stock
1/2 teaspoon salt
1/4 teaspoon pepper
1 3/4 cup water
2/3 cup milk
2 cups boiled blackbird meat, cut up
1/2 cup cooked peas
1/2 cup diced cooked carrots

PASTRY:
2 cups sifted flour
sprinkle of salt
5 tablespoons lard
cold water

DIRECTIONS:
Heat lard over low heat until melted. Stir in flour, onions, chicken stock, salt and pepper. Mix until smooth. Add water and milk, stirring constantly. Heat to boiling and boil one (1) minute while stirring. Stir in meat, peas, and carrots. Set aside. Prepare Pastry: To flour, add salt, and enough cold water so that, via finger-pinching, the mixture just holds form without crumbling. Add just enough more cold water to

make the whole mass form a non-sticky ball (if too sticky, add a bit more flour). Let ball of dough sit in cool place for one (1) hour or more. Divide in half. Roll out halves for top and bottom of one pie. Line plate with one rolled-out half of pastry dough and pour in the filling. Place remaining rolled-out half of pastry dough over the filling. Fold under edges of pastry dough at the edge of the plate; flute. Cut slits in top covering of pastry dough and bake at 425 degrees for 30 to 35 minutes, or until browned.

-- Old World recipe

"Okay, I'm sorry," I said. "I thought you were pulling my leg, or were speaking figuratively, not literally. Like in the Bible. You know? Where Moses isn't really a man but a symbol for something else. Where seven days might not be seven days, as we know them, but some time scale only known to those on some heavenly level.

"I mean, like, face it, I'm supposed to have taken that nursery rhyme seriously? Likewise, to have figured there was actually an Old Lady who lived in a shoe? Really a Jack-be-nimble who jumbled quickly over a candlestick? See where I'm coming from?

"Besides, all those birds baked in that pie were still alive when the pie was opened. Lousy chef, yes? Maybe, a bird lover. Maybe, some-one who didn't have an oven with the temperatures you seem to have managed from a bit of mud and a mere campfire.

"And, it's not as if anyone ever said to me, 'Hey, man, let's go shoot a few crows!' I mean, not to fill the family larder. As a kid, I only remember black birds landing in our yard and cawing and eating the peanuts we threw out for the squirrels. My mother telling me to shoo the birds away every time, not once telling me to go out and get a couple of them, or a couple of the squirrels, for that matter, for supper, you know?

"And, what with you being a Crow Indian, named Tom (Black Bird) Thomas ... well, Tom Tom ...

"I don't know if I even ever considered crows truly edible, you know? Might have, if I'd ever thought about it. I mean, I suppose there were once crows in China and, the way I hear it, there isn't a bird in the sky over there, these days, every last one of them, crows included, having been recruited for some peasant's cooking pot, so ...

"It doesn't taste like ... you know? like ... I imagined crow would taste. Might as well be chicken. Except, that's what they always say, isn't it? I mean, I know a guy who once ate rattlesnake and said it tasted like chicken.

"Hey, do you suppose I'm eating 'the' bird that inspired Poe to write 'The Raven'? You know?: 'Once upon a midnight dreary ...' and all of that. Sorry! Of course, you've heard of it. No way was that meant to insinuate I see you as some kind of stereotypical book-ignorant Indian. After all, I know for a fact that you're headed for college next week, don't I?

"All of this boiling down, I guess, to my being sorry for not having taken you at your word. I should have believed you, seeing as how I certainly know by now that you're not likely to take anything any way but dead-seriously.

"Come on, Tom Tom, I didn't mean that as derogatory, either. It's just that you haven't exactly been Mr. Lighthearted on this little expedition of ours, have you? Not that I needed, or expected, a court jester along to keep me amused. In that, you've turned out to be one helluva a surprisingly great guide.

"Come on, Tom Tom, I didn't mean 'surprisingly' to come off negatively. Come on back to the fire. Have another piece of pie. It's fucking-A delicious. Really, it is. Best meat pie I've ever tasted, bar none."

-- eating crow, 2 August

Eating Crow, 4 August:

I have a hard-on, in that I've always had this thing for American Indians, in general. Don't ask me why, because I haven't a clue. All I know is that it goes back a long ways, my having found myself, more often than not, playing Indian in all of those kiddy cowboy-and-Indian games.

Lately, I have the hots for this one Crow Indian, in particular, name of Tom "Black Crow" (talk about redundancy) Thomas. It has been my attempts to keep secret from him just how frequently he causes the stiffy at my groin that has had me acting like a virgin, ever since Jed

"Grey Wolf" Thomas told me his nephew would be the guide accompanying me through Yellowstone, this time around. Jed having accompanied me just after the fire burned so much park acreage that the majority of ecologists predicted the end of Yellowstone-as-we-know-it! My assignment, at the time, was to photograph the devastation, wrought by Mother Nature, for "Mother Nature" magazine.

My assignment, this time, is to photograph the very same area, a second time, for the very same magazine, in proof-positive of the remarkable recovery made by the park. Photo shoots one and two, part of a projected trilogy that the magazine's editorial board sees as emphasis for their, and the majority of ecologists', newly adopted contention that Mother Nature, and we're not talking the magazine, has the best know-how for successful management of Her territories, without interference from meddlesome, no matter how well-intentioned, humans.

Jed Thomas was fifty-two when I first met him, and he'd still had enough of the "noble savage" about him to put a bit of starch in my pecker, although never so much that I found my arousal unmanageable. Meaning, I even succeeded, sometimes more easily than at others, to strip down for occasional mutual baths (welcome as hell in the stifling heat of any Yellowstone summer), during which the coldness of glacial and snow run-off streams was my constant accomplice in keeping my hards-on from becoming a bone (play on words) of contention between the obviously straight-as-an-arrow Indian brave and this hopefully not-too obviously queer photographer/journalist.

This summer around, Jed with his broken ankle, his nephew in substitute, I knew from the get-go that control of my dick was going to be a helluva lot more difficult. To the point where, early on, I decided that not even frequent dousings of my dick in ice-cold water was going to keep Tom Tom from quickly realizing I coveted more of him than just his expertise as a guide.

Let's face it, Tom Tom isn't in his fifties, and he won't be for several decades. He's young. He's hung. He's handsome. Nor, does he carry around any of that never-lost-baby-fat smoothness of muscle tone that's so often found on those modern-day Indians seen on television and in the movies who play their more rebellious and better-conditioned ancestors. Either Tom Tom comes from an entirely different gene pool (his blue eyes insinuating one or more white man somewhere within his family gene pool), or he spends a good deal of his time in the reservation equivalent of a gymnasium, or some combination of the two.

I mean, the kid is studly, from the word "Go". Even if I didn't have this thing for American Indians, it's hardly unlikely my pecker would remain inattentive to his well-muscled body, completely devoid as his body is, except for the short-cut black thickness tousled on his head, and the equally black hair of his small pubic vee.

He has high cheekbones. Rugged jawline. A Roman nose more like those seen on Roman statues, as opposed to those seen on the backs of some old-time American nickels.

He has square pectorals, mirrored across a deep and narrow pectoral cleavage; nipples the color of non-patina copper. His belly is scalloped, his navel not so much an innie as a mere dent in its abdominal landscape. His arms and legs are powerful accompaniments to the whole: biceps, triceps, gastrocmemius, soleus ... et al, unlikely to have attained their present perfection without help from some kind of supplemental weight training. Although, the overall impression isn't one of muscle-bound jock who spends way too much time clanging barbells but, rather, of someone who has had the good sense to stop without overdoing.

You possibly note how I've steered clear of any descriptions of Tom Tom's cock, balls, and ass (his pubic vee as far as I've gone) -- at least until now. Just thinking about those, his more intimate parts, separately or together, makes my cock go all the harder, assuring me that, this -- my last late super-heated summer afternoon with my Indian guide on the Yellowstone trail -- isn't any more likely to see me join him for his nightly swim than I'd joined him on any of his other previous dips.

Under other circumstances, I would assume he has me pegged as some maniacally modest white man, what with my successful endeavors always to bathe in private. It having been infeasible not to bathe, for the whole two weeks of stifling heat that has accompanied our trek together (although I had originally contemplated that alternative), lest he think I eschewed good hygiene altogether. However, Tom Tom, having been thoroughly briefed by his Uncle Jed, as regards the routine of my previous expedition into the parkland (such briefing likely to have at least mentioned one of the times Jed and I had stripped for mutual bathing), likely assumes my new-found modesty is the final in a series of assumed personal affronts.

William Maltese

Assumed personal affront, number one: My fear, at the outset, of finding myself for two weeks, alone in the woods, with a straight teenage American Indian stud who'd keep me in constant heat, having made me come off unabashedly disappointed when told Tom Tom had been substituted for Jed as my guide. The degree of my fear, as regarded all the temptation Tom Tom has, indeed, offered, was mis-read by the kid, I'm sure, as my doubting his capabilities as a guide. Pretty much confirmed when Jed showed up at my motel room, the night prior to departure, to offer additional and personal assurances that his nephew was thoroughly qualified for the job for which I'd hired him.

Assumed personal affront, number two: My conscious efforts, on the trail, to keep my distance, having found out, early into the trip, that the hardness of my cock increased in direct proportion to how close I was to the object of my desire. Even I see just how easily my avoidance of him came off as unsociability, my having gone to such lengths to bathe separately and keep the camp fire between us, whenever we were eat-ing or sleeping. When, in truth, I was merely fearful that my desire for Tom Tom would see me doing something really stupid, if I dropped my defenses for even the briefest moment.

Why, you may ask, did I so masochistically rein in from at least some attempt to seduce such an attractive young man, especially since he represents the epitome of all I've ever found sexually attractive in the American Indian male? Especially when, more than once in my life, having seen someone I liked, I've gone right on up and said, "Hey, want to go home and fuck and suck each other's brains out?" The answer is that I, from the outset, didn't want to do anything untoward that would screw up so obviously an important photo-shoot. The editorial staff of "Mother Nature" having already blocked out an entire issue for my pho-tographs (sight-unseen) and supporting text. My in anyway failing in my contract with them to give them the photos they've requested bound to reflect badly on my hard-won and sterling reputation as a profes-sional in my field. Therefore, any kind of pass made at this handsome Indian guide of mine, tempting as it might have been, and still is, risks Tom Tom taking offense and hightailing it off to tell the tale of the pho-tographer-pervert, thereby possibly drying up all future access to the guide I'm still going to need when I return for the last and final shooting of the Yellowstone Fire-and-Its-Aftermath Trilogy.

Assumed personal affront, number three: My having made light of Tom Tom's efforts to provide me a traditional Indian meal of crow pie. I simply hadn't taken his crow pie seriously. The very idea of crow as a game bird having never crossed my mind -- not even once. So, when he bragged of this crow-pie specialty, passed down through his family, on his mother's side, and proceeded to serve something up, I'd ... well, I'd ... I'd ... likely hurt his feelings by as much as calling him a liar by refusing to believe I actually ate what he said I ate. Until, of course, he produced the plucked feathers to prove it.

And, now, this, our last night on the trail, filming completed and in the bag, he'd come right on out and asked, point blank, whether I'd like to join him in the swim he now enjoyed, and I, after quickly contemplating the effect on him of my stripping to reveal my raging hard-on, had declined.

He swims the crystal-clear water of the icy stream-fed pool, and I watch, hot as hell (actually pretty much stewing in my own overheated sweat); this time, no other bathing facility to which I can conveniently retreat. My cock goes all the harder as Tom Tom's muscular body streamlines beneath the surface with the grace of an otter specifically designed for such underwater maneuvers.

When he reaches the shallow end of the pool, close-by, surfaces and stands, his body drips cool liquid, some of which catches a stray ray of light, that has managed the maze of pine branches in the distance, and shatters into the myriad colors of the rainbow.

His large hands go to his face to wipe at residue water. I can do little more than watch from the sidelines and marvel at what my body tells me is a thoroughly sensuous display, as I grow all the more sticky with unwashed sweat.

Which, once again, brings me to Tom Tom's exceptional cock, pendulous balls, and exquisite ass.

Amazing how the cold water never seems to phase the impressive dimensions of his cock and/or balls. The former, a good ten inches before submersion, including foreskin that never quite completely shawls his mushroomed cockhead, may actually gain a few fractions of an inch during each dip. My cock, nine inches of flaccid meatiness, when soft and cuddly warm, literally does a disappearing act within my crotch hair whenever exposed to such wilderness-area liquid iciness (no matter what the horrendously high summer temperatures steaming my blood outside the water). Not Tom Tom's dick, though. Nor his balls, which stay loose and low-hanging enough to swing left, then right, to slap both of his thighs as he now slowly sloshes toward the shore from the water.

His ass, presently turned slightly from me, has to be one of the wonders of the Modern World. Never have I seen two such perfect buttocks so perfectly mated along so perfectly snug a crack.

My dick is swollen into a genuinely uncomfortable impasse within my trouser crotch. I would grab hold, from the outside, and shift it into a more comfortable alignment, but Tom Tom, now turned and headed straight for me, will see for sure -- and wonder what?

Don't get me wrong: I've more than my share of willpower. In evidence, I cite my past couple of weeks on the trail with Tom Tom, not to mention glimpses of his stark-naked bathing every night. I've made it through without once making a grab for his big dick or rubbing my stiffy up against his hard ass. But if ever there's temptation pretty much impossible for me to resist, it's Tom Tom stark naked, his body glossed with water, his big dick and his cum-fat balls walked right up beside me, within tongue-licking distance.

"My uncle told you I was gay, didn't he?" he says.

Of all the things he could have said ... of all the things I expected him to say (like, "Why are you, as usual, trying to hide that incriminating queer boner of yours, white man?!') ... what he has said is something that leaves me pretty much speechless, except for my guttural, "Huh?" that can just as well pass for my clearing my throat.

"I know Uncle Jed dropped by your motel room the night before we left," Tom Tom says. "I figure he told you, then, right? Giving you the chance to pull out or look elsewhere for another guide? So, why didn't you pull out, or look for another guide? Any fantasies I had about you being interested in a little wilderness cock and ass, on the side, has certainly proved mere wishful thinking."

"You're gay?" I say, and it's a question, no matter what in the hell I think I've just heard him say. Any notion that he's queer is completely out of the question. I mean, for Christ's sake, I'm gay and would have noticed a "fellow traveler" when I saw him, wouldn't I? Especially after having spent almost two weeks alone with him in the woods.

"Tell you about the picture, did he?" he says, apparently figuring my response, lame as it was, was no more than rhetorical.

"Picture?" Just call me Little Sir Echo.

"You and my Uncle Jed camped at Swillhil Springs."

What in the hell is he talking about? I haven't a clue as to any picture of Jed and I at ...

Wait a damn minute! There had been that park ranger. Jed had asked him to snap a picture of us, using the camera the ranger was using to photograph indigenous wild life for identification purposes. Jed had said something about picking up the print later. Except, I'd never seen it. The only photos to which I'd ever paid any attention were the ones I'd taken.

"Uncle Jed used to keep the picture tucked in that issue of 'Mother Nature' that had your Yellowstone pictures in it, between the pages where you mentioned him as being your guide. Kind of his proof-positive that the Jed 'Grey Wolf' Thomas, in your layouts, and the Jed 'Grey Wolf' Thomas, my uncle, were one and the same."

I'm confused and still pretty much tongue-tied. If Tom Tom has indicated any connection between his being gay (did he really say that?), and some picture taken by a park ranger, I've missed it.

"I used to get the picture and take it into my room," he says. "Never saw a white man quite as good-looking as you. Can't remember ever getting horny enough by just looking at any photo, especially of some white man, to jack-off as much a I did over that picture of you. Finally, one day, I got so excited that I wasn't as careful as usual, and I splattered the thing with several very copious slugs of my heartily squirted cream. You know what cum can do to a photograph? Or, rather, do you know what my cum did to that photograph? Granted, if I'd wiped up the mess immediately, the damage might have been less than it was, but I'd beaten my dick to such an A-bomb explosion that I was left exhausted, afterwards, to the point of taking several minutes to realize just where my spermal fallout had landed."

"You're kidding!"

"Recently, Uncle Jed came looking for the photo, didn't he?" he says. "When you sent word that you were headed in our direction again. Couldn't for the life of him figure out what happened to it. Didn't have a clue, up until the day of your arrival, when he suddenly remembered having once seen me with the (pre-cum stained) photo, in my room. Went looking. Found it, eventually, under my mattress, cum-stuck to the springs. You ever see shit hit the fan?"

"Your Uncle Jed merely came by the motel to assure me you were as good a guide of the area as there was."

"Naw!" Tom Tom doesn't believe I word I've just said; I can tell.

"He never went near the subject of your sexuality and, believe me, I would remember something like that." Of course, were I straight and had just discovered my nephew was queer, would I, no matter what I threatened, actually go on out and broadcast the fact to the world (i.e. to some Mother Nature photographer)?

"Said he was sure you'd want to know you were going to be alone in the woods for two weeks with a fucking queer," Tom Tom says, "and, despite my father being his favorite brother, he was damn tempted to tell you."

"Tempted or not, he didn't," I say. "Either your uncle changed his mind, or he realized if you could fool him for so long you could fool me for two weeks, or he decided one queer wasn't liable to be all that upset in having another queer guide him around Yellowstone."

I'm not the only one who can lose his voice. Although, I find it very hard to believe that, as eager as I've been to conceal my sexuality, I've been quite as successful as Tom Tom pretends I've been.

"No way does my uncle figure you gay," he says. "His suspicions would have come out by now, certainly the times he's been drunk and gone over your time together for the first shoot. And I'm talking more than just one such major drunk. Unless, of course, you and my uncle ..."

"Never happened," I say. "Not that I didn't fantasize it happening at the time."

"Well, I certainly never had a clue."

"You've seen me walking around with a perpetual boner, for two weeks, even sprouting one now..." I emphasize the latter by opening my closed thighs for him to have a peek of the painful bulge my curlicued dick makes in the crotch of my pants. "...and you've thought what?"

"That you had/have a girl friend somewhere. You always so eager for privacy so you could/can jerk-off and fantasize fucking her pussy without this queer around to interfere with your masturbatory fun and games."

"You have to be joking!" It's simply too incongruous that he assumed me pining for pussy all the while I pined for his sexy, and sometimes even naked, manliness.

"You are pulling my leg, right?" he says. "About being gay, too, I mean."

"The only thing I'm pulling ...." I say and reach to take firm hold of his big dick. "The only thing I've wanted to pull ... these past two weeks ... is, guess what?"

I'm excited by his cock immediately swelling against the curl of my palm and fingers.

"You know," I say, suddenly sceptical any of this is anything but the beginnings of a wet dream, "I've never seen this cock of yours hard, while my dick has seldom been soft the whole time I've been with you."

The notion that he may prefer sex with a photograph of me, to sex with the real me, is more than a bit disconcerting.

"If you've only seen it soft, that's only because I've spent every spare moment out of your sight beating it to softness," he says, "just so my turns-on wouldn't be obvious. Sometimes, hiking along the trail, your tight buns dancing in the seat of your pants right in front of me, I'd pull out my prick and whack it off while walking, just wishing you'd turn around and, maybe, just maybe, forget whomever that boner-producing girl friend of yours you'd left at home."

My mind's-eye view of him watching my ass on the trail, his dick out of his open fly and being pounded by his fist, his big dick eventually even creaming to fill the very footprints I'd just left on the ground between us, silly-assed me being none the wiser (more concerned with keeping all evidence of my latest hard-on aimed in the opposite direction), makes me frustrated at opportunities lost, makes my cock go all the harder.

My stiff dick is presently swollen so cockamamie into the confines of my trouser crotch that I'll need both hands to shift it into more comfortable alignment. Only reluctantly do I turn loose of his Tom Tom's prick (fearful my letting go will see me less likely to retrieve it), to perform the deed of alleviating the increasingly painful pretzeling of my dick in my pants.

"What a helluva lot of time wasted," he says, and his eyes watch each and every repositioning movement of my hands at my lap.

Without any additional assistance from me, his cock converts to castle drawbridge, spanning the space between us. I anchor its free-swinging end not with my hand, this time, but with my puckered lips and a hearty suck. My reward is a siphoning of slightly salty preseminal lubricant, and a good view of the wide expanse of his cockback extending between my mouth and his cock's anchorage at his lower belly.

"I've been waiting for this one helluva long time, white man," he says and gently rests both hands atop my head. His fingers actually comb my short-cut blondness.

Within my hand, his balls are as hairless and smooth as billiard balls. None of the usual stubble found on guy's who purposely shaved their scrotums for one reason or another.

Though my face keeps his dick locked in place, I can tell, by the feel of his just-captured cockhead, that the rest of his prick gains additional stiffness. It's as if the mechanism that controls the lift of his particular sexual drawbridge still works, but the lock-down at my mouth's end prevents any additional rise. To test that perception, I leave off sucking and let his cockhead flip free.

"Oh, sweet-sucking white man," he says. Hardly able to know that my temporary release of his dick has been nothing more than purposefully playful, he's quick to manhandle his seemingly recalcitrant cock for its return to my mouth for immediate recommencement of sucking.

For the brief moment, though, before he'd been able to capture it, his dick gave all appearances of having been raised to protect its castle from siege. The weight of it, somehow uplifted by inner stiffness, was a miracle of physics that defied all known laws of gravity. Spit-wet cockhead, shot totally through the cuff of his foreskin, extends upward as far as his navel. His cockbelly a wide slab of meat that provides a view of filigree veins unnoticed from any other but that particular angle.

I swallow another two inches of his cock which prevents his cock's escape as I simultaneously maneuver to my knees. Normally not the most comfortable wilderness position, the discomfort of my rocky kneeling mat, in this case, in combination with the hardness of his cock within the padding of his uncut foreskin, only gets me all the more excited. I don't even pay all that much attention to the drools of sweat profusely running my skin beneath my shirt.

I'm frankly embarrassed by just how hot and excited all of this makes me. Normally, kneeling over some guy's dick, I'd be simultaneously fishing my own hard prick out of my pants. Something too pleasurable, though, keeps me from even exploring the possibilities of unzipping my fly, fishing for my hard cock, taking hold, and trying to pry my extreme phallic steeliness from its pants-crotch prison. Intuition, born of my having fucked and sucked around often enough to know the telltale signs sometimes telegraphed by my body, tells me that my passion-primed cock, having waited around so long for just this moment, is keyed enough to start pumping goo with the least bit of outside interference.

I wonder if Tom Tom's wait has made him equally hot and horny. His recent bath in the cool pool surely must have somewhat tempered both the heat and his horninesss. Therefore, I'm hopeful my labors over his dick aren't going to send his cum rocketing up his stiff penis, into my eagerly feasting mouth and throat, before I have as much time over his crotch as I really now want to be stationed there. I'd go so far as to ask him, "This want to make you blow your nuts, prematurely, red man?", but any such words will come out garbled around his dick, especially as I proceed to swallow up even more of him.

"You know just how close your bit of sucking has this Indian brave's nuts to blowing?" he answers my question with his question, ESP if I've ever been confronted by it.

I decide to make this last as long as my expertise at hanging from hard cock will allow. Meaning, no fancy stuff, this first time around. I'll save the loud and soupy gobbling, the head-whipping tactics that'll have his cock fucking my face every which way from Sunday, the vacuum-tube gone amuk suctioning that'll take even the hardest cocks and stretch them to half again their normal length. I have all intentions of eventually getting around to those advanced techniques, if just sadistically to show my handsome Indian guide how much he's missed by having been so overly subtle as to what he's been prepared to offer, all along, but they'll have to wait. Those tricks will be better put to use when his reservoir of cum has been almost drained dry, and he needs extra incentive to refill his nuts and provide the hydraulics necessary to pump more of his male cream through a pipeline already, by then, overly used and abused.

So, I provide his cock with a slow and easy slide of my ovaled mouth, down the entire length of prick. My gumming lips not nearly as tightly gummed as I can make them but enough so that they make him shiver in visible response.

My hands run up the backs of his naked legs and check out each and every muscle grouping found there. His calves and thighs are as rock-hard as his cock, the latter now completely buried inside my face. His butt is a marvel of how perfectly stony buttocks can provide handfuls for the palms and fingers I cup over them.

His hairless balls elevate farther and offer additional pillowing for my chin. My nose pugs against the hairy scalloped hardness of his lower belly. My mouth goes all guppy-like in a final attempt to gobble the very last fraction of an inch of his dick, except the very last fraction of his dick is already claimed by me.

"Oh, you cock-sucking white man!" he says.

I let his reflexive hip-strokes perform a complete out-in fuck motion that momentarily travels my mouth back to the flare of his cockhead with a quick return to his cockbase. I still provide only the barest of suction and pressure and suspect he's too keyed to know that what I provide is nothing compared to what's going to fill the rest of our short time together.

"So fucking, fucking ... white-man fucking ... face-fucking good," he says.

As if to realize the importance of reticence in order to make this beginning feast of his cock last its possible limits, his next slide of dick out of my face is a slow one, although the control he needs to proceed without posthaste, into a wham-bam, thank-you, white-man finale, is relayed to me by the additional tautness of his now very sweaty buttocks against my very sweaty hands tented on them. My lips once again cock-swallows all of the way down to nestle among the surprisingly straight black hair that composes his very small pubic push.

Tastes and flavors, male and heady, washed free of his body by his recent swim, are renewed now, in the sun's continuing heat and in his body's increasing sexual heat. His studly Indian-brave-in-rut essence oozes every part of his skin.

"Eat this Indian's big dick, white man," he says. Then, echoing my own take on the exquisiteness of the moment, he adds: "Slow ... easy .. making it last ... white-Jesus ... last ... slow ... easy ... slow."

Except, I'm not a trained yogi, although moments like this more often than not make me wish that I were. I'd once unsuccessfully tried to land a photo-shoot in India just to get a few lessons in yoga-control.

Tom Tom's young legs are all a-tremble, his ass so hard-locked along its crack that I couldn't have broken through a finger to probe his asspucker, even if that had been on my immediate agenda.

Tom Tom stops all fuck motions, suddenly seemingly content with my face simply buried totally, yet again, over his dick. His cockhead thrusts so far down my throat that swallowing seemingly rolls my Adam's apple along a good length of his prick.

I swallow again. He groans.

I swallow again, and I'm rewarded with such a hearty gushing of pre-seminal goo that I think he may actually have shot his wad, then and there. It's only the smooth oiliness of the natural lubricant, no attending rich nuttiness of flavor, no gluttonous lumps and sticky strings in accompaniment, that provide the clues as to the real identity of the porridge his cock has provided.

Not that I'm going to have to wait all that long for the main course.

"Jesus, white man, I'm close," Tom Tom tells me, as if the sudden additional swelling of his whole length of dick, inside my face, isn't indication enough.

He might well be able to stand where he is, stayed put for an additional minute, maybe more, masochistically relishing his need for orgasm but keeping it in abeyance, like an Indian shaman, but I'm no longer in all that much control. Actually, I've managed to let this drag out far longer than I've humanly thought possible. My needs have finally gained dominance, no matter what extreme effort of self-denial and self-control my conscious mind might think it can muster at times like this.

I want hot, spewing Indian cum, and I want it now. Not seconds from now. Not five seconds from now. Right ... right ... Jesus, yes, right ... cum you red-skinned hunky sonofabitch'n bastard ... now!

My face is up his cock and back down it, that same route repeated in so fast a replay that the bobbing of my head can't be more of a blur as ...

"Eat my cum-spewing dick!" he says.

His hands clamp my head so firmly over and onto his crotch that my mouth is no longer going anywhere but right where it is.

His asscheeks dimple deeply beneath my hands. The compression of his buttock against buttock, collapsing inward along the shared ass-crack, becomes so intense it's impossible to believe his anal crevice even exists.

His hips swing more tightly forward and his pelvis gives a roll that torques his passion-swollen meat deeper inside me.

William Maltese

"Oh, fuck ... merciful fuck," he says, and it's only then that all the tension locked up inside his studly Indian body genuinely reaches its limit of endurance and lets go.

His cum is a raging flood suddenly turned loose and channeled into a space way too small to contain it. The farther engorgement of his already cum-bloated dick momentarily has me thinking, even with my own intense degree of pleasure, that his dick might well explode in my mouth, like a balloon force-fed too much water too fast.

His seminal bullets release in a white-hot barrage that splashes the back of my throat with hot spermal glue that soon merges and commences a volcanic flow that threatens to make me choke.

"I'm coming ... fucking coming!" he literally shouts, his head thrown back, as if he's a wolf howling at the moon.

I swallow and keep on doing just that, although he feeds me so much cream that its saltiness stings my sinuses and has me wondering if I won't actually drown in the deluge I've been so hot to have set loose inside me.

His cock keeps right on spewing, and I keep right on eating. I'm in yet another mid-swallow when my cock creams its own explosion of pearly mess into the tight confines of my imprisoning trousers.

COMES A NAKED STRANGER

As I open the door, I expect Lou who said he might pop over. The air-conditioner at his place is on the fritz. The air-conditioner at my place is on the fritz, too, but at least it manages a faint breath of coolness that occasionally makes for better than nothing.

Lou, though, in my opinion -- if not in his -- would be damned lucky to have the good looks of this youngster-on-my-doorstep, let alone have this kid's full head of tousled blond hair and trim little body. Hell, even I, hardly a gnome or too decrepit an old fart, at twenty, would welcome a rewrapping in similar packaging to this one.

If I'm not mistaken, I may have seen this kid before, in one or more of the gay bars I've visited lately with Lou; Martin and I having gone our separate ways. Although I might be mistaken in thinking I recognize this kid, because I seldom wear my glasses in look-conscious gay "society" and, without them, usually see things pretty blurred if they're anywhere beyond a two-foot distance from my face.

I've one of these borderline vision anomalies that has me, whenever I wear contact lenses for distance, unable to see close-up without putting on glasses. So, I'm pretty much stuck with glasses, no matter which route I go. I guess there's a laser eye surgery now available to solve my problem, but I'm not willing to risk it until there's a far larger backlog of success stories of people who haven't gone blind in the aftermath.

Not all that comfortable, anyway, back in the cruising rat race, I've pretty much opted, at least for the time being, to remain content with merely seeing the beers put before me, prepared to graduate to seeing people later.

However, I'm close enough to this kid, now standing in my open doorway, to recognize him as pretty much a perfect specimen. Judged not totally perfect only because he needs at least another inch in height. And who knows how many more flaws I'd discover if I ever lucked out seeing him naked?

What I find more fascinating about him is the why behind his Cowboy

William Maltese

Bob get-up: Stetson hat, red bandanna, western shirt, large Colt 45 belt buckle, faded blue jeans, cowboy boots complete with spurs. I mean, the ongoing heat wave has me stripped down to just my pants, and I put those on to answer the door; Lou and I being close but not so close that I'd want him tempted by my cock which I know for a fact he still hungers after. I find myself looking for the definitive piece of stray hay caught in this kid's hair or clenched between his teeth to tell me he's just, this moment, arrived on horseback from the barn and/or farm.

Most importantly, what hard-worked miracle, performed by God up in heaven, brings this vision of stereotypical youthful Montanan ride-'em-cowboy Mr. Studly to my big-city door, on this particular hot ... hot ... too-hot ... summer afternoon?

"Happy Birthday to you, Happy Birthday to you," he bursts into spontaneous song, telling me immediately that this is one of God's miracles sadistically gone awry. "Happy Birthday, dear Jean-Michael ..."

Major fuck-up confirmed (he obviously has me confused with a character in "Boys in the Band")! Nonetheless, I let him finish, because he has a genuinely pleasant voice. Not exactly choir-boy caliber, unless the choirboy in question is courting puberty and a permanent voice change, because he definitely sings slightly off-key.

"Which I do appreciate," I say, "except I ..."

"No, no, no!" he says and pushes right on in, without a by your leave. "Whatever you do, don't interrupt."

He does an about-face back toward me, hooks his thumbs in his belt, his fingers in a downward parenthesis of his obviously well-bulged crotch.

"Interruptions confuse me," he says. "Sorry about that. It's just the way it is. Royally fucked up my first gig, because I kept getting interrupted. Fuck up this time, and it's good-by Joe -- although my name is Parker, by the way. Parker Westen (rhymes with Western). Anyway..." He does a quick look-see at the layout of the room. "...sit on down over there, in that chair."

"I really think..."

"Please, please ... please," he says and washes his hands like Pontius Pilate wanting to be rid of all talk about Jesus. "Just let me see if I can get through this, one time. Once I do, I'll be A-OK. I know I will."

He's already A-OK, as far as I'm concerned. So, if all the kid needs is a little practice ...

I pull the door shut to the outside, head on over to the indicated chair, and sit down. Only after I'm down do I wish I'd detoured to a chair closer the piss-poor stream of cool air hopefully still emanating from my protesting air-conditioner.

"Great ... great!" he insists. "Just stay put. Don't do a thing."

He pushes his hat back, completely off his head. The hat's rawhide cord catches his attractive young neck.   He runs a nervous hand through his thick thatch of blond hair and tousles already attractively mussed strands. For not the first time, I check the carpet for a scattering of dislodged hay.

Once again, he launches into song. Something vaguely familiar, about an old cowhand from the Rio Grande. Can't say as I'm paying all that much attention to the words. He just looks so damned picture-book cowboy-cute, standing there, singing his little heart out, all the while striking poses that would have been laughably preposterous if they weren't so damned charming. I'm particularly fond of his on-horse-back charade that has his slim hips bucking back and forth, more fuck-strokes than giddys-up.

"Sorry ... sorry ..." he says suddenly, having stopped singing.

Obviously, he's distraught, but I haven't a clue as to why.

"I've forgotten the rest of the damned words," he says. "But don't say anything. Just hold a quick second, because the words are right on the tip of my tongue. This damned thing I've here seems too much a distraction."

"This damned thing", as it turns out, is his cock, which he manhandles for additional emphasis, squeezes, twists, pets, prods, paws, with an accompanying little dance, complete with knee squats that finally, it would seem, provide his hard prick with a better-than-original alignment. As well, I might add, as making it all the more evident that the kid is not only cowboy-cute but cowboy-horse hung.

"Here I thought I'd have trouble getting stiff," he says, back to a full-standing position, his thumbs belt-hooked, his downward-aimed fingers parenthesizing and defining his boner. "Figured you'd likely be some ugly old fart. Not that I've ever had any trouble getting a hard-on, even for a knothole. Proved that by getting it on with Mr. Ugly who runs the agency. Still, my first time out, the Birthday Boy, not all that bad looking, when you come right down to it, got me so confused I almost forgot to provide him my dick as well as the last two versus of a song.

William Maltese

Speaking of the latter ..."

He takes off singing anew, possibly from where he'd left off, but you couldn't prove it by me. From whenever, whatever, however, it's a thoroughly enjoyable performance. When he begins clod-hopping, line-dancing, toe-tapping, body-moving, I almost laugh out loud and clap along in sheer pleasure.

I can't remember a more fun few minutes. Not, anyway, for a long time. Lou would be surprised to see me actually smiling. He's convinced I've been permanently screwed, figuratively and literally, by my wasted years with Martin. Lou having never liked Martin, although I never did hear Martin say a bad thing about Lou the whole time Martin and I were together. Martin and I together for two years, housekeeping (playing house?), right out of high school. "Prime years down the tube!" is how Lou puts it. Although, it had been pleasant enough, at the time, to have someone always handy for mutual sex exploration. Martin and my separation hardly traumatic. We both just woke up one morning and realized whatever it was we'd had, we didn't have it any longer. Whatever it was we both now wanted wasn't likely achieved in the same rut we were in. So, Martin headed off to Seattle. After which, Lou began trying to teach me the intricacies of cruising the local bars, after first trying, for not the first time, to get into my pants. I'm sure he finds my resistance, not to mention my ineptness, frustrating as all hell.

Two final clomps of Cowboy Parker's booted feet against the floor, so forceful I suspect it dumps ceiling plaster to the white rugs of the apartment below, and his singing once again stops.

"Now," says Parker, surprising me by unbuttoning (no zipper on his pants), his fly. "If I can just get this monster of mine out without breaking it off at the base. You just too fucking handsome for this poor cowboy's own good. I suppose you're told that, all of the time, though, aren't you?"

"Not recently," I say and give an audible gasp when his large and golden cock springs out of his pants like an arrow shot by a well-strung bow.

I hold up a whoa-pardner palm in his direction.

As fun and erotic as I admittedly find all of this ...

"I really think you might want to leave off just a minute to at least let me explain that ..." I try again.

"No leaving off!" he interrupts. "No few moments. No small talk.

'Cause, studly, I'm on a roll."

"But ..."

"No ifs, ands, ors," he insists. "And, although, the butt is admittedly mighty tempting, I know what you want."

Jesus, but I do doubt that very much. I haven't had a boner the size of the one presently in my pants, since ... well since ... my very first times with Martin.

"I've been clued in," he says. "Given the skinny. Been provided the details. Have had the dope laid out as to how this is all going to go down. All you have to do is sit there. Right? Right!"

"Lou sent you, right? Right!"

"My boss is Mr. Ugly, remember?" he says. "Not Lou, in any case. Guy who paid the bill was John something. You know any John Cleaver, Deaver, Reaver, Greaver?"

In final analysis, no way Lou arranged for this bundle of goodness. Already the kid exhibits too many characteristics Lou finds wrong in the overly look-conscious gay life-style. Cowboy Parker is too blond -- according to Lou. Too pouty lip. Too snub-nose. Too just about every-thing. Parker certainly looks too young. Lou simply can't fathom what there is that has young-appearing studs like Parker attracting guys ... well, like I'm attracted to them ... as easily as raw meat attracts flies. "If one wants skinny, pretty, waifish teens to screw around with, one should screw around with women and/or girls," is how Lou puts it. "You want a man, he should walk like a man, talk like a man, look like a man. At the very least, he should be old enough -- or look old enough -- to have sprouted a couple strands of pubic hair."

"You old enough to have pubic hair?" I hear myself asking Parker. Lou would approve of my asking. Likewise, Lou will want to know the answer, when I tell him this little tale, and it's kind of hard telling what does or doesn't fuzz Parker's crotch as long as it's only the kid's impressive cock that's poked out for viewing.

"Sure do," he says, "but if you're one of those guys who prefers hair-less wonders, although that wasn't indicated at the outset, I can get completely hairless with a safety razor and bit of shaving cream -- both of which I suspect you have around."

"I like pubic hair just fine," I say. "It's just that you look so young."

"You looking like an old man, you mean?" he says. "In fact, maybe, I should ask if you have pubic hair."

"Jesus!" I say and actually laugh. "You have to be kidding!"

"Only because Mr. Ugly wouldn't risk my revealing my dick to anyone underage," says Parker. "Likewise, I guarantee you, he wouldn't risk hiring anyone to entertain you whose balls hadn't legally dropped."

"I'm relieved," I say.

"I'm losing 'the flow'," he says. "I told you talking would do that, didn't I?"

I mimic zipping my mouth.

"Right," he says.

He squats slightly, scoops into the fly of his pants and hauls out two exceptionally nice testicles. I'm reassured by the way their containing scrotum comes complete with more than a few blond strands.

He strikes a pose. I think of a Madonna video.

He faces me straight-on. His are legs slightly apart, as if he were bull-legged, although he's not. His hips thrust slightly forward. His cock juts from his pants, its impressive head aimed more toward the ceiling than toward me. His balls droop halfway to his jean-clad knees. He takes a deep breath.

"Now," he says, "if I can just manage this without being so turned on by your studly good looks that I'm not prematurely creaming, like a kid for his very first time, I've got it made."

"You planning to do just what?" I ask, in spite of any previous insinuation that I was finally prepared to keep my mouth shut.

"I know how you like it," he says. "Your John Cleaver, Greaver, Beaver, Deaver, or What-eaver, provided explicit details on how this should be done."

I should be so lucky as to have just such a friend as this John Whateaver. Unfortunately ...

"You just watch," Parker says and begins beating his cock. "Don't say a fucking word, either, because even your voice is a fucking turn-on. I want to get this right."

What? I'm going to argue? Insist upon looking this gift horse in the mouth? It's not as if I haven't tried my best to tell him he's turned up on the wrong doorstep. Convincing him of that, though, at this late date, would be tantamount to cutting off my nose to spite my face.

Why not just sit back and enjoy? It's not as if I don't deserve a considerate friend, like John Deaver, Cleaver.... It's not as if I don't deserve the sexy, charming, command performance, like Parker is giving.

Besides which, it's just too fucking hot to put up any kind of additional protest.

Okay, I do harbor uneasy feelings that Parker, sometime soon, will be back on my doorstep, less friendly than he is this time around, all as a direct result of repercussions when he's checked in with Mr. Ugly, this all over, informed he's missed his scheduled performance before whomever the real Birthday Boy. Will Parker adequately be pacified by my puny excuses that I was simply too taken by him, by his cowboy air, by his horse-like cock, by his bull-like balls, by the heat (mine and the weather's), to deprive myself of any and/or all of the well-deserved pleasure he'd been mistakenly prepared to offer up? Of course, I'll volunteer to recompense Parker for whatever monies he's out, as a result of the mix-up, hoping to hear him ask me into bed as my just rewards for, albeit belatedly, coming clean.

"This handstroke of mine, over my dick, too fast for you?" he asks.

"It's just fine. You're just fine. I'm just fine," I assure him.

I manhandle my dick to get it laid out in a less bent into a cul-de-sac position in my pants.

"It's kind of hard to pump my dick any slower," he says, "when you're so fucking sexy, but I could try."

"You're doing just fine," I assure.

"May have to stroke faster in a few seconds," he says. "I'm not really in nearly as much control as I'd like to be. I see someone studly as you and, once I get my cock in my hand, it's like my brain sends out instructions to slow down but the message never gets through."

"You're more than providing me John's monies' worth," I say. And that's true, no matter how many dollars John What-eaver has paid to have this young stud mistakenly delivered through my doorway.

I want to pull out my cock and join in. I want to pull out my cock and put in. I want to drop my pants and have him poke in. Except, if that were what Parker expects, I'm sure he would have gotten that across before now. Unfortunately, or fortunately, I'm trapped in the role of someone who gets his rocks off by sitting back and watching. I include "fortunately" only insofar as it's a definite pleasure -- masochistic, admittedly, in the extreme -- to force myself to do nothing but watch.

"See, look at that!" Parker says. "You think I consciously told my hand to start whipping my dick twice as fast as before? Hell, no! I'm on automatic pilot. Sorry about that. Maybe you can persuade John to send me around again, only keep a sack over your head, so I can pretend you're uglier than sin. Possibly, then, I could make this last longer. Then again, knowing what I know, seeing what I see, it would be hard imagining you anything but the stud-muffin you are."

Jesus, is that how people talk nowadays? Maybe I've simply been out of the loop way too long ever to adjust to being back in it. There's a whole new vocabulary out there, spoken by a whole new generation of young gays who, with few qualms, arrive at your door, whip out their dicks and, after a few lively country-western tunes, blast their teenage spunk all over the place.

Anyway, Parker now started and thoroughly into his masturbation, I'd be disappointed if he doesn't whip his delicious dick all of the way to climax. In fact, any attempt by him to veer from that inevitable conclusion, at this crucial point, would likely see me metamorphosed into one frustrated teased-to-blue-balls maniac.

"I'm getting there, buddy," he says. "A lot faster than either of us might possibly like, but you're going to see me cream. No doubt about that, if ever there was. And..." His free hand cups his elevated nuts. "...by the feel of my hefty gonads, I'm going to give you a large enough eruption to satisfy even a man of your discriminating tastes."

"I'm counting on that, cowboy," I say, relieved he and I totally agree on where he's headed with all of this.

His hand goes into even faster rhythmic cadence over his dick. I hear the sounds his fist makes as it travels up and back ... up and back ... up and back ... along the impressive length of his hand-held pecker.

My hand wipes sweat off my forehead. Even without the hot summer weather screwing up my air-conditioner, this kid would have me near boiling over with my accelerating appreciation of his show.

"Getting close," he says and walks in closer. "You want to know when, right? You want me to tell you exactly, so you can fondle my sweaty balls, at one and the same time, yes?"

Goddamn, I actually get to touch him? Reach out, take hold, squeeze down? Watch his cock spurt teenage goo, feel the way his sexual hydraulics pump cum from his perspiration-sheened nuts and blast it up and out the length of his dick?

"Yes?!" he says.

I can't tell whether it's a yes to announce the onset of irretrievable orgasm, or if it's a yes to command me to take hold, now or never.

I don't take any chances but extend a hand, palm up, his ball-fondling hand pulling away for my eager fingers to replace it.

"Any sweet second, now, stud," he says.

How marvellous his testicles, pooled in my hand. His nuts so mysteriously heavy and light, at one and the same time; both made tacky by sweat.

"Ready?" he says, obviously breathless. There's an attractive pale pinkness that flushes his damp face, his damp neck (beneath his kerchief), and even that small vee of damp and hairless chest beyond the unfastened top two buttons of his shirt. It's easy to imagine a similar color tingeing his whole body, maybe even making his nipples go dark purple and rock-hard.

The head of his dick can now pass for the nose of Rudolph the red-nose reindeer. His cockshaft has been made equally colorful from constant self-abuse and resulting friction.

"Oh, fuck, stud, fuck," he says, and shoots comet-like streamers of creamy teen cream to splash the front of my pants and run the sweaty bareness of my chest.

Reflexively, I squeeze my handful of his nuts and delight in another explosive release of his sperm. Hard and fast, I clamp my free hand to the compact mass my own nuts make at my own pants crotch. My nuts let go and hose the inner crotch of my cotton shorts.

"Christ ... oh, Christ!" he says and literally pants. His cock-fisting fingers are soaked with his own gooey discharge.

He lets go of his dick which droops to the parallel, possibly in a halfway stop before depletion to complete flaccidness.

Reluctantly, I release his scrotum which flows free far saggier than when I'd grabbed hold of it.

Inside my pants, my cum-depleted scrotum proceeds into its own passion-released sag.

Parker unthreads the knot on his kerchief and extends the released bandanna to me.

"Looks like I made a mess," he says. "John said you wouldn't mind."

"Let me get us both a towel." I return the bandanna and head to the bathroom where I secret myself behind the partially shut door long enough to stuff a washrag down my pants in order, hopefully, to control my deluge of cooling cream that so thoroughly webs my softening pecker.

I head back out and hand him a towel, while I do my best to wipe clean the spermal spray with which he's rained the front of me.

Once I've done as much as I can, at least until left to the privacy of a more thorough cleanup, I helplessly bring the balled towel I've just used to my nose and sniff the essence of young man with which Parker has saturated the material.

"You want this in a hamper or something?" Parker refers to his own gobbled towel.

"Here," I extend my hand, and he tosses his towel to me. I walk both towels into the bathroom for deposit within the tub for later sniffing.

"That was great!" Parker says when I reappear. His cock is back in his pants, his pants buttoned. Faint rills of sweat trail his left temple as far as his sweat-satiny throat. "I didn't do too badly, did I?"

"Why don't I give you my number, and you have Mr..." I stop, because no way is there likely a boss with the real last name of "Ugly".

"Why don't I give you my number, and you call me," he says.

I'd genuinely like that, but I'm not sure he's going to be nearly as friendly when he finds out he's wasted his time and cum on the likes of me, when he'd been prepaid to perform for someone else.

"I'd like that, but your boss just might insist ..."

"That I should have been sure from the get-go that you were Jean-Michael Carles, not Wynn Baylor?"

That gets my attention.

"No problem, since there never was a Jean-Michael, nor a Mr. Ugly, nor anyone called John," he says. "Only me with the hots for you. And, since the couple of times I've seen you in the bar, with you friend, you never once sitting up and taking notice, I figured a more dramatic way to say hello was in order." I should wear glasses," I say and feel damn vain in making so lame an excuse for having missed him.

"I've got nothing against glasses," he says, "as you can very well test the next time you see me."

"I see just fine up close," I say.

"It being up close and personal that I intend to be," he says.

From his pocket, he produces a piece of pre-folded paper which he hands over.

"My phone number," he says. "But be forewarned: you don't call me within two days, and I call you."

"I'll call. Promise."

"And know this," he says, walks in close and puts a hand to either side of my face to plant a too-quick kiss directly on my mouth, "I find you more than worth the bother it has taken me to get us this far."

He leaves before I overdose. Smart kid, as well as good-looking, as well as well-hung, as well as ...

I plop into the chair nearest the air-conditioner and wish for a return of the sexual heat generated by my little cowboy stud.

The phone rings. It's Lou who says he's on his way over. I tell him not to bother. I tell him I'm tired. I tell him I feel like I'm coming down with a summer cold (does he really want to risk being exposed to that?). I tell him I want to make it an early night.

It's too early to tell Lou of the new boy-man/man-boy in my life. Lou won't approve of Parker, anyway. Parker is too attractive, too blond, too young, too aggressive ....

Goddamn, but I'm one helluva lucky guy!

CHANGING OF THE GUARD

"Jeeez," says Sid Lane. "You ever hear of blue balls? Ever hear how they're caused?"

"You ever hear of black eyes?" I say and maneuver my ass up and off his teenage dick. "Ever hear how they're caused?"

Which shuts the fucker up, because I suspect he suspects I'll follow up with an exhibition as to just how black-eyeing is done. In that, yes, I can't abide a whiner.

However, what Sid, here, may not comprehend, what my fellow cops at the precinct certainly didn't understand, my partner, Candy-Ass Bill Naffy (rhymes with taffy) included, is that I never hit anyone who doesn't genuinely deserve it. Sid perfectly safe, because his whining is to be expected. He's a fucking teenybopper, albeit of legal age, isn't he? His big cock doesn't make him any the less one, either.

Not that I have this sexual thing for look-like-little-boys with big cocks. I'm no pederast size-queen. I've had some mighty good times with older average-hung hunks, even older small-weenie wonders. Sid's teenage cock is merely the closest I can come, on short notice, by way of match-up with the dildo I've used for the initial phases of this particular bit of sexual experimentation.

The problem of my not having achieved full penetration of the kid's cock up my butt, where the dildo, at least most recently, managed every time, has been my underestimation of Sid's body fat. I should have calculated more residual baby-fat, left over from pre-puberty, in that his thighs are far less solid than I imagined.

Nothing, by way of frustration here (Sid's and mine), that can't be ratified by my taking away a couple of books from each of the piles on which I've been precariously balanced in my gymnastics split.

"Think, maybe, I could just fuck you dog-style?" says Sid.

"Think, maybe, you could just guess how many guys would pay big bucks to be where you are now?" I ask. "Guys who wouldn't be so complaining?"

I'm not just blowing hot air out of my asshole, either. A guy doesn't have to be egotistical to realize he looks good. Like I look good. Damn good. Fucking good. Prime, A-1 good. Improved upon, as usual, by the way the intensive summer heat provides my naturally olive complexion with its genuinely attractive glow.

What you do is take a great tousle of blue-black hair, green eyes, Roman (but not too Roman) nose, sensuously full lips, dimples (one in my right cheek, two in the other), deeply cleft chin, hunky-muscled chest, washboard belly, big-enough cock, firm ass, great legs, and that bit of sweet summer sweat that provides the icing: put them all together and you've got me. Although not all that far into my twenties, I look all man. I looked all man at eighteen, for that matter; where Sid looks about twelve, probably will for some time to come, albeit with the mouth of a truck driver.

Besides which, you're not likely to come across any guy as sexually versatile as I am.

"Quit playing with your dick!" I say. "You think I want you squirting as soon as you're back up my ass? You think that, and you're going to be sadly sorry."

My right hand forms a fist and produces a satisfying smack against the open palm of my other hand.

No one should figure that just because I beat up on Willis Crawfold I'm as likely to beat up on Sid. Willis was a no-account wife and child puncher, threatening to knock around his wife and kid one final time too many. That's why I stomped his shitty ass. That's why his wife and son can sleep peacefully these days. That I got booted from the force because of over-excessive use of force, saved from worse by Willis wisely deciding to skip to another state, doesn't make me less glad that I did what I did.

It's a helluva lot safer and a helluva lot more lucrative working security detail for Klise Linehan, as I am these days. Now, if I can just figure out a way to shed Henry Henry (Jesus, yes, just like the echo!), my immediate asshole security-force supervisor, I'd be sitting pretty.

"Christ, Struan, are you reading those fucking stacks of books, or what?" asks Sid and brings me back to the here and now.

"Or what," I choose from the selection given.

"Funny. Not!" says Sid.

"You want funny, picture yourself with a broken nose."

"I love it when you talk mean."

"The only thing you love is the idea of being with the one stud from the Y shower room with whom everybody wanted to go home."

"That too."

I laugh. Can't help it. Maybe he's not as afraid of me as I think. Then again, maybe he's a masochist. If he's the latter, and I've attracted a few, he's in for a big surprise. He wants popped, he'll have to get married, have a kid, beat his wife and kid to pulp, threaten to kill them, then get caught by me.

"There," I say, satisfied with my readjustment of the mirror-image book piles that parenthesize Sid's sitting-on-a-cushion-on-the-floor naked body.

Sid's legs are extended in front of him. His feet, by the way, are big enough to be proof-positive that big feet equal big dick. His genuinely tiny nose, however ...

My intention, almost successful our first go-round, is to do the split, over his dick, one of my feet on each pile of books. Actually, my split, in finale, always ends up more an inverted vee in that my legs go several degrees beyond horizontal. The split I've had down since high school. The beyond-split having taken considerably longer, especially since everyone's body -- mine included -- has a decided tendency to stiffen up, with age, not get more limber.

"Can we get this show back on the road?" asks Sid who defiantly grabs his big dick and strokes it twice before he turns loose.

"You kids, today, are too much into quick fixes," I say, as if I, unlike Sid, am of a generation uncorrupted by TV sound bytes. "Sometimes a thing is made better by ample preparation and lead-in."

"How do you figure, when each of us could have had our nuts blasted twice in the time you've been fucking around trying to manage a 'just-right' first time?"

"How many teens you figure get a split lip before getting their teeny-bopper dicks off up the ass of a guy doing the split?"

"You may well provide me with a split lip," says the ballsy little prick, cruise'n for a bruise'n, "but I'm more and more doubtful of ever getting any promised blast-off up any ass lowered over me by your split legs."

The trick, of course, is for me to achieve my beyond-horizontal split without the piles of books shifting, spilling, and/or otherwise fucking up the maneuver. It helps that I've used only large coffee-table books to build two pretty stable stacks.

William Maltese

"I'm encouraged," he says when I'm again mounted into an elevated partial-split position, facing him, although I'm not quite lowered far enough for his cockhead to make target against my dropping asshole. "Except -- stop me if I'm wrong -- weren't we this far before? You actually having had most of my dick plugged inside of you? Or, what?"

"For Christ's sake, put a lid on it!" I say and wish I'd taken the time to find someone more mature and appreciative of what I'm attempting. How many guys, after all, get the uniqueness of screwing an ass from Sid and my positions?

The advantage in my having picked someone as immature as Sid is that he's less likely to try and take advantage, because of my being so obviously butcher, bigger, stronger and older. He may bitch, he may complain but, in the end, he'll likely do each and every thing I tell him to do. Had I taken on someone with a bit more will of his own ... someone who even suspected he was in the presence of the reported bad-boy ex-cop, Struan Mackelby ... I may well have risked being taken advantage of, in my split-beyond-the-horizontal, by someone out to prove something. Although, admittedly, the very fact that I make myself vulnerable is part of my turn-on.

"Well, miracles do happen," says Sid, his rubberized cockhead once again maneuvered directly against the slight pout of my descending asspucker.

"Elevator coming down," I say.

"Believe it when I see it," he says. Cocky as he pretends, he groans damn loudly and gutturally when I lower my asshole right on over a good inch of his stiff pecker.

I perform a series of up-and-down bounces, and each downward bounce slides my feet, calves, and thighs, more and more right-angles to my torso.

"Can we please, please, take your ass all of the way to the bottom this time?" Sid begs. "I've bluer balls than Babe the Blue Ox."

"Read of Babe, have you?" Frankly, I'm surprised.

"Big statue of her and Paul Bunyan on Highway 101, where I vacationed last year," he says.

Which confirms my suspicions that the cock in my butt doesn't belong to any member of the literati. Which doesn't mean Sid's cock feels any the less good stuck where it is.

It hard for some people to fathom how a guy, butch as I look, butch as I act, butch as I am, actually likes it up his ass, on occasion. It just damned hard for me to find someone who won't take advantage when tough-guy me is willing to show a bit of his softer, more feminine side.

"Doesn't that hurt?" Sid asks, my split slightly beyond horizontal, most of the kid's cock up my butt.

"I've had bigger cocks than yours up my asshole, kid," I say and I'm not just whistling "Dixie".

"I don't mean my dick up your butt, shit head," he says. "I mean you playing wishbone with your lower extremities."

"Yeah, it hurts a bit," I admit. "However, when that little-boy brain of yours matures, one of these days, you'll come to realize how a bit of pain can do a whole lot by way of supplementing pleasure."

"You're genuinely weird," says Sid.

"You're genuinely someone who likes a bit of weird, right?" I can tell.

"Damn right!"

I drop my firm and tight asshole so far down around his cock that my pucker finally -- objective achieved! -- gums the very base of his erection.

"Makes me look like I've got a new cock, on backward" says Sid, but only after a few goldfish-like gulps for air. He refers to my dick now seemingly jutted upward from his lower belly, his cock nowhere in sight.

I put a hand to each of his shoulders, my fingers making indents in the baby-fat still found there. I use my handholds as leverage to increase the natural bounce provided by the natural spring of muscles along the entire lengths of my legs.

My ass rises. It comes down. It rises higher. It comes down lower. It elevates all of the way to the flare just beneath his cockhead. It ...

"Mag ... ni ... fi ...cent!" he says and grunts softly.

"You want to use my hard cock like you would use the handle of a butter churn, feel free," I suggest. Only in retrospect do I realize the kid probably doesn't know a butter churn from a hole in the head. That I know the difference is only because I once saw one in a museum.

Frankly, I don't know how much pleasure his manhandling my dick is going to give him (although, I always get a charge out of masturbating the guys I fuck), but it's sure as hell going to add a bit of something to my side of the pleasure equation.

Not only does the clever little fuck wrap one of his hands around the thick neck of my dick and use that to help lever me down, solidly, on my next descent, but his other hand grabs my balls and gives them a sensuously painful squeeze.

"Not too shabby," he says, and my ass heads back up his dick. "Not at all."

I agree. His dick is much better up my asshole than the dildo I've used for practice. But, then, I've yet to find a dildo that correctly duplicates the steely-hard softness of real male dick.

"Maybe this is actually worth the wait," he says, after a few more bounces of my asshole over his dick.

"Surprise! Surprise!" I say sarcastically, always having known his impatience the sure sign of a kid who hasn't fucked nearly enough times to know the advantages of proper leads-in and correct preparation. So many kids, these days, prefer fast foods over gourmet meals, fast sex over gourmet sex, only because the "fast" part of everything is the most familiar. Well, this kid is getting force-fed a genuinely gourmet fuck. Or, rather, I'm converting his fast-food dick into a gourmet meal for my butt.

My ass, once again, is down to Ground Zero. I've got the height of the books just right, this time, so that I'm down as far as humanly possible over Sid's boner. The cushion beneath his ass can't compress any farther. His baby-fat thighs, this go-round, are scrunched as far possible beneath the weight I've sat atop them.

I feel far less discomfort, as the fuck progresses. Probably because, once my legs are accustomed to their positioning, they adjust to it. Partly, though, it's because pleasure counters a lot of the discomfort.

Speaking of pleasure:

"Oh, that does feel good," Sid says, as I, once again, use the springlike flexibility of my leg muscles to ride my asshole up, then down, the entire length of his sticking teenage dick.

A few more of my bounces, and Sid's masturbatory strokes of my dick become erratic. Even the way he fondles my balls is less-concentrated.

"You get your rocks off without my joining in, and you're going to wish you hadn't," I say. Sometimes, by threatening, I get guys to hold off longer than they ever think possible. Then again ...

"Oh, sorry ... Jesus, fuck ... sorry!" he bellows and, no more warning than that, his dick lets go with powerful spurts of his teenybopper cream.

"You fucking little shit!" I say and, keeping one hand on his shoulder, put my butt one final time down completely over his lap ... wrap my hand over his suddenly inert hand on my dick and commence some hearty flogging to get my rocks off.

He's already quit growling pleasure when my dick finally spits its fountains of cream to splatter our bodies, mid-bellies to chests.

"I should knock you silly," I say, recovering from my orgasm. Although our timing had been more than a little off, the intensity of my ejaculation was helped by my exotic positioning and by Sid's cock locked in my butt. "I thought I'd picked up someone with a bit more self-control."

"It was all the fucking waiting," he says. "You must have seen how all the starts and stops had my balls literally blue."

"Jesus, fucking amateur!" I say.

As far as any thoughts of actually knocking the kid around, just because he beat me to blast-off, they're purely baloney. Kids, as young as Sid, no matter how many butts they've fucked, don't have the maturity for mustering the same kind of control that comes with years of experience. The exotic way he's fucked me has to have been more of a turn-on for him than he seems willing to admit.

Besides, once again, I didn't thump all over on Willis Crawfold because he couldn't help himself when he beat his wife and kid. I beat on him because he could control himself but didn't.

"Look, gotten off once, my cock lasts longer leading up to seconds," Sid says and leads me to confirm he's had a really fine time. "It never takes my cock all that long to resurrect, after first blast-off, either."

"That's a mighty tempting offer, kid," I say, "but I've got to get to work." I hoist my ass to freedom. "How about I give you a rain-check?"

Although, another time with Sid isn't all that likely. He's way too kiddy-boy for my trouble, legal fuck or not. Next time, now that I'm a bit more self-assured of the mechanics of my get-fucked-in-split position, I'll feel little less vulnerable assuming the position with someone a bit older and more experienced than Sid.

I send Sid on his way; the little shit, I'm sure, fully convinced his time with me has been well-spent.

I shower, shave, put on my security guard uniform (any uniform making me all the more sexy), and drive to the Linehan estate for night duty.

I've beamed open the estate gates and am on my way through when the ambulance passes me from the opposite direction.

There's a cop car in front of the main house. There's no cop in sight, but Jules Madison, fellow security guard, isn't that far from where I pull my car to a full stop.

"What the fuck's up, Jules?"

Jules has mousy brown hair. He has dish-water skin. He has puce eyes. He has a way-too-thin body. None of which does all that much for me. His big pecker and equally big scrotum, the latter complete with his huge testicles, say all there is to say about why his old man named the kid "Jules" after the only family jewels the Madisons were legally ever likely to come by.

"Mr. Linehan got the shit kicked out of him," says Jules.

"What in the hell was Henry (echo) Henry doing all this time?" My stupid-shit (echo) stupid-shit supervisor.

"Jesus, Struan, get real!" insists Jules, like some teacher talking to a pea-brained adolescent. "Who the hell do you think did the ass-kicking?"

I know Henry Henry is a loose cannon , but even I figure he should have had more sense than to put his own boss in the hospital.

"Where the hell is Henry?" I want to know. Hopefully, he's already locked in the squad car, although I don't see him. Maybe the missing police officer/officers have him in custody inside the house.

"I figure he's hiding in the wine cellar," says Jules.

"You tell the cops that?" I ask, and a uniformed policeman heads out of the house and in our direction.

"You out your fucking gourd?" says Jules.

After which, the cop says, after checking a clipboard, "You Struan?"

Thank God, he's not some flatfoot I know from the old days. Thank God, he doesn't seem to connect me to the much-publicized Willis Crawfold incident, or he would probably be out to blame my innocent-ass for what's gone down between old-man Linehan and Henry Henry.

"He's just checking in for night shift," says Jules.

"Someone may want to talk to you later, Struan," says the cop whose name-tag says -- swear to God! -- "Dicks" (as if he has more than one of them).

"I'll be here," I say.

"A few words with you, Mr. Madison," the cop says to Jules.

"Sure," agrees Jules, and I make my exit.

I head around the house, unlock the outside access to the basement and head on down. Underground is a maze of hallways and store-rooms. I head for, and arrive at, one particularly blank expanse of what-looks-like cement wall. Know just where to press down -- and I do -- and a panel opens in adjacent floor boards. Know the correct combination to input the key-pad revealed beneath -- which I do -- and the seemingly cement wine-cellar door slides open with a breathy sigh -- which it does.

Revealed is one mighty surprised Henry Henry, guzzling the con-tents of one bottle of Mr. Linehan's probably finest French Bordeaux.

"What the hell you want, Mackelby?" Henry says by way of hello.

"Rumor has it that you've put old-man Linehan in the hospital," I say.

"None of your business," he says. "So, just fuck off, why don't you? Unless you're up for a few days of hospital time, yourself."

He's not dealing with old-man Linehan, here, nor with someone even vaguely scaredy-cat impressed, like Jules so obviously is, with Henry's he-man posturing.   I prove just what kind of an adversary he's got by providing the sucker punch, to Henry's obviously glass jaw, that puts him out faster than a candle flame snuffed by a hurricane. After which, I use his dip-shit body as a punching bag until I'm damned good and sure, when he wakes up, he's going to feel and look like he's been run over by a fucking freight train.

I haul his sorry ass out to the Range Rover we use for patrolling the perimeter of the estate, and I chauffeur Mr. Henry to a back road, where I unceremoniously dump his unconscious body in an obliging ditch.

Back at the main house, I join Jules in his, "Gee, I haven't a clue as to what's gone down here" act. Although, I'm better at it, because I wasn't around when the assault on our boss went down.

Next evening, I return to the back-road ditch and find it empty. Either Henry has crawled his sorry ass out on his own, or some carnivorous bit of wild life has hauled it out for him. Either way, I figure he has the message that he'd better not show himself in my bailiwick, ever again.

Two nights later -- another night in a long series of hot, hot, summer nights -- Mr. Linehan is back from the hospital and, he assures, looks far worse than he really is.

"Mr. Henry seems to have left my employ," says Mr. Linehan, having called me in for a chat. "No notice given. No reason offered as to why. I thought maybe you had some ideas."

Is the skinny old fart pulling my dick, or what?

"Duh!" says I, like I'm a turnip fresh off the truck. "Could it be because he put you in the hospital?"

"He knows I know he didn't mean it to go that far," says Mr. Linehan. "There has to be some other explanation."

Beg my fucking pardon!

"Henry and I are close," says Mr. Linehan. "Surely you know that."

"Close?" (Echo) "Close?" says I.

"I mean, Marcos must have at least dropped a hint."

Marcos being Marcos Ramez, the pimp who got me this job. And when I say "pimp", I mean pimp; although, Marcos refers to himself as a manager. What he does is pimp young men to older men who take advantage of the young men's cocks and asses. That Marcos's kids don't peddle their asses on the street, but out of a condo on Blenshire Boulevard, makes Marcos think he's something more highfalutin than the pimp he is. Nonetheless, I've a soft spot for Pimp Marcos, because he was right there when I was bounced out of the force on my ass. He told me that Mr. Linehan was gay, but that no part of my job description, should I take the position open for me at the Linehan estate, would include my sucking or fucking the boss, or vice versa. All of which has been true. Probably, I see now, because Mr. Linehan didn't need me servicing him as long as he had Henry, and vice versa.

"Surely Henry, or Mr. Madison, must have mentioned something," continues Mr. Linehan.

"You and Henry close?" I can only repeat myself.

Unbelievably -- Jesus fuck! -- he starts to cry. Real, true-life, god-damn, honest-to-goodness tears, big as chandelier crystals.

"What am I going to do?" he sobs between wet hiccups.

"For Christ's sake, the bastard punched your lights out," I argue, in attempt to put some degree of sanity into all of this maudlin cocka-mamie. "With your money, how hard is it to buy another cock, or piece of male ass, come complete without fisticuffs?"

Summer sweat makes my neck sticky under my collar, and I put a finger between my shirt and my neck and give a tug, in order to feed my chest some air. I wish to hell I wasn't required to wear this stran-gulation tie.

Linehan looks up at me. He's teary eyed and still blubbering. His black eyes makes him look like Rocky Raccoon.

"Cock?" he says to me, eating his tears and snot. "Ass? God, if it were only that simple."

"So, if not cock or ass, then ... whatever," I include the whole gamut of sexual possibilities. "God gave the world plenty of cocksuckers who ..."

"Oh, Jesus!" he interrupts and manages a laugh through his tears that sounds more like a cackle. "What kind of dumb-fuck are you?"

"Wait one damn minute, buster," I say. I try my best to provide a sympathetic ear for this sorry piece of shit, and he calls me the dumb-fuck?! "You want dumb-fuck, you tell me who got himself two black eyes and had his ass hauled off to the hospital."

"Henry was supposed to hit me!" literally shouts Mr. Linehan. "I asked him to hit me. You think I paid him what I paid him to guard the premises? Hell, he stole more from me than he ever guarded. I didn't care. I don't even care that he put me in the hospital. It's the one and only time he got really carried away."

"You sick sonofabitch!" I say, and he can feel free to include Henry (echo) Henry in my assessment.

"Pot calling the kettle black!" he suddenly screams at me, as if he's a whore just refused his/her recompense. "Pot calling the kettle black!"

"Willis Crawfold was a scum-bag," I say, because I know just where old-man Linehan's pea brain is coming from. "My breaking Willis's nose, jaw, and whatever other sundry bones, doesn't begin to compare with your invitation for Henry Henry to put you in the hospital."

"Look, Mr. Mackelby," says Mr. Linehan, wiping his snotty nose -- on his shirt sleeve, for Christ's sake!; obviously, money doesn't buy good manners. "I need someone to take up the slack until I can find a per-manent replacement for Henry. I've always hoped you might fill in, in just such a situation as this. Actually, I had the foresight to hire you with just that in mind."

"Wait a damn fucking minute, here, you sorry butt-fuck! Your sick mind somehow had me figured for ...?" I'm too fucking speechless to finish.

I'm all hot and bothered. My blood pressure rises. I sweat like a stuck pig. Given a few more seconds of this bullshit, and I'm likely to see a return of my childhood stutter.

"Hit me," he says. "It doesn't have to be very hard, you'll see. Make it a love tap."

William Maltese

"Love tap?!" The guy is fucking out of his mind!

"I know you want to hit me," he says. "I can tell. You may want to hit me even more than Henry ever did. You might be surprised just how long it took me to persuade bully-boy Henry to land his first slap. The first slap always the hardest."

I feel one helluva fool, let me tell you. I go off and pound Henry Henry into a pile of mush mush, to the point where he's probably only barely able to crawl crawl from the ditch ditch in which I dump dump him -- if hungry bears didn't carry him out, first; and, it turns out old-man Linehan isn't a victim at all. Now that's a good piece of .... What's the fucking word I want? Irony! Yeah. A ... good ... fucking ... piece ... of ... irony.

I'd beaten the shit out of poor Henry who had not only been paid to wallop Mr. Sick-as-shit Linehan but had been begged to do it. By all rights, I should give this old fart that quick slap for which he asks. Mother Nature isn't the only one who doesn't like being fooled.

"Hit me," he says.

So, I hit him -- a good one. Then, for good measure, I hit him again.

For which, I'm given a job promotion with one very large increase in benefits and salary.

CRAPSHOOTS

Life is a crapshoot.

Lose some. Win some.

Uncle Leroy a winner. Big time!

For the very first time in my life, I actually know someone who wins a state lottery.

Thirty-eight-million bucks. Not that it comes out nearly that much after Uncle Leroy decides to take his winnings in a lump sum, instead of in monthly installments. Then, of course, the tax man takes his huge dollop, right off the top. However, even after all of that major cash depletion, Uncle Leroy ends up an undeniably rich man.

What's more, he's generous to his extended family, except for Cousin Maynard whom Uncle Leroy seems to loathe, with a passion, and vice-versa. I suspect their dislike for each other has something to do with sex, or lack of it. In that, maybe, Uncle Leroy asked for sex, and Cousin Maynard refused. More likely, Cousin Maynard asked for it, it no secret Uncle Leroy is gay; Uncle Leroy the one doing the turning down. Uncle Leroy has always been exceedingly generous toward certain young male members of his extended family, by way of providing memorable cum-vacuuming blowjobs (yes, I speak from personal experience), but his type has never been the likes of chub-tub Cousin Maynard..

What with Uncle Leroy's financial windfall, he buys my mom (who's his youngest sister), and my dad, a new home and a car.

I turn eighteen and drop out of school, exceptionally well-timed if I do say so myself, in that Uncle Leroy (who dropped out of school even younger than I did), decides it's an opportune moment for me to stretch my wings and get out on my own. Whereupon, he plunks down the considerable cash to get me a condo. Nor does he do so without obvious forethought, because he picks a place on the beach, just a short distance down the boardwalk from where all the exhibitionistic body-builders daily work out in their small rectangular playpen of sand.

If Uncle Leroy knows his preferred body-type, for fun and games, he has, likewise, paid particular attention to how my tastes have evolved over the years. Actually, not all that long ago, he came right out and told me, point-blank, that he considered himself lucky to have been around before I decided toward tricks with all that hard muscle. Uncle Leroy, like most of his tricks, is super-thin. Mom says he possesses a marvellous metabolism that's destined to keep him skinny forever ... and ever ... Amen.

Uncle Leroy's skinniness something I hadn't minded when he first got into my pants. After all, what horny young kid, my age at the time, just beginning to realize his boner's potential, and always seeming to have one standing at full attention, is going to be all that picky?

Although, I once had a guy tell me that he knew, from day one, what he specifically wanted, by way of male partner, for first-time gay sex -- namely, a blue-eyed, blond-haired, big-cocked, skinny, me! -- and hadn't succumbed to temptation, even through years of raging hormones, and then some, until he'd found me. Lucky for him, I'd been around long enough, by then, to have decided he met my preference for body-type. He not only my high-school gym teacher but someone whose studly body proclaimed his enjoyment of sports, as opposed to the undeveloped body of someone having just been dumped into the job-position because of budget cuts that fobbed off PE classes to any Tom, Dick, and/or Harry whose schedule made him available.

Speaking of my coach, Harry (hairy) Klynsdale, he has sexy whorls of coal-black fuzz completely covering his chest and belly. He has a great mane of pubic hair so puffed from his lower belly that it makes his genuinely big cock seem tiny, except, of course, when his accordion dick gains an additional four inches in erection. He has a sexily small vee of hair grown at the exact spot where his spine meets his buttocks, and spillover hair cascades the entire length of his asscrack.

Studly, sexy, hairy Harry Klynsdale, though -- who I still see sexually, although he's become a lot more promiscuous after having waited so long for a first-time with me -- is another story altogether. So ...

Getting back to Uncle Leroy:

"I got you this pair of binoculars and this telescope," he says, "so you can enjoy the view."

Still early morning, there are already a couple of mostly naked guys in the exercise area. Even without the aid of Uncle Leroy's generously provided optics, I can see muscled and tanned male flesh gone glossy with sweat from early-morning exercise and early-morning sun-shine.

"I do hope you know what you're doing, Peetie, my boy," says Uncle Leroy. "It would scare the shit out of me to have one of those Cro-Magnons in bed. One could as easily maul me as a grizzly mauls salmon. You not exactly Arnold Schwarzenegger, yourself, you know?"

Uncle Leroy is right. Just because I've developed a penchant for well-muscled bodies doesn't mean I have one myself. Actually, I figure I've inherited not only Uncle Leroy's gene for homosexuality but the one for high metabolism.

I'm not as skinny this year as last, though, and I've gained ten pounds over the last two years, but there's not much I find all that sexy about my musculature (or lack thereof). Stripped bare-ass naked, I'm all sharp angles, although you can no longer actually count my ribs and/or play them like a xylophone -- which was pretty much the case when both Uncle Leroy and my high-school gym teacher first advan-taged my physical charms.

"Ohhhhhh!" says Uncle Leroy with a noticeable shudder and a finale "guttural" that sounds very much like a horse whinny. He still gazes out my condo window, toward the beach enclosure wherein sunlight and sweat now provide a highlighted display of one body-builder's large pecs, washboard belly, and humongous thighs. Too much of a good thing, actually, even for me. As for Uncle Leroy's sense of anatomical aesthetics: "Too ... too ... reminiscent of our ancestors whom knuckle-walked!"

After which, Uncle Leroy gives me a big hug (my albeit small weight-gains having removed me from his preferred list of teenagers he lusts to suck), and he leaves me to enjoy my new digs and their view. He has a few last-minute things to take care of before he heads off on a world cruise with scheduled embarkation date of next Thursday.

It takes me one week of playing Peeping Tom, through the window of my condo, to fall in love. Or, more appropriately, to fall in lust. The really weird thing being that Mr. Perfect has been there, from Day One, but I'd somehow kept skipping over him. Perhaps having fooled myself into believing my tastes had progressed more toward Arnold Schwarzenegger stereotypes than they really had. There being plenty of would-be Arnolds displaying their wares in posing trunks so skimpy and tight that I can tell the size and shape of any dick down there, whether it's cut or uncut, without ever bothering to see it unveiled. For seven days, I concentrated on these human behemoths. Rejecting one because his torso is too veed. Rejecting another because his thighs are too brick shit-house. Rejecting a third because his shoulders are so damned broad they can out-Atlas Atlas in offering support for the world or, at the very least, are so wing-like as to provide their owner the capability to become airborne.

I'd about decided the very best was Blond Boy, with his militarily-cut blond hair; with no trace of an I-shave-for-effect stubble on his handsome face or on his impressive chest and belly; with his perfectly squared pectorals, each with its pink nipple centered just above a pectoral fold. By far, Blond Boy seemed to offer the most potential for fantasies to accompany my daily multiple whacks-off of my stiffy dick.

I mean, Blond Boy is exceptionally good-looking. Also, he's exceptionally well-built, while maintaining, for the most part, an all-important all-around body symmetry so most everything about him pretty much perfectly balances with everything else. Reference how he's seemingly chiseled from warm gold ... how his muscle delineation is cleanly defined, with deeply crisp edges ... how his biceps well-balance his triceps ... how his hard ass fills out the butt of his posing trunks like a hand fills out the contours of a custom-made glove ... how his cock ....

Frankly, his cock -- or, rather the all-too-obvious evidence of it -- is the only thing vaguely off-kilter about him. His monster prick, such a ropy bulge in the crotch of his posing trunks, is frankly distracting.

It was while I compared Blond Boy's massively-bulged crotch to the suddenly seemingly more perfectly to-scale cock-bulged trunks of the guy who always chums with Blond Boy, and who helps the kid hand-press free-weights, that I experienced my first really long and falling-in-love/lust look at the real honest-to-goodness Mr. Perfect. Apparently, up until then, I hadn't been able to see the one perfect tree in the forest because of all the surrounding growth of inferior (albeit one near-perfect) male-of-the-species timber.

I mean, on closer examination, they don't come any better put-together in my book than Mr. Perfect! He has it all, and all of it fits. Initially overlooked (obviously due to my sheer carelessness, I might add), it's okay that he won't likely win any Mr. Olympus contests. He doesn't have the necessary bulk for the professional circuit, although he does have just enough bulk (in the body and cock departments) for me.

That he's damn good-looking to boot is frosting on the proverbial cake. He comes complete with cut-short but not-too-short black hair, black eyes, and a black shadow of a beard (no actual mustache or beard). Combine all of that with his square jawline, his high cheekbones, and his slightly dimpled right cheek, and -- wallah! -- an undeniably he-man handsome man just made for my creaming my jeans.

Suddenly, I'm jacking off just looking at his face. His exceptional physique and readily defined (perfectly proportioned) cock momentarily forgotten -- or at least shuttled to the back of my mind.

For the next three days, I think I've found my sexual calling: voyeur, pure and simple. Well, maybe not so simple. As long as I have Mr. Perfect in focus, my dick is stiff. No matter how many times I cream -- twice, thrice -- my dick is always ready for more. Whenever I stop whipping it, it's not because it loses its starch, not because I'm drained of all cum (my cum, in fact, miraculously seeming never-ending), but because my cockshaft gets too sore from chafing to touch. Eventually, I get around this setback by using a vibrator. The only thing that for certain brings each of my daily multiple-marathon squirtings to their collective conclusion being Mr. Perfect winding up his workout and exiting the scene (usually with Blond Boy).

I'm not sure when I realize I want more from Mr. Perfect than just what he offers by way of voyeuristic thrill. Maybe I've wanted more from the very beginning but tried to be content with pretty much all I figured I was ever going to get.

I don't head on down to the beach enclosure, make myself known, blatantly let Mr. Perfect know that I'm there, interested, available. Hauling my bean-pole physique and skinny ass on down for inevitable comparisons, with and by the members of that physique-oriented clique, just too much for me to ask of myself. Also, Mr. Perfect's ongoing chumminess with Blond Boy (he of my earlier fantasies), has me convinced the two (who continue to arrive and depart together, as well as partner for workout routines), are lovers. At the very least, Mr. Perfect and Blond Boy's obvious relationship insinuates Mr. Perfect's ideal of physical perfection. Studs involved in the body-building scene, when not too narcissistically hung up on their own bodies, often tend to gravitate (sexually and otherwise) toward guys of their same ilk.

As frustrated as I become by the prospects of the status-quo lasting indefinitely, I'm not kept from another morning of trying to beat my dick into submission. So what that, as usual, I only succeed in getting my prick to hang its weary head when Mr. Perfect and Blond Boy pick up their gear and head off to ... heated sex? ... mutual gropes in some shower? ... meetings of their two-man mutual-admiration society?

I need a rest and head for the bed.

I'm naked as a jay, having found little point in early-morning dressing, considering what occupies my time during my morning hours.

For not the first time, I glimpse a mirror-reflection of my too-thin body, complete with finally drooped prick. I pause to give myself another critical once-over. This time there's the question germinating in the back of my mind: "Does what you see reflected back to you from that mirror, Peetie, really have to be the final say?"

I turn full-on toward the mirror.

My lightly tanned skin stretches tightly across my chest. My belly concaves, with its innie-navel in punctuation mark, between my prominent hipbones. My arms are thin. My legs are thin. Turning slightly, my ass reflects as downright skinny. Want to talk off-kilter anatomical symmetry, my cock is way too large for the rest of me, way too thick and way too bulky, coming off more as an afterthought appendage, probably a leftover from some larger product, but tacked on me, complete with large balls (left nut forever hanging half again as low as the right), like some kind of creationist's joke.

Who says, though, I can't be improved upon? Only a very few men come miraculously provided with natural musculature that looks workout-refined though it isn't. Most guys, myself included, are less lucky. Sometimes we merely think ourselves beyond help, when that isn't the case at all. As some previously skinny studs have discovered via the benefits of fine-tuned exercise programs.

Granted, up until now, I haven't made any real attempt to change, because, up until now, I haven't seen the need. I've fucked and sucked just about everyone I've ever wanted, looking just the way I do. The few muscled studs who may well have slipped through my want-you fingers, because I wasn't sufficiently beefed up, hadn't rated nearly so importantly in my book that I ever contemplated going through the bother of the personal exercise program that just might have given me access to them.

My increasing hang-up on Mr. Perfect, though, soon sees me standing before some guy in Darbey's Gym. The guy's name tag says "Mr.

Kenner", but he says "Call me Bob."

"I want to pump-up a bit, Bob," I say. "I'm way too thin."

Darbey's Gym is a no-nonsense place across town from where I live. I figure Mr. Perfect lives near enough the beach so that if he ever heads to an indoor gym it's one in my condo neighborhood. I don't want to run into Mr. Perfect until I've the body that will make him sit up and take serious notice.

"How much pump-up you talking, kid?" asks Bob.

"I want my body to look like yours," I say and hope flattery will chock up some points.

Actually, I know full well that I don't likely have the God-given basics to end up as picture-perfect body-wise as Bob, let alone have the willpower to stick with whatever the shed-sweaty-gallons workout regimen probably needed to give me even an echo of his kind of superb muscle-cut.

Bob's tight muscles are poured into his form-fitting Darbey's Gym T-shirt and short-shorts. He's red-headed, with a lightly freckled peaches-and-cream complexion. Downright perfection, if you like all of that with big feet, big hands, all of which presumably insinuates a big ....

"Some guys just have to wait longer than others," Bob says. "A lot of the time, muscle definition is just dependent upon the greater physical maturity that comes with age. Likely, I could work you to exhaustion, seven days a week, and nothing would happen if your muscles aren't ready."

"I, at least, want to see if they're ready."

"A lot of muscle-bound guys would give their left nuts to have back the kiddy-svelteness you have."

"Well, if I didn't already have a left nut, or needed an extra, I'd possibly be tempted to make the trade."

"How old are you?"

"Eighteen. What's more, I have the money, if that's what you're worried about." The latter thanks to a little extra cash handed my way by Uncle Leroy ("You need a bit of free time before facing shitty real life, Peetie!"), before he recently sailed off into the wild-blue yonder.

"You gay?" Bob asks as if it's a standard question on his check list.

"Look, I'm not applying for the position of your trick."

"Good, because I don't mix business with pleasure."

"So, who asked you to?"

– 137 –

William Maltese

He smiles his -- I know and you know and everyone knows -- I'm-irre-
sistible smile. Granted, it's a nice enough smile, if you like full pink lips
and small white teeth in a pale and freckled face that comes with eyebrows and lashes so pale-red they seem almost nonexistent.

"I've a couple morning hours free, Monday through Friday," he says.

I prefer my mornings saved for jacks-off while watching Mr. Perfect
do his sit-ups, curl-ups, and leg-lifts, but my dick, still raw from its last
few mornings of beatings and batterings, tells me I need a break from
my current routine. Besides, I refuse to admit I've become so addicted
to my morning creams that I can't do without them. Of course, there's
also a decidedly masochistic pleasure in planning such major depriva-
tion. And, what's the old bit about absence making the heart (and/or
pecker) grow fonder? The last thing I want to do is overdose on Mr.
Perfect, seen through telescope and binoculars, before I can access
the (his) real thing.

Bob Kenner, sadist, soon has me in and on a variety of torture imple-
ments that are better suited to a dungeon than to a gym. After which,
for days on end, I'm too sore to give Mr. Perfect anywhere near his previous due. Every time my willpower to stick with my new exercise routine seems on the brink of failing, Bob always cajoles me into or onto
some other damned machine, and off I go again for another ride of pure
agony and unadulterated hell.

Results, despite all my hopes and prayers, refuse to materialize
overnight. If I'd started out knowing just how long it would take to spot
just the merest beginnings of genuinely recognizable results, I likely
wouldn't have started in the first place.

In that, I'm not talking days here, even weeks. I'm not talking one
month ... two month ... three ....

"Finally!" Bob says, at the completion of yet another week of sweaty
supervision; though, he'd likely be enthusiastic no matter what, his personal clientele, like I, providing the bulk of his income. "From here on
out, I want us to start working more on your diet, get you into heavier
weights, maybe think about steroids."

I'm thinking: "Right, steroids!" Like I want to get into Mr. Perfect's
posing trunks so much that I'm willing to risk short-circuiting a lot of very
vital brain cells.

No denying, though, that my endurance has increased, during my
months of workouts with Bob. These days, I've actually a bit in reserve

every morning, expended in looking out my window and, whenever spotting Mr. Perfect (alas, as usual, with Blond Boy), managing a jack-off in quick long-distance hello (and good-bye), before I head out the door for another rendezvous with Marquis de Bob-Sade.

"Maybe we can try a few supplemental workout sessions some evenings," Bob says. "Mr. Darbey says it's okay and even gave me the key to the gym."

All I need is a return to twenty-four-hour days of drag-ass!

However, since by now there is improvement I've actually been able to see, and since additional sessions just might hurry things along ...

Bob begins devoting several nights a month toward working me pretty much into a state of exhaustion before herding me into the sauna, where, one night he says:

"You've never -- ever -- wanted to get down and dirty with me?"

Our sweat is reminiscent of Mr. Perfect's sweat in summer sunshine.

"Down and dirty with Mr. Don't Mix Business With Pleasure?" I say. "Sure I have, but somehow -- don't ask me how -- I've managed to control myself every single time."

It comes out just as facetious as I intend.

"You sure as hell a lot more sexy now that we've managed to put some meat and muscle on your bones."

"Obviously spoken by a guy with a meat-and-muscle fetish," I say.

Lines of sweat flow diagonally across his bas-relief pectorals and drain through his deeply serrated cleavage to spill on his abdominal plain.

A towel sits slightly askew his crotch. I see a bit of his left ball, as well as the damp puddle it makes where plopped atop the wooden tier-bench.

It has been a helluva long time since I've had other than self-masturbatory sex. Been too busy ... exercising ... exercising ... exercising ... at Bob's insistence.

"About that policy of mine -- not mixing business with pleasure," he says. Trying to be nonchalant, and failing, he moves his towel slightly to uncover all of his left nut and part of his right. "I, sometimes, make exceptions."

I've seen him completely naked. Seen all eight inches of his circumcised cock looking pink as any dog's prick. Usually, his peaches-and-cream complexion makes his bright-colored dick all the more noticeable. Now, though, the heat of the sauna blushes all of him, so his cock, if and when fully unveiled, will likely come across far less uniquely neon.

"Don't start doing me any favors," I say.

On the other hand, just because I'm doing all the shit I'm doing in order to bed Mr. Perfect doesn't mean I've vowed celibacy until the big date. Before Mr. Perfect came into my life, through the lens of a tele-scope and the lenses of binoculars, Bob would have been a prime can-didate for seduction. Now?

"Actually, it would be doing me the favor," he says.

Between his legs, his towel tents big-time Big Top.

Instead of asking him to define "it" and "favor", I say: "Bob, I haven't the energy to suck your cock." A statement not likely to hold up under closer scrutiny. Actually, I might even manage something more adven-turesome if either of us can come up with a rubber.

"You didn't happen to bring a condom?" I ask. I suspect he's been this route before. Just substitute me for any number of his muscle-'em-up-for-fucking clientele.

"I don't need a rubber, and you don't need much energy, for me to suck your big blond dick, kid," he says.

"Maybe not, but do I even have the energy to feed you a proper meal for your efforts?"

"Obviously, you can't even begin to imagine just how hungry I've got-ten for you over these past few months."

"Seems my cock may have some notion," I say and unwrap my peck-er which is standing tall. I sit, kind of scrunched, my back against a wall. The head of my dick presently wears my innie belly button as if my navel were a hat.

I scoot more toward the front of my tier-bench, and I sit up straighter. Suddenly hatless, my cockhead and its accompanying neck sway metronome-like in front of my belly. Meanwhile, my scrotum smarts with having been unceremoniously dragged onto hotter wood.

Bob doesn't need any more invitation than that.

Amazing, how quickly he sheds his towel, goes to his knees, facing toward me on the tier just below mine, his hands on my thighs and pry-ing my legs wider.

Nor does he waste any time in achieving an initial total face-fuck of my sizable erection. Doing so, I might add, without even one hint of gag-reflex.

His lips quickly secure the very base of my sweaty dick, but he doesn't rest on those laurels. He wants even more of me and proceeds to have at it, his hand elevating my nuts, one at a time, to where he successfully pop-feeds them, one after the other, into his face with my dick.

"Christ!" is pretty much all I come up with by way of response to the combination pleasure/pain of my testicles so completely sucked up and so thoroughly mashed, one against the other, and against my cock, in such stuffed confines.

His deep-throat groan sends my cockshaft vibrating, like a tuning fork, my gonads trembling in sympathetic harmonic response.

I've a good view down the nape of his neck. Rills of his sweat converge along the sexy curve of his back; drool his muscled asscheeks; run the entire length of his sexy asscrack; gloss his calves, his ankles, his large feet.

Along with his sound effects, his marvellously increased vacuuming challenges the seemingly stalwart steeliness of my erection and actually lengthens my prick -- the head of my dick sucked deeper and deeper into Bob's throat, my cockbase remaining firmly anchored by his pursed lips to my despite-all-my-exercise still-slightly concaved lower belly.

I lean against the wood wall my sweaty back has only recently vacated, and I almost hear the sizzle of my sweat turn to steam upon contact. I raise my feet to accompany my ass on one-and-the-same tier-seat, and I fillet my thighs. My new position elevates my crotch into high relief.

Don't ask me how Bob keeps my genitalia contained and sticks out his snaky tongue whose slippery tip progresses so far between my thighs and up into the lower crack of my ass that I imagine it eventually reaches my asshole and slithers right on inside.

"Cock-sucking cocksucker," I say, full of compliments.

This guy does things with his mouth, throat, and tongue, that I've never thought possible, and I've sucked my share of cock and had my cock sucked more than a few times in turn. Bob's focus, during his body-building years, undoubtedly has been as much on honing his skills as a cocksucker as on molding his muscle structure.

The vacuuming of his throat increases and decreases, stretches my cock and releases it, so I literally fuck his face without providing any accompanying hip movements. I do believe I can sit there, not moving a muscle (except the cadenced suction-forced lengthening and return-to-normal shrinkage of my love muscle), and get my rocks off. If I'm, likewise, inclined to do just that, more primitive control centers inside me say differently. In no time, I'm helplessly bouncing my butt against hot wooden seat.

I'm on an upward bounce when Bob's hand, palm up, takes advantage of my elevated ass to slide between it and the tier-seat. When my ass drops, it rests atop his cupping and sweaty fingers. When my butt, ever so slightly, lifts again, Bob's fuck-finger finds my asshole which his tongue only just missed. My next sit-down, my asshole opens and swallows most of his jabbing finger.

"Uhhhhhhgh!" I say and dribble my chin, although it's hardly unlikely I actually distinguish my drool from all my sweat.

It's hotter than hell in the sauna, and it's getting all the hotter by the second. Any normal human being would head out, about now, for a cool-down shower. That said, I'm not going anywhere. The twist of Bob's finger against my prostate, his hand a platter beneath my butt, tells me he's staying put, too; as does the way his face twists around my dick and torques my stiffness on my impressive cockbase.

No doubts why Bob initially came off so reluctant to mix business with pleasure. Once experiencing his skills at cocksucking, anyone (I included), who has his cock sucked even once by him, would be hard-pressed not to make an attempt for seconds, thirds, fourths ... ad infinitum. Actually, I wonder if Bob can make more money sucking hard cock than trying to harden other than the love-muscle on the likes of yours truly.

When my nuts audibly pop, spit-drenched, to freedom, from between his pursed lips and the upthrust of my erection, I don't need genius IQ to know Bob is about to begin, in earnest, his eating of me to full eruption.

His head becomes one of those California oil-well pumps gone quite ... up, down, up, down, up ... out of seeming control. His face downs to my cockroots, then ups to my cockhead, then downs again, all so bloody fast it's amazing. The whole length of my prick undergoes this remarkable squeeze and caress that sensuously slides and re-slides my loose outer layer, albeit circumcised, of cockskin up and back, up and back, along my sturdier inner cockcore.

His fuck-finger doesn't leave off playing my prostate, either, although his hand must hurt beneath all the helpless smashing and grinding of my sweaty ass.

I've so much perspiration running my body that someone who doesn't know better would swear I stand in a full-blast shower. Rills, rivers, streams, oceans and seas of the stuff, have me completely cocooned in a watery womb on-the-move. In my ears, it makes for swimmer's deafness. In my eyes, it burns. On my tongue, it tastes salty.

Christ, I'm on fire. I'm burning up. One would think all of the liquid my body oozes would shield me from the holocaust, except it doesn't. Every drop of my sweat is gasoline at flash-point. What manages to evaporate, with a sizzle, is immediately replaced by more volatile seepage from heat-opened pores.

I've a genuine fear of being sucked bone dry, of converting to desiccated mummy, right then and there, like sand-buried bodies in Peruvian and/or Northern African desert.

Even the virtual gallons of liquid a-slosh in my balls aren't destined to be of much help, in that they plan, even now, to exit and convert to steam. My gonads are pressure cookers that need desperately to pop their loads, or pop their seams.

"You've about sucked and finger-fucked me to coming, stud," I say.

Bob so good at what he does that he likely already knows just when and where my scheduled ejaculation will occur in the scheme of things.

I put my hands on his head, although there's no way I make his cock-bouncing face go any faster. My fingers merely clamp his sweaty scalp and go along for the ride.

I'm so strung out on passion, I bite my lip. I feel the pain, but I'm no longer able to distinguish the salinity of my blood from the salinity of my perspiration.

"You're about to suck me dry," I say. Not by way of warning but by way of yes-please. I'm so far up the pleasure scale, so far walked out on the plank, I've nowhere to go but ....

He gives no quarter but continues to gobble like sixty, his fuck-finger doing battle with my bruised and battered prostate.

My scrotum is passion-compact. My balls have seemingly disappeared into my lower belly, as far out of sight as when Bob had them swallowed.

Every muscle of mine is in high-relief. Had I the wherewithal to give the total results, as far as to the present display of my physique, an appreciative once-over, I would conclude to never having looked so good, so buffed, so ripped, so chiseled.

Orgasm, though, or rather my increasingly desperate need for it, is what predominates my each and every thought. I can't understand why I'm not already creaming, suspicious it has something to do with Bob's expertise at giving head.

"Please ... please ... let me ... let me ... come, please ... please!" I plead.

I whinny: a wounded horse begging its rider to pull the trigger and put the poor animal out of its misery.

"I'll have to pull out and whack myself," I threaten, torn between my need to climax and my desire to have the pleasure/pain go on and on and ....

"Mmmmmmmmmm!" His sounds vibrate over and along my submerged stiff dick.

It's as if he provides sound effects for an incoming bomb; I complement by providing the explosion.

The massive exit of all my existing cream out of my super-hyped body causes a vacuum behind it that, swear to God, threatens to turn me inside-out via fire-hose intensity that seemingly spews not only my cum but my guts through the small hole in the head of my dick.

"Fuck, suck ... fuck, suck ... fuck, suck ... fuck ... SUCK!"

I squeal. I mewl. I grunt. I groan.

I bounce. I weave.

I sweat. I drool.

I cream. I Cream. I CREAM!

I ram his head one final time down the total length of my erupting inches. I hold him there and grind my lower belly into his face so his nose pugs against my pubic bone.

What seems an eternity later, I gently tug his head up and off my geyser-drained cock.

He looks up, his face handsomely flushed and sweaty.

I put a hand to each side of his face, one thumb to each side of his nose. Like miniature windshield wipers, my thumbs squeegee sweat from his cheekbones and from his cheeks.

There's a bit of white residue (my cum?) couched wetly just within the left corner of his sexy-lip mouth. I lower my face and place my lips to his. I kiss deeply and taste his sweat, my sweat, and the lingering essence of my so recently blasted cream.

It takes me a year, to the day, after that, to make the walk down the boardwalk from my condo, to unlatch the gate of the weight-lifters' playpen, and to step inside. Although my body still isn't as ripped, buffed, well-toned as most of the guys in attendance (Mr. Perfect and Blond Boy included), I'm confident enough to take off my shirt before I begin a few sets of arm-curls.

Actually, I could have made my appearance a helluva lot earlier. The delay came because, by the time I figured I was ready, in mind as well as in body, I found myself so locked into the routine of morning work-outs with Bob that I couldn't bring myself to stop them. I'm not talking morning sex with Bob, by the way, which rarely occurred during a.m. sessions; usually, there were simply too many other people around. I'm talking the pure adrenaline rush I started getting early on from my exercise regimen and which I continue to get to this day. If I don't get a regular dose of pumping iron, I miss it, as was well-proven those couple of times, during the last year and a half, when I was sick and couldn't make it to the gym.

It was only when Bob had an opening in his afternoon schedule, a client moving to the East Coast, that I finally cleared my mornings, once again, for Mr. Perfect.

If I've come to the beach workout area, though, expecting Mr. Perfect to fall all over the "new" me, like a bee falls all over honey, I'm disappointed. Pretty much all I get out of everyone present is a brief nod. As previously, Mr. Perfect and Blond Boy leave together.

The next day, I have better luck, only with the wrong person. Mr. Perfect provides only another brief nod, it Blond Boy who's downright friendly.

"Name's Jeff," Blond Boy says and finally puts a Christian name to his face and body. "You just move into the area?"

"Pete," I say and return his firm but thank-God not bone-crushing handshake. "I've a place just down the boardwalk."

"Welcome," Jeff says. "You need any kind of an assist, just ask. Some of these guys can be real jackasses until they get to know you."

I'm going to ask if Mr. Perfect is just one such jackass, but I think better of it. You don't make friends by bad-mouthing friends of potential friends. And, I genuinely like Jeff. He, after all, my first pick from this muscle-bound litter. My covert introduction to him, via binoculars and telescope, didn't do him justice. Close-up, he's blonder, handsomer, even more studly. He's one of those rare blonds who take to sunshine like a fish takes to water and tans attractively instead of turning bright red with burn.

I don't ask him to spot for me, but he's right there, anyway, when I decide to bench press a few sets. Instead of watching the barbell from the head of my bench, he straddles the bench (and me on it), mid-center. Facing up my torso, he provides me an undeniably sexy and exciting look-see of his weighty crotch suspended above me like a posing-trunk-sheathed sword of Damocles.

As it turns out, I'm glad he's there, and not just because of the improved view. I try to show off and lift my load of weights one attempted rep too many. Were he not there graciously to add his heft to my final lift, I would end up with barbell and weights down and locked embarrassingly against my chest.

It just about then that Mr. Perfect comes over and sets my heart to beating like sixty. He gives me another noncommittal nod and says to Jeff:

"I've that appointment."

"Right," says Jeff.

For one of the very few times, since I've observed the studly duo, Mr. Perfect and Jeff don't leave together. Problem is, I'm left with the wrong one of the twosome.

I go through some additional look-at-me, aren't-I-the-muscled-stud?, motions, even a bit of narcissistic posing for a couple of giggling female adolescents to whom I normally wouldn't give the time of day. I prepare to make my hopefully nonchalant exit when Jeff joins me at the unlatched gate.

"How about a drink at my place?" he suggests.

"Orange juice and wheat germ? Protein supplement and goat milk?" I've learned from Bob that these people can talk an entirely different language than the rest of us.

"I have a friend at the health-food store who just sent over a couple comp cases of Energy Boost. Does that get your old taste buds singing?"

Not really, but ... hey ... Jeff may end up my best access to Mr. Perfect.

One of the reasons I don't come right on out and ask if Jeff and Mr. Perfect are officially "an item" is because I'm afraid he'll say, yes, and thereby deprive me of any excuse of ignorance when I make my grab for his other half and Jeff gives me his hang-dog, didn't-you-know-we-were-a-couple?, expression.

At Jeff's place, the Energy Boost isn't as bad-tasting as some of the shit peddled to and consumed by members of the muscle-culture.

Jeff is friendly, funny, attractive, sexy, and, last but not least, a Monopoly-game fanatic. I'm not at his place for fifteen minutes before he has the game board and pieces out, set up, and has coaxed me into play.

"Kane hates Monopoly," Jeff says.

I've not a clue as to whom Kane might be, but I pretend it's Mr. Perfect, because he looks like a "Kane".

"I go to the Monopoly-game nationals every year," Jeff says. "Got as far as the semifinals last year. This year, they're being held in Las Vegas, and I plan to play my way all of the way to the top."

I certainly don't offer him much by way of competition. His piece, the silver motorcar, isn't around the board but twice before he has both Park Place and Boardwalk.

"Luck," he assures me.

"I thought we beginners were supposed to have that."

He laughs good-naturedly. Will he, though, be nearly as cheery when not winning? It's my experience that game enthusiasts play to win -- always.

As expected, my exceptionally speedy bankruptcy puts him in high spirits. He offers to lend me money from his own copious and multi-colored reserves, offers to let the bank out-and-out-give me some cash, offers to trade me New York for Baltic so I can have at least one monopoly.

I decline and head on home.

Next morning, in the body-builders' playpen, there's a repeat of much of the previous a.m., including Mr. Perfect's almost begrudging hello nod, his early check-out, and Jeff's suggestion we have a drink.

Not really up to more Monopoly, however, and since my place is closer, I suggest Jeff and I go there.

"Give me your address and about fifteen minutes, and I'll met you there," he says.

Fifteen minutes later, he's on my doorstep with a new Monopoly set still shrink-wrapped in cellophane.

"A little something, by way of house-warming," he says. After all, I have given him the impression that I've only just moved in.

He persuades me to break in the new board and pieces by having a game. During which, against all my expectations, and actual efforts to lose, I end up with all four railroads, Park Place (able to keep him from "the" all-important monopoly), and both utilities, Jeff yet to acquire any two pieces of the same color.

When he shakes a three that lands him on my Reading Railroad, he doesn't immediately drive his little car along the edge of the board to the pay-me spot. I figure he's about to show his first hint of I-hate-to-lose pique.

"I badly ... badly ... badly ... want you to fuck my ass," he says instead.

No doubt about it, if I had him, then and there, down to his last Monopoly dollar, I would concede the game to him, in order to take him up on his offer. Obviously, he has discovered exactly the secret of playing himself to the very top of the nationals.

"Fuck the game!" he says. "Fuck my ass."

We've played over a glass-topped coffee table. I'm on the couch, and he's seated on the floor. He stays put, takes off his tennis shoes, peels off his socks, lifts his T-shirt. Suddenly naked to his waist, he rolls to his back, unfastens his shorts and, faster than any professional stripper, does away with everything from his waist on down.

I just sit, any sense of his money-owed for landing on Reading Railroad long since forgotten.

I'm seeing his cock unveiled for the first time. I've known it was long. But this long? I've known it was big. But this big? I've known it was thick. But this thick? I've known it was circumcised. But this perfectly deprived of its foreskin? His cockcorona is web-free, bulbous, and slit-mouth perfect. His outer cockshaft is veinless, perfectly smooth, like a newborn's ass, and perfectly straight, without nary a bend, twist, turn, or even minute variation.

His blond-fur scrotum is a tennis ball lobbed securely into the base of his dick. There's no discerning its two separate nuts within the looks-like-one total package. The compaction of his sac's wrinkled skin is uniform, and shrinks the whole to seemingly smaller and smaller circumference even as I watch.

The only thing that distracts me from his cock and balls is his speedy assumption of a fuck-me-dog-style position on the floor. Buck-naked (butt-naked?) his two solid asscheeks, with their tightly squeezed mutually shared crack, aim invitingly in my direction.

"I want your cock up my butt," he says, his head turned in my direction, as if he invites me to sniff his ass. "I've wanted it from the start. Sorry if I can't be more diplomatic about it. It hasn't been for lack of trying."

My cock proclaims its own hardening by how painfully it protests impasse within an inconvenient fold of the briefs I'd immediately donned upon reaching my condo; my exercise-funky jockstrap having been relegated to the dirty-clothes bin. I palm my cock-bulged crotch, and my fingers maneuver the underlying lumps into better alignment. Already, there's a pre-cum spot of dampness leaked from my cock, through the white cotton of my underpants, through the darker cotton crotch of my trousers.

I'm on automatic pilot as I stand, step my bare feet out of my loafers, pull out the tail of my Polo shirt, cross my arms across my chest and belly, hand-hook the freed material of my shirt, pull upward, and proceed to turn my shirt inside-out as it comes up over my bared muscled belly and bared muscled chest, finally to pull completely free above my head.

"Jesus, you are beautiful!" says Jeff, muscular Adonis to simple-wanna-be.

I open my trouser fly. I drop my pants, step out of them, except for the portion I hook with one foot to shift to one side.

The flats of my hands slide beneath the waistband of my briefs, and my thumbs hook the elastic. I attempt to drop my underpants straight down my body, but I'm momentarily frustrated by cotton material getting hung up on the head of my dick which leans outward precariously from my belly.

I pull out the crotch of my shorts and disengage all entanglement. I bend at my waist and pull down my shorts, over my cock, over my thighs and ass, around my ankles, to my feet which step out of them.

Jeff grabs his asscheeks. Still dog-fuck position, he yanks his buttocks open along their mutually shared crack and shows me a line of pale blond hair that targets his pucker like radar pinpoints a bomb site.

"There's a rubber in the right front pocket of my gym shorts," he says.

"There's one even closer than that," I say and head for the Japanese ginger jar on the closer-at-hand mantle.

My fingers are uncoordinated as hell as I rip open a condom packet and free its ring of unlubricated latex inside.

There's KY in the bedroom. There's Vaseline in the bathroom. There's Crisco in the kitchen. I decide on my own spit to ease the passage of my cock up his asshole.

I drop to my knees directly behind him, between the backs of his open calves.

He gives me one final view of his awaiting asspucker, then he releases his handholds and falls forward on his forearms to leave his ass elevated and ready for sexual mounting.

"Fuck me ... fuck me ... Jesus, fuck me!" he says.

"I'm not Jesus, but I'm sure as hell going to give it the old college try," I say and hit his ass, one open palm to each asscheek, just to hear the exquisite collision of his flesh with mine.

Immediately, my handprints materialize, pale pink, against blond skin which has been kept a good two shades lighter than the rest of him by having spent so much time beneath posing trunks.

"Go all the way down on your belly," I tell him.

"I want you to fuck me dog-style, kid," he says. "Or, haven't you noticed?"

"I'll fuck you any way you want me, but unless you really want me to fuck into you dry, I need a better go at spit-drenching your rear."

He collapses all of the way in a quick second, then he humps his butt upward from the floor just enough so his balls hang freely rather than pool on the rug beneath him.

I clamp his asscheeks, dig my thumbs into his crack, pull his buns open like I'd halve a ripe and rosy-fleshed peach. I bow my head to the widened crease, position my nose and chin within the deep indentation. The flick of my tongue misses his ass altogether and pokes, instead, his compact scrotum from behind.

He smells sexily of sweet summer sweat, of heady, musky, aphrodisiacal male-in-high-rut.

My nose burrows deeper, pinpoints his asshole, prods it, and greedily sniffs its concentrated essence-of-man

His asspucker tastes like it smells, and I enjoy it so much that I want to lick it forever. Too quickly, though, I replace its wondrously ripe flavors with the blandness of my spit.

Everything about Jeff's body is so tight that his asshole won't likely be any exception. Suddenly, I'm not at all sure I have enough spit in me to prepare him for taking my sizable cock. Still, I make every attempt and roll my tongue into a spit-feeding funnel to probe the moued entrance/exit of his anus.

"Oh, Jesus, yes, tongue-fuck me!" he says. His ass rams my face, his asscheeks hard pillows that momentarily smother.

I leave so much drool on and in his pucker that the goo backs up to leak his crack, run between his legs, bead the wiry hair of his balls.

Despite all the spitty lubricant, my attempt to poke my finger up his butt is like trying to poke through the resisting rind of an unripe melon.

"I try fucking this tight asshole of yours without it being greased with more lubricant, and it's destined to rip for sure," I warn him.

"Stay put," he says. "It'll be fine. I promise."

"Your asshole ever been fucked before today?" I finally get my finger worked to its first knuckle up his ass.

"Flattery will get you one helluva ride," he promises.

I'm still uncertain it's going to work the way he's so insistent it will. I've fucked more than one asshole in my time, and I pretty much know what can and can't be expected from a combination of my cock and any asshole offered up for service. Jeff's asshole simply comes off too naturally small to take a dick my size without a resulting tear from the base of his spine to his spit-bead balls. I can only guess the frictional damage that'll end up being done my cock.

"I've really got to get more lubricant, buddy," I insist and prepare to do just that. "I've more than a few oiled-up rubbers in the ginger jar. Just our momentarily bad luck that I came up with a dry one."

He rears up, turns, and gets hold of my balls to keep me from going anywhere.

His face is attractively flushed. His eyes are sexily dilated. There's a small run of summer sweat along and into his left eyebrow.

"Trust me," he says. His hold on my nuts isn't so forceful that I fear permanent damage, but it's sufficient to convince me of his determination to keep me right where I am. "We can do this. You and I. Your cock, my ass. I know we can. Who better to know than I? You think I'd risk ripping my ass for some masochistic kick I figure to get from it?"

"I've finger-fucked your tight butt, stud," I say. "How am I going to get my cock in a hole that barely manages to take my finger?"

"You want more lubricant?" he says. "Here."

His face is down over my cock as quickly as Bob ever managed that first time in the gym sauna.

By the time he finally comes up for air and leaves the whole length of my latexed cockshaft bubbly with his saliva, I wish he'd stay put. I've never been blown while wearing a rubber, and it's surprisingly more pleasurable than expected.

Then again, my dick so thoroughly wetted down, his asshole still tacky from the spit with which I've washed it, my horniness increased tenfold by the short time he's been down munching my dick, I suddenly see fucking his tight ass as not nearly the impossibility I once did.

He releases my threatened gonads.

Once again, he's on all fours, doggy-style, his ass aimed directly at me.

Knowing his determination to have my cock up his butt, recognizing my growing determination to have it there, too, and knowing full well that spit has a rapid rate of evaporation, I make my move.

My left hand, fingers and thumb in an inverted vee, opens his ass-cheeks along his crack. My right hand painfully pries my stiff dick away from my belly and points my cockshaft parallel to the floor for easy alignment against his anal pucker. My hips exert pressure in follow-up, and my dickhead pugs against the entrance of his butt, no other immediate indication his butthole isn't going to roll open for it.

It's a backward thrust of Jeff's ass that force-feeds three inches of my dick into his anal slot to leave me momentarily so caught up in the agony and ecstasy of so tight a squeeze that I'm now totally convinced I've found a butt simply too tight to be screwed.

"Yes ... yes!" he says triumphantly, and surprises with an even more forceful ram of his ass toward my belly.

My cockshaft actually bends, almost to a sharp right angle, before it straightens, in spring-reflex, and sinks an additional three inches up Jeff's butthole.

"Easy ... easy ... easy," I insist. The buried inches of my dick feel caught in pinchers, and I'm not at all sure I'll survive my whole boner subjected to the same degree of intense pressure.

I curl my torso down over his: yin to his yang.

"I want all of your big blond muscle-teen cockinches inside me," he says. "Jesus, fuck, I want them."

"And you'll get them all," I say. Miracles have happened to get me this far, and a couple more, if given the time, might do the rest of the trick. "But, I really do need a minute, here, stud. I really ... really ... do."

"Ohhhhh, but your dick feels so ... so ... good," he says.

If I think his vising asshole is clamped down with maximum intensity, I'm wrong. It squeezes even tighter and literally takes my breath away.

"Oh, Christ," I say, my cheek against his back. The flats of my hands curl reflexively to try and clamp a hold on his chest and belly. His chest and belly prove too slick and too solid for me to maintain a sufficient grasp.

I try to pull a bit of my dick free. It's useless. Jeff and I are as stuck together as two dogs at fuck. We'll either stay this way forever, to orgasm, or we'll stay this way until someone obliges with a pail of tossed cold water.

I sense him more and more impatient with my seeming inability to give him all the cock that he wants. Having already been responsible for his butt gobbling two-thirds of my cock, he is probably more than prepared to feed his butt the rest of me.

Hopefully to exert just a bit of control over the situation, my right hand slides his body, bangs his stiff dick on the way by, and takes hold of his large balls. I recall how quickly just such a maneuver by him, to claim my nuts, kept me from searching out additional lubricant, and I now think it a fair turnabout, on my part, to exert some calm-down influence on him.

However, my fist quickly around his tennis-ball scrotum only gets him more hot and excited. His trembling is a detectable vibration relayed throughout my body so closely mated to him.

His asshole gives another maddeningly tight squeeze.

"Sweet, sweet Jesus!" I say, as helpless as I feel.

Unabashedly, his ass bucks to claim the very last fraction of my sizable dick. My scrotum, noticeably more compact that when I first began, is still flaccid enough to make a loud "whack" as it collides with the undercurves of his rear.

If I'd all along suspected that, of the two of us, I was never the one -- ever -- in control, that's now fully confirmed. Like a rodeo cowboy, I've climbed on, the gate has been thrown open, the ride has begun, with nothing more for me to say except "Giddy-up, cowboy!", and hold on for dear life.

I'm not even sure which of us does the actual fucking, in that it's mostly his bucking hips that drag his asshole off my dick and sink it right back again. His ass is into so many gyrations that my dick pretty much assumes the curlicue characteristics of a screw.

Having early on realized his muscular chest and belly are simply too solid, and too slick from sweat, to offer me adequate handholds to maintain any semblance of balance, I make due with clinging to his scrotum and to the stiff jutting of his prick.

It takes no more of my concentrated effort to jack-off Jeff's cock than it does to fuck his ass. In that, once again, it's Jeff's grinding and bucking and heaving and rearing and twisting that whips his dick back and forth within the masturbatory corridor my curved fingers provide.

Inside me, pleasure multiplies with each succeeding second that I remain in the saddle. It being a damn ... damn ... damn ... good -- and getting even better -- ride.

Helplessly, I mutter guttural bits of indecipherable garble against the muscles of his sweaty back. Just as helplessly, I drool enough spit to provide lubricant enough for seconds -- not that either of us seems likely to survive mere firsts.

There's another massive smack of his ass into my sweaty belly, another massive undulation of his full-stuck butt to twist -- swear to God! -- my submerged dick a full three-hundred-and-sixty-degrees along my cock's linear axis.

The momentary delay that occurs just before my actual eruption is merely my body's suspicion that my dick is too corkscrewed, up Jeff's ass, to let any blasted cum come on through. As soon as Jeff's butt reverses gyrations and lets my cock unwind, my nuts let go.

Jesus ... H ... Christ, do my nuts let go!

We're talking a flood of Biblical proportions ... tidal wave .. tsunami. A roaring, steamrollering, rushing, cataclysmic gushing of spermal goo, straight from my exploded testicles, out along the still torqued and twisted, bent and broken, length of my squeezed to nothingness dick, out through the pulsing mouth of my friction-reddened cockhead, and into a rubber ballooned to a capacity never dreamed necessary when its prototypes were tested under laboratory conditions.

My handhold on Jeff's balls, and my fist of Jeff's cock, are all the more difficult to maintain when his dick lets go its steamy ropes of cream that, despite binding my fingers to his exploding penis and balls, with thick hawsers of cum, can't keep my fingers from slipping and sliding and milking.

When my last almost-painful pulses squirt the very last of my drained juices into the cock-plugged rubber so deeply imbedded up Jeff's butt, his cock spits its final slugs of mess to puddle the carpet beneath his overhanging belly.

As good a shape as I'm in, I can't get my breath. I gasp for more oxygen, like a fish out of water. A cum-depleted Jeff does the same.

Finally, all over and done, I regain enough of my senses to worry that his tight ass will, in grand finale, keep my cum-stretched rubber, while my cummy cock pulls free of his butt and from the used condom, at one and the same time. Only a concentrated clamp of my fingers, to hold the open end of the rubber securely about the thick base of my softening dick, assures me that my cock exits with its rubber sheathe still intact.

The sweat that still wet-ties us together, when forced to separate, by our efforts to come free of each other, provides sound effects reminiscent of cows extracting their hooves and legs from muck.

"I think maybe I need a shower," Jeff says, still more than a little breathless.

"I think we both need a shower," I agree.

Each of us too exhausted to manage any semblance of additional sex play and/or grab-ass amid our shared rush of hot and soapy water.

We're toweling off when Jim checks his watch left on the edge of the bathroom basin.

"Jesus, the time?!" he says. "I'm supposed to meet Kane in ten minutes."

Had I even a vestige of energy left, I'd persuade him to stay. As it is ...

"Kane?"

"Hasn't the shit gotten around to introducing himself, yet?" Jeff asks. "He's that brooding, dark-complected hunk I usually arrive and leave with."

"Oh, yeah," I say innocently while Jeff hurriedly -- at least as hurriedly as his sex-exhausted reflexes allow ... gathers his things. "You know,

I actually had you two figured for lovers."

"Kane and I? Jesus!" He laughs.

He makes it sound genuinely absurd that I've come to such an untenable conclusion.

"Oh, we did trick a time or two," he backtracks, "but that was genuinely back in the Dark Ages. Certainly not since I started lifting weights, and I started doing that in junior-high school."

I hope my lack of comment provides a vacuum he'll spontaneously feel the urge to fill with more details.

"Obviously, you've never seen Kane with any of his little playthings," Jeff obliges, "or else you'd really know just how far off base you were. They're all -- every one -- skinny as rails. Not a well-defined muscle to be found among them. Skeletal arms, skeletal legs, sunken bellies, skinny asses." He visibly shudders. "Kane no more likely to fuck the likes of me, no more likely to fuck the likes of young and studly you, than he'd likely fuck Michelangelo's studly David come to life for no other reason than to offer up, for Kane's screwing enjoyment, a turned to flesh and blood marble-muscled butt."

He shakes his head as if Kane's taste in men is genuinely beyond his comprehension, and he heads for the door. He detours at the last minute to come on over and give me a quick and playful kiss.

"Promise we'll do this again," he says.

"Let's see if my pecker survives this go-round."

He's laughing as he leaves.

I sit hard on the couch, lean back, feel the frustrations, of what he's just told me of Kane's long-standing sexual preferences, sink ... all ... of ... the ... way ... in.

I come forward on the cushion, and I clear the unfinished game of Monopoly from the coffee table with one full sweep of my arm. The board cartwheels across the carpet, the air fills with the flutter of airborne funny-money. Metal playing pieces, wooden hotels and houses, splatter noisily against the wall.

Dice ricochet off the window with a clatter and come to wobbly rest two inches apart on the floor within kicking distance of my feet.

Snake eyes!

ONE... TWO... THREE... OUT

Delivery-room nurse:
   "Too pretty to be a boy!"

Woman in grocery store:
   "What's her name?"

Photographer:
   "I couldn't help noticing your child. I'd like to snap some pictures for an agency that's always on the look-out for new faces for ad campaigns and the like. I suppose you well know you've an exceptionally good-looking little girl, there?"

My Father:
   "So what, my kid gave yours a black-eye? Teach your ugly little brat a little something about going around calling my kid a sissy just because we've got better looks in our family than you do in your family of trolls? You want me to follow my kid's good example and give you a black-eye, you fuck-ugly bastard, you just keep raving on about your poor little Johnny and his broken nose!"

One:
"Come on over, kid, and I'll give you a piece of candy. Come on, don't be afraid. I know your parents probably told you not to talk to strangers, but you don't have to say a word. Just take the candy. Unwrap it. Wrap your angelic pouty lips around it and chew it all the way on down. If you don't like this kind of sweet, I've a whole selection here in the front seat of my car. At least, come on over far enough so that you've a better look. Yeah, that's the way. Maybe even a little closer than that? No? Well, at least you're close enough to see this? Know what this is, kid? It's my man-sized lollipop, just for you. You don't know how much pleasure it would give me, if you'd just step on up and give this manly lollipop of mine a quick kiddy-lick or two. As a matter of fact, if

you'd do that for me, just step on up, climb on in the car, give a suck or two, I'll gladly give you all of the candy I have. Okay? Ah, come on, kid, don't be that way, pretty please! Kid? Where you going, kid? Goddamn-it! Get your pretty little ass over here, and ... Fucking little tease!"

My mother:
"Someone as attractive as you will have to get married or people will talk."

High-school slut:
"My God, that was good. And most of our know-it-all classmates think you're queer."

Prostitute:
"Hey, handsome, for you I'll do it free! No? How's about I pay you for it?"

My uncle:
"My God, if I were a woman, I could go for you."

Opposing high-school varsity quarterback:
"You fucking queer!"

Two:
"Scare you? Sorry! Just me. Or is it, 'Just I'? What's an old jock like me (like I?) know about correct English? Only know I stuck around tonight to take care of some last-minute paperwork for our gymnastics meet next week. Figured to save some time by showering and changing here. Supposed to meet the wife tonight for a dinner with her always-have-hated-me parents. Can't wait. Saw you practicing horizontal-bar dismounts with Kerry. So, where is Kerry? He didn't leave without showering, again, did he? Guess, I'm going to have to have that long overdue talk with that kid about personal hygiene. I can understand his reluctance to strip down during the school day, what with a shower room full of juveniles towel-whacking every naked ass that goes by, but with only the two of you ...? Well, three of us, here, counting me. Confidentially, Kerry's main problem is that he's too self-

conscious about being so goddamn skinny. He has one of those naturally bony bodies that never takes on muscle definition all that easily.
Where you ... well ....   It certainly not helping Kenny, not that you can
help it, that you look like perfection by Praxiteles. You learn about
Praxiteles in any of your classes, have you? A Greek sculptor. Known
for his marble representations of the perfect male body-beautiful. Even
I have to admit it's a bit daunting stripped down, you here for comparison. Not that I'm that old. Not that I'm in that bad a condition. I've
always had pretty good natural body definition, and my steady exercise
regimen, what with coaching you teenage studs, keeps me in pretty
good shape; and, thanks for the compliment, but you don't get higher
grades because of it. Nonetheless, I have to admit, I never looked as
good as you do. My only consolation: very few men, young and/or old,
ever have, or ever will, look as good as you do. Were you a cute baby,
or were you one of those Munchkins who turned cute later? Cute
babies, the way I hear, usually turn into genuinely ugly teens. You
about as far from an ugly teen as anyone can get. I'll bet I'm not the
first person who ever told you that, either, am I? Because .... Hey,
need some help soaping your back, there? Know such a thing would
be frowned upon during regular school hours, but, hey, I'm your coach,
right? Come on, no big deal, I'll just .... Jesus, do you believe I
dropped the damn soap?! I sure as hell don't. You tell anyone I played
drop-the-soap with you and I'll .... There, that should have been a quick
enough recovery to avoid any suspicious minds. So, turn around and
let me soap down that really difficult spot between your shoulder
blades. Not afraid, are you? Because, what's to be afraid of? This is
your coach, here, buddy? Remember me? Wife and two kiddies at
home. Only showering to save a bit of time, and .... Right! Easy as
pie, and .... Jesus, but you've the softest skin. You rub down regularly with baby cream? No? Can't remember when I've touched skin as
soft as yours. Don't think the baby-ass of any of my kids was ever this
soft. Just farther proof that you have it all, kid. Did I tell you what I
thought when I first saw you naked? I thought: how in the hell did God
manage to give one kid so fucking damn much? So damn much! Like
this ass of yours.... Hey, kid, don't take offense. I'm just telling it like it
is. You ever backed up to a mirror and taken a gander at what's back
there? Buns of steel! As for that monster cock you have between your
sexy legs .... Where you going, kid? You aren't done showering yet.

William Maltese

You've still got suds between your shoulder blades. Come on back into the water. Just for a moment. Just to rinse all that soap off. Can you do that for me? Yeah, I know my cock is getting kind of stiff. You telling me this is the first stiffy you've ever given another guy? Because I don't believe it. You're boner-producing material, from the word go. That the real reason Kerry didn't stick around. I've always figured the kid a closet case, and you naked in the shower is probably way too much temptation for him to handle. Me now (I now?), I'm just appreciative of the male body, in general, and your male body, in particular. Come on, kid! Okay, then, be that way. Except -- hey, one bloody moment, stud! A word to the wise. Don't go telling everyone you showered with the old coach and gave him a boner, because I'll deny it, and you're the one everyone thinks is queer."

Fraternity brother:
"I could be a better judge of you if you were ugly."

Spanish exchange student:
"You're truly an angel by Bernini!"

Girl friend:
"I could never be sure you loved only me."

My aunt:
"A man ever proposition you up for sex?"

Drill sergeant:
"You went to one of those all boy-fucking-boy private schools, didn't you, pretty-boy Private smart-ass?"

Korean prostitute:
"Hee, hee. She say you pretty."

Sergeant-major:
"You can thank your lucky stars, Corporal, that you somehow managed to get it up for a prostitute, or you'd be out of here with the rest of the queers. Way it is, there are still a bunch of ignoramuses in authority around here who figure a guy who sticks it to pussy won't go near

male butt, but you and I know differently, don't we? The only difference between you and me being that you know from experience. And, although I can't prove it, you'd better not give me any kind of real evidence that you're a faggot, or I'll have you out of here for a 209-discharge on the very next plane."

Old Army buddy:
"Remember that closet-case sergeant-major who used to follow you around with his eternal hard-on?"

Three:
"Need a lift? Glad to be of service. I'll drive you even farther down the road, if you want. I'm headed all of the way to LA. Although, yes, I do kind of recall an auto repair shop, up here, just off the next exit. Funny, but I don't remember seeing your stalled car pulled off to the side, back the way I've come, and wouldn't I have driven right by it? Oh, well, if it broke down off the freeway, you're right that it was probably easier for you to get a lift on this side of the cyclone fence. Even the cops probably would have given you a lift, instead of arresting you for hitchhiking where you're not supposed to. I sure having had you figured for a hitch-hiker, though. Although, there aren't as many of those as there were in the good old days, not that you'd remember. How old are you, anyway? Jesus, you look younger. You so good-looking young what should have been the clue to tell me that you weren't the one-and-the-same guy a couple of my buddies, separately, picked up hereabouts. I just automatically assumed ... although I'm sure they would have mentioned having lucked out with someone as exceptional as you. You do know that you're exceptionally handsome? I mean, people like you have to know, don't they? You can pretend otherwise, but, let's face it, even the least vain of us occasionally stand in front of a mirror and get the feed-back. Right? You, swear to God, honest-to-goodness movie-star material. What is it you do for a living? Naw! You're kidding? Just discharged? Korea? Don't you dare tell me you were there for the war, conflict, or whatever, because I won't believe that for a second. Right! I guess we do still have forces over there. A little rest-and-recuperation for you, then, before you get back into the grind of civilian life? Except, you really should head directly for Hollywood. I know the town has it's share of good-lookers but, kid, you'll have the best-looking of those

paled-by-comparisons green with envy. Every indication that what you have underneath your clothes as impressive as what's out. I only mean, military life has obviously kept you fit as a fiddle and then some. And, let's face it ... unless you've a sock stuffed in your pants ... well ... kid ... I could drive many a mile of highway before I came across a cowboy toting that size six-shooter. Or, should I say seven-, eight-, or, hell, more likely, twelve-inch, shooter? Don't mind that kind of frank talk coming from me. I sell rubbers, and not the kind you wear on your feet. Which kind of makes me a connoisseur of cock. Cross my heart. Prophylactic companies having their on-the-road reps, too, don't you know? A lot of stiff competition in our business, as we like to say, when we're all gathered around the conference table. Well, we like to say it other times, too, but that's another story. And, speaking of stiff, you need your rubbers special-made, or what? Just kidding! Help yourself to whatever free samples of extra-extra large-large you can find in the glove compartment. Not that I don't sell a helluva lot of the giant-size, usually to guys, unlike you, whose illusions of grandeur are bigger than their dicks are. Few bona-fide big dicks out there, kid, and take that from someone who knows. Or, would you rather I shut up all this cock talk? I'm just a guy who gets excited about his line of work, and it's so very seldom I run across a real dick the size of the one all the visible evidence says is in your pants. It is real, what I'm seeing signs of there? Not that I won't take your word for it, but what are the chances of you pulling it on out for me to get a good look-see? You actually blushing? That all the more a turn-on for yours-truly. Swear to God! Unless, of course, your military service taught you all that kung-fu shit for beating up on queers. Because, I'm queer as a three-dollar bill. And, as if you looking like a movie star isn't enough, you come complete with mouth-watering cock likely bigger than King Kong's dong. But, no way you've gotten this far in life without knowing the effect you have on guys like me, right? Right! Sure as hell, I'll pull over, but let's wait until a convenient spot that'll afford us a bit of privacy. Because, nothing I'd like better than to suck up every last damn inch of that wonderful damn cock of yours. If you could, maybe, just pull it on out now, though, and .... Hey, damn-it, what the fuck are you doing?! Let go the wheel, you fucking shit! Want to get us both killed? Jeeeeez! Fucking Christ! What the fuck? Where the...? What the ...? What'd I say? What'd I do? Get on back in. Okay, okay, no need to get all upset. How in the hell was I supposed to know? You can't fault a guy for trying, can you? So, get back in and I promise no more come-ons. Truly! I made a mistake, that's all. Give a guy a break! I've never forced my attentions on anybody. Besides, you look big enough to take care of yourself if I have another relapse. Okay, I promise there'll be no relapse. Just get the fuck in. Passers-by are staring. Fine. Great. Stay scrunched as far over on that side of the car as you like. And, while you're there, take a word of advice from me about how you should learn to handle, far more calmly, propositions from queers like me. Hell, I can't believe you haven't already learned, all the experience you must have had, with women and men, turned on by the way you look. All you having to say, nine times out of ten, is a simple, 'Thanks, but no thanks!' Another thing -- You might try not getting a hard-on, because that hard-on in your pants definitely sends the wrong message."

Member of a health spa:
"Why in hell are you wasting your time in here with us old farts? No way God, let alone a gym, is going to improve on perfection."

Friend of a friend:
"You don't have to prove anything with me; I know you've been to bed with Ann."

Starlet:
"You have more men in this room hot for you than I do."

Friend turned enemy:
"Beauty is, after all, only skin deep."

Enemy turned friend: "I wouldn't have your kind of good looks for all the tea in China."

Fashion critic:
"It's hard to give all that much notice to what he's wearing when it's his exceptionally good looks and obviously exceptional body that immediately catch and hold all attention."

William Maltese

Film critic:
"He looks good, no doubt about it. However, whether or not he can act, is something more difficult to determine, in that it's hard for me, even after having been so exposed to Hollywood's gamut of beautiful men, to get past his exceptional handsomeness and exquisite physique long enough to concentrate on his mastering of, or failure to master, the nuances of acting."

Roger:
"Sorry. Sorry. You took me by surprise! Or, is it: I took you by surprise?! My name Roger, and I frankly just wasn't expecting anyone to be sunbathing, in the nude, way out here, in the virtual middle of nowhere. Obviously! Hot as it is, most people prefer staying home scooted up to their full-blast air conditioners. I, though, don't mind the heat. Actually, I like it. Mother Nature still gives a better sauna than you'll ever get in any of those little Scandinavian wood-cubicles. Besides, whatever the weather, I like to get out and generally commune one-on-one with nature. You, too, yes? All that innocent-first-man stuff, sans Eve. Although I don't suspect Adam, albeit naked, really ever got as aroused as you now see dick-out-of-my-pants me; anyway, he likely didn't before Eve turned up. I'm certainly not always as turned on by Mother Nature as my ... well, my ... present state ... might indicate. Actually, my present condition has more to do with my having been on the trail quite some time now, and ... well ... man to man ... if I don't pull out this old hog and flog it, every now and again, like you caught a glimpse of me doing as I so nonchalantly strolled around this bend in the trail, I can very well go ape-shit. I suppose I could just take more frequent leaps into icy-cold mountain streams, like that one over there, in that that usually does it for me, but ... sorry, don't mean to stare ... but the stiffness of your giant-size whang is truly impressive. God, listen to me. Suddenly Mr. Chatterbox, just because I've walked my boner around a bend in the trail and found a naked and sun-bathing Adonis with equally giant stiffy. Truly embarrassed, I guess, that I was so occupied I didn't realize you were even here. I mean, what if you'd been a bear? Although, you certainly are bare. Nice of you to smile. Fuck, I feel like such a dip-shit! Had I only known, I'd have tucked in my dick and zipped up my pants, at least making a bit of noise so you could hear me coming over the noise of the stream. Well, not really

coming, because it never got as far as that. Jesus, did I really say that? Me here. You there. It being so fucking enjoyably summer-hot. And .... Jesus Christ, but you do know who you look sooooo fucking like, don't you? Come on ... come on ... I can't believe I'm the only one who's ever seen the resemblance, because the two of you could be brothers. Except, he's supposedly in Borneo, or New Guinea, or somewhere, escaping all his adoring fans after finishing his last movie. No way, out here in the middle of an American wilderness area, right? Yeah, that's what I thought. Still, if you're not in the movies, you should be. I've been on the trail for close to three months, now, and all the hiking up and down Pacific Crest hills hasn't gotten me nearly in as good a shape as you. I mean, you are really one ripped dude, aren't you? Sorry about that spontaneous bit of jerking you just saw my right hand resume over my boner. That's just a very unsubtle way my hand and cock had of saying hello. Actually, my cock pretty much has a brain all of its own, in situations like this. Next, it'll be bursting into preseminal tears. See: no sooner said than done. That's just the way it is. It having been hot for men even before I consciously awoke to that fact. Probably not too smart an admission by me, out here in the wilderness as I am, alone, with someone obviously big enough, and strong enough, to beat this queer to a bloody pulp and throw him over the side of the trail into that stream, the deed probably never to be found out. It's just that, I woke up this morning particularly horny, thinking merely to do a bit of spermal seeding as I walked along, only to stumble on you with your dick, well ... enough about your dick ... enough about my dick. Just, please don't be angry, okay? You just stay put, and I'll mosey on down the path a bit farther and let the both of us get on with what we were doing, or trying to do. Me genuinely glad you took all of my hot-boy-with-raging-hormones stuff without erupting into some kind of indignant hetero-butch production number. I really should save whatever dignity I've left by .... Thanks, but I really couldn't eat a thing, except .... God, look how beet-red I'm turning because of where that most recent bit of fantasizing took me? Really, I'd better go before I really stick my foot in my mouth. Although, I'd rather have something else in my mouth, seeing studly you. You being a genuinely good sport about this, and I want to thank you for it, but my sticking around isn't a good idea for either of us. Not for you, because you'll probably soon tire of my helpless inability to keep from coming on to you (coming on you?). I, because I'll probably end up with a busted nose because my run-off-at-the-mouth mouth is suddenly out to chew on more than just the health-food bar you're offering. It's just that, you .... Can you really be this good-looking, close up? At a distance, after all, is one thing, but in close-up? All a guy's flaws are supposed to come out when .... I mean, in the movies, say, or in photographs, they have ways of erasing imperfections, but you don't have any imperfections, do you? Not any that I can see. I'll bet there won't be any flaws to be seen even if I walk in a bit closer, like this. How about if I go so far as to touch ...? Jesus, how velvety your skin feels stretched over all your hard and exquisitely etched muscle! Even your goose bumps are perfection. Surely my touching didn't give you those, by the way, although they weren't there when you were just nakedly toasting yourself in this sweet summer sunshine. Or, were they? Maybe I'm just out to flatter myself, because you're so ... so .... Goose bumps not nearly the half of what I can give you, if you'll let me. That you've let me get this far ... you still sporting that giant-size erection of yours, which is just to die for by the way ... leads me to believe you're not completely turned off by all of this. If I could just ... you know ... slide my hands along your torso to your hips ... and drop to my knees, like this. Oh, yes ... yes ... so ... so ... perfect a view of ... so ... so ... perfect ... perfect ... perfectly hard ... a ... ah ... cock. At this point, it best for you to tell me to stop ... even better, take hold of my hair ... yank me to my feet ... tell this queer to get the hell on out of here, because ... because ... Jesus, I am sorry, but your cock is just too ... too ... too tempting to ...."

Out:
"Ohhh ... ohhhh ... ohhhh ... sweet Jesus, Roger ... but ... I shouldn't ... really ... shouldn't be ... but .... oh, oh, how long I've wanted to, but ... oh, God, you really are ... taking my cock ... all of my cock ... all of the way down too ... sweet, sweet, sweet ... unbelievable, Jesus ... down, down, down ... to my ... oh, you're manhandling my nuts ... swallowing my cock ... squeezing my ... sucking my .... ohhhhh, such unbelievable pleasure that ... if only you weren't so fucking studly ... so hiker-boy young ... so tan ... so sexily summer-sweaty ... so willing ... so anxious to ... suck, eat, gnaw, squeeze ... oh, my cock ... oh, my balls ... oh, your mouth that's ... eating ... eating ... please, eating ...my dick and ... slobbering my cock with wet-warm spit and ... oh, Christ, this is lovely

... unbelievably ... lovely ... so lovely ... which is why ... isn't it? ... I've waited ... waited ... Jesus, why have I waited? ... so fucking ... fucking long ... except that I knew the minute I saw you ... blond hair ... blue eyes ... boner in hand ... hiker-boy stud ... tanned ... so slimly muscled ... so eager ... so, oh, oh, oh ... where did you learn to eat cock? Someone so young. I having wasted so much of my youth to find the guts to get to this ... ohhhh, easy stud, easy ... far ... I not nearly as experienced in this as you might very well think, in that ... oh, yes, yes, that is the way ... no cunt, no pussy ever having ... ever having ... oh, how can it be so ... so good? ... and, why have I waited ... so, so long? ... when, when, when ... Jesus, easy, easy, easy ... oh, please, dear God, don't let it end, because ... I'm fucking this handsome ... hiker-boy's ... face ... fucking his mouth ... being gobbled, eaten, sucked, chewed ... and I need it to last ... just last ... a few ... few ... minutes ... more ... before ... I, I, I ... Jesus, I ... oh, oh, can't believe ... it's so fuck-ing hot ... I'm so fucking sweaty ... sweet-sweet summer sweaty ... and who knows when or if I'll ever ... ever ... again ... oh, I'm going to ... going to ... come ... come ... Going To Come ... now, now, now ... oh, Jesus, kid ... now ...my balls ... even now ... oh, ohhhhhhh .... aghhhh ... aghhhhhhh .... AAAGGHRRUHHHHH! Take it! Take it! Take it!"

ABRACADABACUS

I hate air conditioners. Never, ever, have I been in a natural setting, and that includes some ice caves, with breezes a-blow'n through, where the real thing comes anywhere close to the fake chills produced by those damnable machines.

LA having this love affair with air conditioners that has driven me crazy from the first day I stepped off the air-conditioned bus that got me here. I mean, just look around: air conditioners everywhere, even in the fucking dog-houses (and I'm not talking just the mutt-homes of the rich and famous, either!).

You want to know how a whole gamut of upper-respiratory problems can be solved overnight in this city? Just turn off all the air condition-ers. Nothing clogs my sinuses faster, or gives me a summer cold any quicker, than a few hours of going from ice-box buildings, that require I wrap myself in a coat, out into the blast-furnace heat of an LA summer, where I can't get cool if I strip stark naked.

Presently, the came-with-the-lease air conditioner at my place is blessedly on the blink, the result of my having thrown a heavy and very-well aimed (thank-you, very much!) boot at it. That's the plus side of my life. As for the minus ...

I'm fucking depressed.

"Fucking" a key word, here, seeing as how, and the irony doesn't escape me, that's what is literally being done to me at the moment. A big fat pecker, albeit not all that long a one, works like sixty up my ass-hole which I've presented for servicing by having lifted my legs and locked my heels atop Mr. Kinney's less-than-in-fit-form ass.

Mr. Kinney doesn't care the room is air-conditioner-on-the-blink warm. Once, he mentioned having spent a good deal of time in the tropics. "LA summers," if I remember him correctly, "compared to what goes on three-hundred-and-sixty-five days a year in places like Burma, aren't likely to see me suffering heatstroke, under whatever weather and/or fuck conditions this city might serve up."

"Fuck me, daddy!" I say to Mr. Kinney. Depressed or not, I've a job

William Maltese

to do. If I won't be doing any of this for much longer, I still have a certain pride in giving the client his monies' worth. "Yes, daddy ... yes, daddy ... yes."

Mr. Kinney isn't my real father, of course. My real father is in Turnkey, Montana. And, don't try to find Turnkey on any map. Even while driving through, you blink and you've miss it. I'm not looking forward to going back there, either, although I'll be welcomed with open arms. And, since you probably wonder, my mother and father don't have a clue as to what their only son does for a living in LA, or they'd likely have coronaries and drop dead. Love the both of them, but moving back in with them, into my own room, and resuming my role of cowboy for the city slickers who check into the family dude ranch, isn't something I await with bated breath. On the other hand, I made myself a promise the day I came to the big city, and ...

"Tell, daddy just how much you love it," Mr. Kinney says, his putty-like chest laid across my skinny one, his breathing slightly minty against the side of my face, the cadence of his beer-can-thick dick, up my butt, a bit erratic in his spiral toward orgasm within this young stud's saddle.

"None better, daddy," I say on cue. I really have to pay more attention. Mr. Kinney, after all, has paid big bucks to jump my bones and to have me pretend, for a few short minutes, that the two of us are involved in some kind of lovingly incestuous relationship.

Once, made curious by how Mr. Kinney's conversations never go much beyond the banality of the very few words geared to his fantasy, and/or to comments on the weather, I asked Gary if Mr. Kinney had any kids of his own. I'm talking Gary Handlin, not Gary McCoy. Gary Mc knows nothing except that Gary Mc has a big prick coveted by a whole coterie of old farts willing to pay out money to get at it, most of whom first have to take out their false teeth. Anyway, Gary H said, and don't ask me how he'd know, that Mr. Kinney is single.

"Probably afraid to get married and have kids, because he figures he'd be riding their asses from six-months of age on and be hauled off to the Big House in no time," said Gary H. "Or, more likely, he could never keep it up for pussy long enough to seed any of those kiddy-making furrows."

Mr. Kinney's butt-banging pelvis starts pumping his cock up my ass all the faster, as he provides little grunts in accompaniment, all of which has me trying damn hard to get back to concentrating on the business at hand.

I look upward, beyond Mr. Kinney and above our sex-locked bodies, to where there are forty curtainless curtain rings, thirty-nine to the far left of an otherwise bare rod, only one remaining on the right. I figure the bed was once a four-poster, since downgraded to a two. The rod and curtain rings probably supported part of the headboard end of a now long-gone canopy.

The curtain rings, and this one particular fuck, are responsible for my present downer. Although, I've always rather enjoyed Mr. Kinney's purely little-poke-poke big-barrel cock-fucks of my ass. Maybe if his dick were as proportionately impressive in length as it is in circumference, it could do me permanent damage. As it is, it's more like a bully trying to crash a party but not quite making it all of the way inside.

I haven't a clue what fucked-up stuff goes on in Mr. Kinney's head. Can he really be the sweet older gentleman he appears, when he always ends up busily pumping my ass, calling me sonny, and insisting I call him daddy?

Wherever Mr. Kinney is coming from, I could have Graff Miller riding my bones and still be depressed. And that's saying a helluva lot, because my all-time ultimate fantasy is Graff in bed with me. Just in bed, his not having to do anything but lie there, perfectly naked. Fucking and sucking icing on the proverbial cake, because Graff is my biggest and best turn-on. He's only two years older than I am, but his body is all man-stud, while mine is strictly slim-teenager. I hear Graff has one helluva muscle between his legs, too. That info courtesy of Gary H who claims to have "gotten word" from someone called Teddy who supposedly gets it off regularly with Graff for the watching pleasure of some old fart who only likes to look.

"Sonny ... sonny ... tight-ass sonny!" says Mr. Kinney and, once again, brings me back from self-indulgent reverie.

I'm giving Mr. Kenny short shrift. Though, I suppose, that only becomes important if Mr. Kinney knows it. If he does know, will he complain? Will I end up leaving this business on other than my sterling record up to now? Oh, I suppose my first fucks for money might not have been the best ever, but even they were okay, because the guys who handed over the dough were balling me just because I was a novice at getting humped.

"Love me, daddy. Big-daddy cocked daddy ... love me. Daddy ...

daddy-cock ... oh, daddy."

I make another conscious effort to stay tuned. If I want to mope, and I do, I'll have plenty of time after I've seen Mr. Kinney, and his cum-depleted balls, to the door.

"Oh, sonny ... sweet sonny," he says and gives a series of low and muffled grunts that tells me he's pretty much as far gone as he's going to get.

Will I miss Mr. Kinney when he literally comes and goes, this final time -- at least with me as his saddle? Will I miss Gary H? Will I miss ... ?

"Oh ... sweet ... sweet ... boy of mine!" says Mr. Kinney.

I wrap my arms tightly around him. I clamp my fucked asshole tightly around his thick plug of a dick.

"Oh, daddy, yes ... yes ... daddy. Please, daddy, yes!"

He creams. I know, because, he tells me.

"... come ... come ... come!" he chants to final last-drop conclusion and collapses, dead-weight, atop me.

Aside from his pronouncement of orgasm, I've little evidence to go on. He's not such a profuse shooter that he ever balloons the rubber on his dick enough for me to feel a significant difference.

Luckily, he never requires me to come. Maybe because any real kid being humped by his own father might not derive as much pleasure from the incestuous molestation as the older man does, no matter what the kid might be cajoled to utter during intercourse. I'm never so turned on by Mr. Kinney's little fantasy that I manage an orgasm.

"Oh, that was wonderful," he says. Since he always says the same thing, it's hard to tell if he's faking.

I can't help smile at the prospect of any john faking pleasure. Faking it is supposedly the bailiwick of us professionals. Although I'll be the first to admit that women whores have it far easier, in the charade department, than we guy whores do, because of female inside-plumbing.

I unhook my ankles, and Mr. Kinney pulls out and off. He removes and ties off his rubber to take with him: the good little camper who hauls away whatever the rubbish for which he's responsible. I once offered him the use of a handy wastepaper basket, but he refused. Since then, my suspicions as to what he does with his bit of cummy residue is probably more fantastic than the probable reality.

He dresses with his back to me, while I slip into a terry-cloth robe.

"A little something extra, just for you," he says and slips me an extra couple hundred. "And as a special parting gift," he produces a couple more, "in that Harold says you're leaving us. Such a pity you have to go!"

As soon as he's gone, after I've socked away the extra money, I go to the frig for a beer. I know what I have to do now. No big deal, I tell myself, but I've obviously made it one. From the start, I've made it a point to measure my time in this life-style by the number of paying johns I've had in and out of my bed.

I finish the beer, leave the bottle on a counter. I go over to my bed, stand on it, unceremoniously flip curtain ring forty from right to left.

Jesus, forty paying customers in the last six months! No big deal to a lot of male whores, in a business where the more traffic in the bedroom the more cash in one's pockets. Amazing to me, though, because I never thought it would come to this. I was convinced, from the very start, that I'd never throw that fortieth ring, having been genuinely flabbergasted when I'd actually thrown a mere ten.

Selling my body for profit the last thing I thought I'd ever end up doing. Granted, I knew from the get-go that I wasn't leaving Turnkey for LA with the brainpan of a rocket scientist. Still, I'd had high hopes. Maybe not vice-president-of-some-microchip-company hopes but expectations of at least a living wage.

I started out working at a service station where I met Harold Orkey with his emerald-green BMW, his Brioni suits, his Bally shoes, and his whatever other fashion logos overstuff his closets.

It's the same tired old story of country-kid hick charmed by big-city pimp into turning a few tricks for a few extra bucks. A prepaid apartment came with this deal. The curtain rail over my bed having become my, "If I don't get a regular job by the time I throw ring number forty, I'm giving up on the big-city and heading back to the sticks."

I'm not so damn ignorant that I didn't and don't see how I was seduced by the easy cash made from male prostitution. That and the fact that Harold isn't exactly the heavily-chained typical pimp peddling his boys' cocks and asses off some street corner in the seedier part of town.

Each time I fucked, or was fucked, sucked, or was sucked, and flipped one more curtain ring from right to left, I convinced myself that

I'd get a better than sex-selling job in the morning. Never happened.

The last curtain ring is now thrown. My having made the rule that when that last one went, I went -- home. Mom, dad ... and blue-haired old ladies, playing Dale Evans on horseback ... Yuk! ... here I come!

The doorbell rings.

I come off the bed, where I've stood for some time.

It's Harold with some well-dressed, genuinely natty, older man.

It's Graff Miller, though, standing a bit behind, who has me hardly believing my eyes.

"Jordan," says Harold. "You know Graff."

I've said maybe two words to Graff, and vice versa. My fantasies of him have all been from far afield, the result of my having heard all sorts of tales regarding his prowess -- from Gary H. I've long wanted to know him -- in the Biblical sense -- but that's all been a pipe dream.

Graff nods hello and keeps our total life-time conversation to four words.

"This is Orrin Harp," says Harold. "An old old friend."

"Yes," says Orrin, as if it isn't true until he confirms it.

"Mr. Harp," I say.

"Orrin," he says.

"May we come in?" Harold asks.

"Sure."

I suspect Harold has a key, since he pays the rent. Except, he's never used one, always knocking first and waiting for me to let him in, even the time I was in the shower and inadvertently left him standing in the hall for what had to have been ten minutes.

I invite them to sit. Harold and Orrin do. Graff remains standing and assumes a sexy lean against one wall.

"You've heard about Teddy?" Harold says.

"Teddy?" I try to recall everything I've ever heard about Teddy from Gary H.

To hear tell, Teddy is a cute young blond number who looks fourteen but hasn't been chicken for over a year. He has lush eyelashes, pretty green eyes, an attractive ski-sloped tiny nose, permanently petulant lips. His body, if possible, is even thinner than mine.

"Seems Teddy has a genuinely bad cold," Graff says. Which in one sentence more than doubles our previous oral history together.

I suspect Terry's cold has more than a little to do with some air conditioner, but it's Harold who says:

"Goddamn, it's hot in here."

"Sorry, but the air conditioner is on the fritz," I explain, all innocence. "The manager insists he'll be up to look at it first thing tomorrow."

"Orrin?" asks Harold, as if that may change the circumstances of this little meeting.

"I'm fine," says Orrin.

Certainly, Orrin looks as cool as a cucumber. On the other hand, I, having so recently been ridden by Mr. Kinney, have a thin gloss of sweat cocooning my body, my one cold beer not having done a helluva lot to make it otherwise.

"Orrin," says Harold, but his attention is focused back on me, "may have a penchant for snot-nosed kids, but it's purely in the figurative sense. In the literal sense, there's nothing more revolting than someone (AKA Teddy) with a truly drooling nose."

I've always pictured Teddy as coming off so young that he still eats his boogers and licks snot from his upper lip. So, if Orrin genuinely has a penchant for the illusion of that kind of kiddy-type, what in the hell brings him to my door -- with Graff and Harold in tow?

Harold must see me mulling the situation, my giving Graff another thorough once-over as I do so, because he says: "Orrin, likewise, has a penchant for a certain stud-type viewed in combination with stereotypical snot-nose-kid type."

So, what, I wonder, does that really mean, and what does it tell me?

"Orrin, like you, is leaving town, only he's flying out this evening," Harold says. "He's most anxious for a session before he goes, and Graff suggested we might give you a try, seeing as how you're in the neighborhood and Teddy is unavailable." While I'm amazed that whatever this is it has been suggested by Graff who never seemed to give me a second look, I'm frankly chagrined as to how I've somehow been lumped into the same snot-nose kid category as Teddy. Just because Teddy and I both have green eyes and blond hair .... Just because Teddy and I can both use a bit more meat on our bones ...

"We've not interrupted other plans for your evening, have we?" asks Harold who is well acquainted with my fucking, sucking, and packing schedules. He knows not only that my session with Mr. Kinney is over but that I'm not booked for anyone else this evening. "I've explained to

Orrin that you're used to working one-on-one and might not be up to an audience. I, also, told him that you might be anxious to get packing, since you're scheduled to leave us tomorrow. But we thought it wouldn't hurt if we just dropped by to query you, as regards the matter."

"Yes," says Orrin.

"All of this, of course, depending upon Orrin liking what he sees," adds Harold. He wipes sweat from his brow, and I get the distinct impression he has second thoughts about the whole thing, even if Orrin doesn't.

"Oh, yes, yes," says Orrin. "Yes."

Which is a helluva lot of yeses, and I hope Harold can figure out what in the hell they all mean.

"So, if you think you might like to give this a try?" Harold says and sounds God-it's-hot-in-here dubious.

I figure he's asking Orrin if I, and the absence of any functioning air conditioner, pass muster.

"Cat got your tongue?" says Graff.

I realize Graff speaks to me. Likewise, Harold's query had been to me. Orrin apparently gave his okay via one or more of his previous run-on yeses.

"A simple sixty-nine position will do," says Harold. He's always given me a yes-no options on all my johns. Up until now, I've never said no. I suspect that if I back out of this one, Harold will diplomatically usher Orrin and Graff into a quick retreat and leave me to my packing. I've always liked Harold because he's never made our business relationship one where he's all-knowing and I'm to do exactly as he says, every time, with my input counting for shit. "Sucking need only proceed until one of you comes."

"Yes," says Orrin.

"No need to set any endurance records, either" says Harold. "Especially in this heat. Besides, Orrin realizes that your newness to this sort of thing might ... well ...." He leaves the obvious hanging. "So, as soon as you come, no matter how short a time it may take ...."

Suddenly, I've gone from someone so thrown by the novelty of the suggestion that I'll be lucky if I manage a boner, to someone so turned on by the scene that I'll likely prematurely pop my rocks before Graff's handsome face even gets as far as my pecker.

Graff's supercilious grin, complete with sweaty upper lip, seems to confirm how he figures I'll prematurely pop my rocks without his having to expend all that much effort.

I wish now that I'd been able to get off with Mr. Kinney's beer-can-thick dick having massaged only the first couple inches of my asshole. Had my nuts erupted, once this evening, I'd have that grin wiped off Graff's handsome face, in no time, once he, laboring over my prick for its sloppy seconds, was subjected to air-conditioner-on-the-fritz heat that he, probably as much as Harold, wishes would go away.

Graff may well work his studly charms in getting a snot-nose Teddy to cream with hardly any effort, but I'm determined to make this studly bastard sweat buckets for whatever feasting he manages over my cum-spewing penis.

"I need to be top-man," I say. Man-over-man the most logical position for Orrin's viewing pleasure. Side-by-side would likely keep much of the action less visible, unless of course Orrin sprouts wings and hovers over the bed. My initially going down-up, as opposed to up-down, over Graff's hard cock is to my advantage, because the latter position always needs be accomplished while hanging from the top-man's hips, like a monkey hangs from a tree. Graff's experience might give him the versatility to perform equally well, whether on all fours over my supine body, or on his back beneath me-on-all-fours, but I need all the advantage I can get.

"So, you be top-man," Graff says.

The bastard looks and sounds so bloody confident. Would I ever manage the same were I to stay in the business a few more years?

"It's settled, then," says Harold who gets up and manhandles his chair to a position closer to the bed.

Orrin stands, too, but it's gentlemanly Graff who obliges the move of Orrin's chair to ringside.

"You two proceed at your leisure," Harold says and lets Orrin settle in before sitting himself.

First thing, I let them know there's no chance in hell that I'm not up to the performance. I unhook my robe and shrug it off my shoulders. If the boner I unveil isn't the same I sprouted during parts of Mr. Kinney's ride, that one having faded to limpness during the course of my having had a beer and my having finalized the last ring-toss, this erection is more impressive. I'm anxious to take on studly Graff, under whatever the circumstances. I only wish he wasn't quite so aware of his good looks and how much they so obviously turn on guys like me.

I plop on the bed and fluff up some pillows. I expect to enjoy each and every second of Graff's more time-consuming disrobing. Except, Graff has mastered the technique of quick undress more thoroughly than any male stripper. His speed is helped by the absence of any and all underwear. What little his delay is only because of how tightly his studly body is poured into his clothes.

If Graff, with his clothes on, is an impotent man's dick-stiffener, which he is, then Graff naked and already gone slightly all-over sweaty can put the starch back into the pecker of a palace eunuch.

The usual descriptive bit about rectangular pectorals, tanned skin, rippled belly, muscled arms and legs, big cock, large balls, sexy feet, all fits, but it doesn't begin to do justice to the total package.

Literally, I drool at the sight of him, kept from showing how much only because I quickly swallow the evidence. The drool from my cock, though, isn't so easily or successfully hidden. My dick goes so artesian that Orrin likely assumes it's already into cum-spewing phase.

Graff does provide me a couple seconds of pure viewing pleasure while he manhandles his cock in order to work out whatever its kinks sustained during its tight confinement within his trousers. Simultaneously, his other hand fondles his balls and fluffs up his sweat-stuck scrotal fur.

It's Graff's sweat-burnished tan, as he lies down beside me, that's really a turn-on, possibly because I've always found it so bloody difficult to get as berry-brown. Graff's tan is incomplete only because of the thinnest and sexiest of bikini lines.

Determined not to allow him any unfair advantage, above and beyond his having sixty-nined for this very same audience, countless times before, I waste no time straddling his studly supine sexiness, head-to-foot. I deep-dive my face just below Graff's laid-out-along-his-scalloped-belly cock. I put my pursed lips to one of his large and sweaty testicular eggs that are so contentedly nestled within their furry scrotal nest, and I suck.

There's an audible pop ... pop ... as first his one nut, then his other, enters my oral doorway made purposely small to hard-squeeze each gonad during its inward passage. I'm delighted by Graff's resulting breathless grunt, and by the way both his large hands clamp hard and fast to my ass in responsive squeeze.

I compress my lips around the very base of his scrotum. Had I the inclination, I could sever his balls in one hearty bite, my head and nose buried so deeply between his open thighs that I'm close to nose-fucking his sweaty rectum. I smell Graff's emanating manly-ass smells, each one excitingly aphrodisiacal as it wafts whatever its pheromonal essence through his tangled weave of perspiration-damp asshair.

What's good for the goose being good for the gander, Graff uses his handholds on my ass to elevate his head between my thighs. His mouth opens so wide it clamps over and locks onto both of my nuts, at one and the same time.

"Yes!" says Orrin, returned to a familiar theme.

Since I've never known a guy to get off by my merely eating his nuts, I figure it's best I leave off chewing on Graff's nads. Better to concentrate on what's going to make real progress toward getting him to spew his studly cream.

My head pulls up and releases all of his scrotum, except for what continues to Saran-wrap his still-swallowed golf-ball gonads. I'm a robin with a recalcitrant worm that insists upon keeping one end firmly grounded. My head pulls back even farther, and I reproduce the original pop-pop as each of his nuts, one after the other, returns to the outside world. Turned loose, his testicles, and their attending sac of hairy skin, shift and move with lives all their own.

My left hand, palm down, slides his abdominals, gathers a thin line of sweat, and finally stops where the base of Graff's big dick attaches to his belly. I pull his monster cock to perpendicular. I've a bird's-eye view of his pouty cockmouth gone all juicy and wet with a veneer of clear liquid. The slit of his pulpy cockhead is a perfect divider that makes his cockcorona two separate but equal parts united into a whole (hole?); like each buttocks of his ass melds along mutually shared ass-crack to form the sensuous perfection of his rear end.

I suck the blunted end of his cockhead perfection. I drink and savor that delicious pre-cum oiliness that I steal from his deep-gash pisshole. My lips open wider and slide along, then over, his coronal flaring. My moue contracts as my mouth locks within the groove formed by his mushroom-cockhead attachment to the uppermost limits of his thick penile shaft. My view is slightly askew, because I see more than a little cross-eyed down the lengthy belly of his dick to the ocean swells of his shifting still-spit-wet scrotum and balls.

I'm grateful that Graff lets me continue my head start, he seemingly content with his continued oral manipulation of my nuts. Although, I'm the first to admit it probably isn't magnanimity on his part but his smugness in suspecting his experience will see me sucked off before he is, no matter how much initial leeway he gives me. His is the same ill-advised smugness exhibited by the rabbit before the turtle whopped hairy (harey?) ass in fabled road race.

At least, I don't come into this a complete novice at cocksucking. I try to compute how many thrown curtain rings, over this very bed, represent cock sucked to climax. So diverting are those mathematics that I'm able to divert some of my attention from Graff's continuous noshing on my balls.

Does ESP tell Graff he's suddenly more out of the picture than he feels it right for a comparatively innocent, like me, to put him? Or, is it merely a natural progression, from step one to step two, in a time-worn format, all with which he's intimately familiar, that so quickly has him jam one of his unlubricated fingers a good inch up my butt?

"Jesus, fuck!" I respond and know full-well that what I say doesn't come out even vaguely like that, so distorted is it around my mouthful of Graff's erection.

If Graff was out to grab my attention, he has does so. His stuck finger immediately commences a series of miniature fuck movements that tug my snug anal lining right along with them. Were he simply to pull his finger free with a vengeance, I'd likely end up with a good inch of my bowel turned inside-out and trailing my asshole like a ribbon in the wind.

He's perfectly coordinated in his working my balls and my asshole.

I've heard of guys who cream with just the finger-fuck of their butts, but that has never been me. Even those guys who have it happen certainly must need a bit more finger penetration, surely to collision-with-prostate depth, in order to achieve climactic reaction. My best bet is to get on with some serious sucking of Graff's cock and leave him to do whatever he's doing. I only hope his well-spring of expertise provides him the secret of getting his finger back out of my asshole without causing me permanent damage.

Luckily for me, his cock, large as it is, is seemingly just made for my sucking of it. It has no disconcerting anomalies, where I've one regular john whose cock comes with a forty-five degree bend about an inch from its tip. Gary H has a regular who went to the Philippines and had two rows of plastic pearls implanted along the shaft of his penis. "Going down on that," says Gary H, "is like taking on a row of speed bumps."

Graff's cock is slightly wider and flatter along its belly and back than it is along its sides. Its base is greater in circumference than even the impressive flare of its cockhead, but the increase is gradual. When my face completes its ride and my nose pokes his pillowing balls, I comfortably have each and every inch of his penis shoved inside my face. My chin burrows the wiry-hair nest that's his pubic bush.

I scoop my hands between the bed and Graff's muscled ass. One of his solid buttcheeks in each hand, I knead each bun hard and fast, as if I'm making bread. I lift upward on his ass to mate his crotch more securely to my face.

He obliges and bends his legs more fully at their knees. The space between his thighs goes even wider, and my face bows farther and deeper along his asscrack. I see his asspucker. I smell it. A bit more effort, and I can probably pug my nose against its winked anal eye.

What I do, though, is "pull a Graff": my finger, not my nose, hits the doorway of his asshole. Though both my hands simultaneously slid inward into the damp valley between his buns, it's my right fuck-finger, quicker than the left, that wiggles up his butt like a snake wiggles into a gopher hole.

Confident sonofabitch, Graff actually jiggles his ass ever more securely over my probing finger. By doing so, he assures that before I fully commit to my finger's removal, I'll need him to provide some hint, by example, as to how to extract a dry finger from a dry asshole.

In the meantime, I slide my mouth almost all of the way back up the length of his erection and stop only when the flare of his cockhead catches inside my ovaled lips. I've left behind one thoroughly spit-wet dick.

"Yes," says Orrin who I've almost forgotten. Harold hasn't said a damn thing. (Too busy wiping sweat from his brow?!)

"Ohhhh," I say as Graff's finger twists up my butt and pulls out a bit before it pauses to allow my asshole to adjust to his prod's new position.

I suck Graff's cockhead like Lolita sucked her lollipop, and I threaten, as best I can, to purse-lip decapitate his penile monster as thoroughly as Marie Antoinette was ever beheaded by Madam Guillotine. I keep right on sucking, gumming, munching, and slobbering the bulbous tip of his dick until he obliges, whether real or feigned, with a loud-low grunt. Only then do I leave off focus on the head of his dick in order, once again, to claim the total dimensions of his meaty hunk.

Still sucking my balls, Graff slowly, expertly, removes his fuckfinger from my butt. I'm now convinced I can risk an equally masterful retrieval of my fuck-finger from his ass.

When I finally do get my finger out, I put it to the base of his mouth-submerged dick. I slobber an ocean of spit and let the drool escape the seal my lips make around the thick bottom of his boner. No sooner does the ooze appear than my finger rolls in it like a pig rolls in viscous mud.

Quicker than you can say finger-fuck, I not only have my spit-wet digit back to his asspucker, but I've provided a follow-through push that places the whole length of its wetness right smack into Graff's sexy behind. That I actually manage contact with his prostate is relayed to me via the walnut bulge suddenly against my fingertip, and by Graff's surprised whelp that is accompanied by a squirt of preseminal juice from his throat-basted pecker.

Maybe, just maybe, my finger's success at plumbing his asshole convinces the smug bastard he's not dealing with a complete amateur.

He spits out my balls, as if they've suddenly grown puffer-fish spines, and proceeds with a direct attack on my penis.

I give my butt-fuck finger a hearty butter-churn twist and massage his prostate more thoroughly than any doctor during a physical exam. My head moves into quick up-and-down bounces over his pecker, and I genuinely feel I'm well enough concentrated, on what I do, to stand up to any additional assaults he plans on my asshole and/or on my erection.

Of course, I'm wrong! If my finger's workout up his butt, and my mouth's workout over his dick, gets Graff mewling pleasure, which they do, you haven't heard anything like the sound you hear from me when his finger returns up my butt, saliva-buttered this time, and his mouth hungrily lunches on my dick, and his finger and his mouth quickly achieve well-coordinated unison in working me over like sixty.

His finger corkscrews against my sorry-ass prostate, and his mouth torques all of the way to my sweat-drenched balls.

I squeal like a stuck pig, and all of my remaining concentration evaporates in another flash of pure, unadulterated, pleasure. My fuck-finger comes to a dead stop up his butt, and my head stops, mid-bounce, like a piston completely into lock-down. My mouth opens and shuts, opens and shuts, around its mouthful of hard dick, like a python having decided it has taken on prey far too big to swallow. More of my spit pumps out and over the base of Graff's sticking penis. My slick saliva, none of it finger-captured this time, bubbles his pubic hair, both on his crotch and on his balls, like foamy frog eggs on wet seaweed.

His head lifts farther between my thighs and my balls come to rest, one over each of his eyes. His nose sniffs whatever smells his drilling finger brings free of my butt.

I finally begin, again, the bounce of my head over his stiff dick, and the push and pull of my finger up his asshole. Whenever his finger performs some new twist or turn that causes me a particular surge of pleasure, my finger tries to replicate the same up his asshole. No one ever complains I'm not a quick study.

I'm impressed by how little impaired Graff is by having been required to swing beneath my belly, simultaneously to maintain tenuous handholds of my ass, simultaneously to eat my dick and to finger-fuck my asshole. It's more coordination that I could master, seeing as how I have so much trouble maintaining the pretty straightforward dive and retreat of my face over his vulnerable groin, not to mention the dive and retreat of my finger up his ass.

Nor am I particularly pleased when my hips reflexively provide Graff an obviously unneeded assist by their commencement of a spontaneous fucking cadence that coincides with his increasingly more vigorous head bounces, up and back, along and over the length of my erection.

"Yes," says Orrin.

My world pretty much shrinks to exclude Orrin, and whatever his voyeuristic tendencies, as well as to exclude Harold, and whatever he makes of this and the sweat that soaks him. Being so securely contained within the cocoon that includes only Graff and me, I have to be careful that I don't get so caught up in my pleasure that I forget my objective is to provide just as much as I get.

I'm still determined not to give Graff the satisfaction of sucking me to the easy climax of a snot-nose kid getting head for the very first time. It has less to do with providing Orrin a good show, than it has everything to do with pride of professionalism.

Goddamn it, I'm a paid cocksucker (among other things), and that means I'm not your average run-of-the-mill gay, picked up in some bar, or lucked on to in some park after dark. I'm better at this than most, and that's why I get money for doing it. Therefore, I refuse to appear to Orrin, to Graff, to Harold, to me, to anyone, as some inexperienced little shit so turned on by the expertise of major-domo cocksucker Graff turned loose on me that I can't hold my own.

Besides, I'm not likely to get another chance at Graff's asshole or at his pecker, and I'm determined to milk this moment for all it's worth. I'll probably be calling upon my memories, gained here and now, for whatever the fantasies required to keep my sanity back in Turnkey.

A sad fact, despite all my attempts at denial, is that Graff is far more the pro at this than I am. Were there curtain rings hung in a row, along a rod over his bed, I can only imagine how countless the number thrown to the left by now. You don't get to be number-one stallion in Harold's stable without providing the proven worth that gets you there.

All along, I've mainly been the student following the master's lead: the neophyte attempting something only after Graff proves the technique successful on me.

Somewhere along the line, having finally accepted that Graff not only comes into this looking like a million but is capable of performing that way as well, I know he isn't going all-out, never has been, likely in deference to the money Orrin pays to see Graff getting it on with a kid even less experienced than boyishly kiddy, skinny and presently snot-nose, Teddy ever was.

Once I have it figured that Graff probably isn't really out to see me cream my load as fast as he can manage, that maybe we're a team here, each trying to give a client his monies' worth, so the client leaves happy and desirous of coming back for more, I quit trying to suppress my pleasure. I figure Graff is perfectly able to gauge where I'm at, by way of my impending orgasm, either to speed up my climax, or to pull me back from the brink, at his leisure.

Graff never has been some evil knight who picked up the metal gauntlet and whacked me across the face in some kind of challenge to sexual joust. He's merely a teammate, a pro, in employ of the same pimp (manager?), out to achieve the goal of pleasing a client, which should be my goal as well.

I grunt and squeal, more than sure I'm about to cream my load, when Graff accomplices the miracle, don't ask me how, of easing me back from the edge.

"Oh, oh, oh," I say and slobber all the more over his dick and no longer even hold out the promise of a snowball in hell of providing the successful sucking that'll coax Graff's cock to any mutual explosion with mine.

Once again, he pulls whatever the trick from his hat that allows me a few more spitty mouth-pumps of his erection, a few more rises and falls of his head beneath my belly ...

Until the point is finally reached when I'm less appreciative of his skills that keep me from orgasm, because it's climax I want and so desperately need. I've an overload of ecstasy cooped up inside of me, an excess of cum in balls which are no longer sufficiently designed to contain it. My nervous system is about to go completely out of whack because of a sexually electric power surge.

I'm back to suppressing my grunts and groans, afraid Graff will keep on using them as signs to interrupt and begin again yet another abortion of my explosion.

"Ohhhhhh," I moan over his phallic truncheon, as his cock once more sticks all of the way into my mouth and throat.

I'm a time bomb waiting to explode, if only Graff would get the hint that it's time to light the fuse, push the plunger, pull the lever, so that ... once ... and ... for all ...

If he doesn't give me needed release damn soon, I won't be responsible. In frustration, I'll bury my face over his dick one final time, and bite his sexy dick off at its thick base. In further punishment, I'll ...

"Ugh ... ugh ... ugh .. ugh," I perform in guttural mantra to the sudden runaway bounce of his sexy head over my dick.

Finally! Jesus, finally!

Every bit of stored tension inside of me funnels directly to my balls and explodes from there along the length of my dick. Every gallon of spunk crowded into my testicles proceeds, hardily and heartily, along the barrel of my sex-charged sex-hose.

My mouth, down tightly against the base of Graff's dick, opens so wide he must suddenly think his cock fucks wide-open spaces. My lips clamp back, though, just as suddenly. My cheeks concave in the presence of my eagerly applied sucking vacuum. My throat proceeds into major contractions.

Non-stop, his cum begins to feed its steamy bullets to my sucking face.

The miracle of his orgasm, simultaneous with mine, seemingly so perfectly timed with mine, is so unexpected and so unbelievable that I'm completely caught unaware until his hot sperm fills, then overflows, my mouth. My reflex gagging unsuccessfully contains his deluge and my sinuses sting from the flood.

My hips collapse, and my cock nails Graff's sucking head to the bed. His spewing penis slips free of my mouth and sends streamers of pearly mess spiraling into my hair, corkscrewing onto my face, torquing along my cheeks, neck, and chest.

"Yes ... oh, yes!" says Orrin. Or, maybe I say it. Or, maybe Graff says it. It's damn hard to know, hard to tell, among all the onrushing creamy cum, all the grunting and groaning, all the exclamations of triumph and wonder, all of which finally come to a grinding halt and leave me fearful I've strangled on Graff's cock, or strangled him on mine.

My hips heave upward to unstick his head. My cock's withdrawal is seemingly endless before it finally comes completely free.

"Oh, my ... my," says Orrin.

Oh, my ... my, indeed!

I roll completely free of Graff's sensuously sex-slicked body, not because I want to but because I figure he needs room to breathe. I shut my eyes and still pant, determined to check out Graff's well-being as soon as I'm assured of my own.

His movement on the bed tells me he recovers far faster than I do.

I open my eyes to see his ass in retreat. He pauses in route to his clothes to retrieve my discarded robe. Rather than immediately toss me the white terry-cloth, he gobbles it in both hands, reaches it between his legs and wipes from his sweaty asscrack, up beneath and over his balls, to finish along the neck of his cock. Then, he tosses the robe on over.

Whatever his markings of territory, I'm more turned on than off by their being where he's just left them as I thread my arms through the robe's sleeves and fasten its belt.

By which time, Graff has made it to his own clothes, his cock stuffed nonchalantly within the crotch of his trousers as he zips up.

"Do me a favor when you finish dressing, will you, Graff?" Harold says. His handkerchief is out, not to wipe up any of his voyeuristically spilled cum, which is nowhere in evidence (if it exists at all), but to wipe summer-sweat from his face and neck. "Take Orrin down to the car and wait with him for the few minutes more I'll be here with Jordan."

"Sure," Graff says through his T-shirt pulled down over his head en route to its full covering of his exquisitely perspiration-defined chest.

Orrin stands. If I've expected his cock out of his pants, his cum splattered all over the place, that's not the case. He looks as natty and as well-groomed as ever. Not even a trace of damp residue or obvious swelling at his crotch. Has there ever been?

"So very nice to have met you, young man," Orrin says to me and bows slightly. In redundant affirmation, he adds, "Yes."

Graff ushers Orrin out and shuts the door behind them.

Harold surprises the hell out of me by walking to my bed, stepping right up on it. Then, making damned sure I'm watching, amazed and as curious as all hell as I am, he slides one curtain ring from the left to the right.

"See," he says, "how easily they move in either direction? No abracadabra magic required, merely the incentive to lift a hand and perform the deed."

He comes down off the bed with the impressive agility of a humidity-soaked cat.

"What people like you forget, Jordan ..." he says and walks up close but not touching. "And, by people like you, I refer to those who come up with these little games of I'll fuck and suck only until I've slid forty rings from one side of some rod to the other, or I'll fuck and suck only until my favorite television show is canceled, or I'll fuck and suck only until I have such-and-such amount of dollars in the bank. ... is that you make all the rules to your little games but, as often as not, you forget just how easily you can change them. They're not, for Christ's sake, anywhere, chiseled in stone!"

I don't ask how he knows the significance I've placed upon the movement of forty curtain rings from right to left. He might well be as all-knowing, as all-seeing, as many of the guys in his stable believe. More likely, though, Gary H -- who might have heard me mention it -- passed on the word.

"You really want to go home to mom and dad, and the dude ranch, just because of the right-to-left movement of some curtain rings along

a rod, when I've just proven how easily those same rings can be shifted on back?"

He shakes his head, as if in answer to his own question.

"Look at this," he says, full of surprises.

I follow the movement of his hand to his crotch. His fingers splay so
that the hard ridge of his obviously hard pecker is put into bas-relief.

"Hard cock," he says in superfluous identification. "Do you know the
last time anyone or anything in this business made my dick this stiff?
Well, I'll tell you, it's longer than I care to admit. But, here it is, not only
stiff, but leaking, for Christ's sake!"

Only then do I spot the faint smudge of dampness where his cockhead bulges trouser-crotch material.

"I figured that artesian well dried up long ago," he says. "Yet, watching you and Graff go at it caused the miracle at the well." He makes it
sound downright Biblical.

In emphasis, he pats the hard-ridge evidence that's his leaking pecker. Does he know he makes me hornier than hell?

"You think Graff picked you randomly out of some hat?" he says.
"For that matter, do you really think Teddy is out of this action just
because of his cold?"

Hell, yes, that's exactly what I think.

"Want to know the last time Graff had a simultaneous orgasm with
Teddy?"

Hell, yes, I want to know.

"Never. Zilch. Nada. The big goose egg. 'Let's see what I can
come up with, figuratively and literally, with that kid, Jordan,' is what
Graff said to me. 'Orrin lately seems to be getting a bit bored with
Teddy and me.' Well, neither Graff, nor Orrin, nor I, was bored this time
around. And, you're prepared to squander your obvious talents, at
doing so well at what you do so well, by heading back to mom and dad
-- in horse-shit-filled Montana, of all boondocks places, for Christ's
sake! Why? Because one too many curtain rings finally traveled right
to left? Jesus H Christ!" Another head shake.

"What time does your bus leave tomorrow?" he says.

"Three in the afternoon."

"I'll call at four to see if you're still around," he says. "If you are, we'll
make an appointment to have a very serious conversation about how I
see your possibilities for development in this business."

I wonder if such possibilities include my having a go at his leaking-once-again pecker.

"I've Orrin and Graff waiting," he says and leaves.

I plop on to the bed, pull the collar of my robe tighter around my chin and smell more evidence of the funky ball-and-ass sweat, and nutty creamy-cum smears, Graff has left on the material for me.

I look to the curtain rings above my head, one thrown to the right, the others waiting to ...?

As if by magic, the air conditioner clicks into half-life and immediately wafts some of its much-hated-by-me half-ass LA-coolness. The obviously still-damaged machine's suddenly chill-contracting metal guts protest with a din similar to cats rummaging a trash can.

As if on cue, I get up and start packing.

SUMMER SWEAT

It's a very hot day, very near the very end of a very long, very hot summer.

My name is Adrian Basiff. I'm weary, aching, fatigued, numbed, drag-ass exhausted.

I'm so weary that I hardly remember getting into the shower, only vaguely aware of how the hot water momentarily soothes my aching bones.

I'm so fatigued that my numbed fingers insufficiently fasten the damp towel I hang from my waist, at shower's finale; the half-ass knot comes loose and almost trips my dragging feet that somehow manage to shuffle on over.

I'm so exhausted that after I plop unceremoniously on to my bed, I'm unable to summon even the energy needed to conceal any part of my nakedness; my dick gives no response whatsoever to sexy Caldron Rooge who suddenly sits his firm, naked, not to mention black, ass on the mattress directly beside me.

I'm so fagged that ... Well, while that's probably the best description of my state, mental and physical, moral and whatever, at the moment, let's not go there for the time being.

"Feeling like shit, about now, Adrian!" Caldron says; notice his is not a question. He has a low, deep-timbre voice. He has incredibly handsome facial features, an exceptionally well-delineated body, a snake-like cock, a rock-hard ass. All looked as if dropped in deliciously dark chocolate.

"Yes, like shit," I somehow manage.

"Tomorrow will be worse," he says, "but the day after will be the very worst."

"Thank-you for that helpful bit of encouragement," I say.

He laughs. From where does he get his energy? It's not as if I've arrived on this scene a skinny citified kid having missed too many meals at some urban soup kitchen. Hell, I've pretty much had the best nutrition and exercise that money can buy: my tailor-made physique molded and sculpted by a private trainer who charges a hundred bucks an hour.

You want to see a thoroughly "ripped" body, take a look at mine. Even now, my physique looks studly in repose, no effort made by me (no strength remaining) to suck in a nonexistent gut. I have great legs, fantastic arms, washboard belly, and twin rectangular pecs that pretty much mirror one another across a shallow and serrated cleavage. My buns are as solid as any rock.

Is Caldron more buffed, body-wise, than I am? Well, I guess, it all depends upon one's definition of buffed. Caldron's muscles are definitely bulkier, possibly because he consciously wants them that way, where I've made it a definite point, from the very beginning, of saying I never want to come across as someone obviously spending narcistically long hours in the gym.

Not that Caldron has the developed musculature that so easily pinpoints those physique-conscious fanatics who go from one professional Mr. Something competition to another. I mean, while Caldron's muscles are big, they're not big-big. No biceps and/or triceps so pumped that he must always stand with arms akimbo, whether he wants to or not. No pronouncedly veed torso that makes an observer wonder why so massive an upper body doesn't snap at so tiny-tiny a waist. It's all good-big and big-good. As Goldilocks would say: "Not too much, not too little, just right -- albeit built upon naturally big bone structure."

"But the day after the day after today will find you over the proverbial hump," Caldron promises.

Normally, I might read double entendre into his use of the word "hump". This day, though, hasn't been normal. So, my response is merely closed eyes. Actually, I have no conscious control of my lids, in that they droop of their own accord.

As I drift into sleep and wonder if Caldron will now take sexual advantage of me -- preferring he not, only because I won't be conscious enough to enjoy it -- I decide he has better survived the ordeal of the day because he's been through just such a Day One four times before. His muscles have adapted, moreso each year, to the unique physical exertion required of them today, required of them tomorrow, required of them over the next couple of weeks. No way Tony, my trainer, could have come up with any kind of exercise program to prepare me for what is pretty much, by my definition, the equivalent of slave labor.

Not that either Caldron or I is a slave. Although, Caldron's family tree, not all that far back, includes more than a few of those. Go back far enough, and he can also boast a few African kings by way of relations. My ancestral beginnings, in contrast, aren't nearly as illustrious, nor have my family's "ups" and "downs" been as pronounced, between then and now.

"You'll be fine," he promises. Anyway, it's what I think he says. It's kind of hard to tell. I'm so fucking ... fucking ... fucking ... tired. Except, unfortunately, fucking has had absolutely nothing to do with it.

If Caldron's hand is cool on my sweaty forehead, as I completely vacate reality for the far preferable nothingness of slumber, I'm unable (damn-it!) to label his concern as anything more than one final attempt, by him, to convince me that I'm not -- no matter how I may feel -- near death's doorstep.

I nod off and dream of California sugarcane.

Anyone who knows shit about U.S. sugar production likely scratches his head and wonders if I don't mean Louisiana sugarcane, because that's what contributes the majority of mainland cane to total U.S. sugar production. However, it's California sugarcane, albeit only a few acres of it, to which my dreams refer. Just as it has been that very same acreage which has so occupied my day.

Cane sugar, and its by-products, provided the original fortunes of the Basiff family and Rooge family, although that sugarcane was grown entirely in Jamaica. Expansion plans included attempts to cultivate wide-growth sugarcane in California, and land was purchased for that purpose. Little sugarcane was planted, though, before estimates for profit potential ruled, to sugarcane's detriment, in favor of California-growth grapefruit, lemon, lime, and oranges. Income from those diversified fruit crops provided the second fortunes for the Basiffs and Rooges. When the orchards finally gave way to the Basiff and Rooge real-estate developments that, to this day, includes two major motion-picture studios, we reaped even more money and found ourselves no longer sugarcane-connected, at all, except for these few lone acres of California sugarcane kept soley as symbolic reminder of the original Jamaican-grown catalyst that started us on our slingshot way to wealth and respectability.

Caldron and my present endeavor merely a mutually shared and long-lasting Basiff-and-Rooge tradition (AKA rite of passage).

Admittedly, having seen the males of so many generations of our families so willingly off to harvest and process, by hand, and by more hard work than is certainly necessary in this day and age, these mere few token acres of California sugarcane, I've long figured masochism runs in our families.

Six years ago, my older brother took his couple of weeks to head here and do "his bit". At the time, I was convinced I wasn't about to follow in his footsteps (tradition be damn!).

What changed my mind? Aside from my having heard Caldron Rooge, for whatever his reasons, was going be around to join me, his having apparently so enjoyed his regularly scheduled stint "in the field" that he'd taken to repeats? Actually, I'm not sure much more was needed than that. I so looked forward to seeing, once again, that particular young black man stark naked, I was more than willing to undergo a bit of physical discomfort in order to make it happen. It merely coincidence that I would kill two proverbial birds (family tradition and prurient interest) with one and the same proverbial stone.

My first spotting of Caldron in the buff, by the way, having happened very near the very end of his very first tour of duty in this California cane field. The sugarcane, then, had already been cut and processed, by him and by the work crew under his supervision -- raw sugar, molasses, and syrup the result.

I'd, also, briefly been on the scene during my brother's tenure, although I'd not been nearly as impressed by Joe's nakedness, or by his efforts. Which Dad figures has to do with long-standing sibling rivalry that never sees me all that impressed by much of anything my brother does -- and vice versa.

Not, initially, that I'd been all that impressed by Caldron's obviously Herculean efforts in having converted sugarcane to produce. What tipped the scales in Caldron's favor was that clandestine glimpse I had of him getting out of the shower, his large and chocolate penis elongating into sturdy erection, his large right hand beating his stiff truncheon to creamy eruption.

Yes ... it was that exquisite vision of Caldron's chocolatey big cock in eruption ... that man's all-around rock-solid nakedness. Yes ... it was my having just come to accept my predominant sexual attraction to men ... my having heard those long-existent (seldom-mentioned) family rumors that more than one male of the Rooge family had been sexually involved with more than one male of the Basiff family -- and vice versa. ("How else," had whispered one Basiff Grandma, "had mere slaves managed emancipation and key job-positions within a once completely Basiff-held empire?").

Now, having finally succeeded in getting that naked black Adonis in the shower with me, then seated on the very edge of my bed (cool black hand to my sweaty white brow), I'm too damn done in, by the physicality of our workday, to make any attempt at homosexual seduction.

Caldron right when he tells me day two will be even worse. In that, I awake with a total body stiffness the likes of which my cock had never attained, even during my first wondrous days of just-discovered puberty, when my stiffies were their most impressive and their most aggressive-- seemingly forever and ever, Amen.

I get through day two, which consists mainly of our downing more sugarcane with machetes, but I do so only because Caldron is there to set an example. Literally, I shudder as I wonder how much bigger and more difficult the harvest would be had we waited the extra couple of months for a full-growth crop. My Fall freshman term at UCLA has made my participation, at this earlier date, a now-or-never situation. Luckily, none of this has ever been about optimized production. It's never the end that counts but the means to that end. We're talking goals -- of men bonding with the land, of men achieving insight into their heritage, of men personally becoming acquainted with the ins and outs of the crop that provided the groundwork for them to become rich enough to attend the best schools, pledge the best fraternities, join the best social clubs.

Day three, as Caldron predicts, is the very worst yet. So bad is it that I have trouble remembering it, even in progress, except for the very end when, Caldron, once again naked and at my bedside, his hand gently resting on my weary forehead, assures me, over my offered protests to the contrary, that it's all downhill for me from here.

Day four, although my pain never really dissipates, I adapt, and actually achieve a work-a-day rhythm that not only gets me through the day but leaves me with a genuine sense of accomplishment, albeit still pooped at day's end.

Day five sees me so well having survived that day's hours of hard physical labor that I've enough energy left over to be thoroughly disappointed when Caldron doesn't show for his heretofore regular good-night pep-talk.

Nor does he make any appearance in my room over the next few nights, although our days continue together, cutting cane, side by side, with each other and with the itinerant work crew hired to help us.

There is something unbearably sexy about the movement of Caldron's muscles beneath their sensuous veneering of velvety dark-brown skin -- as he makes each graceful swing of machete to down several cane stalks at one time -- as he hoists the resulting lopped cane into piled-high carts for transport to the hand-operated presses whose bigger rollers crush the cane, and whose smaller rollers ooze green and sugary sap into awaiting buckets

Sexy, too, is the way Caldron sweats! Or, is it merely that I haven't paid that much attention to anyone's perspiration, my own included, before it became as much a by-product of my workday as sugar has?

This day, Caldron's sweat pools the lower end of the jugular notch located at the base of his powerful throat. Its overflow runs the scalloped gully between his pectorals and momentarily lakes within the shallow lower cupping of his indented navel.

Cascades eventually drool the remaining part of his scalloped belly.

His abdominals, by the way, aren't horizontally washboard but composed of individual off-set rectangles that fit him like anatomically correct pieces of wrought armor once encased Roman centurians.

His sweat exits the crinkly curls of dark hair at the nape of his neck. It flows his spine, between the flare of his parenthesizing twin shoulder blades.

It soaks the waistband of his trousers and darkens the vee-shape breach where the top button of his four-button pants fly has been popped by some previous exertion -- or, maybe has been popped by the efforts of so little material trying so hard to keep concealed so massive a chocolate cock and balls.

A sweaty line begins at the exact spot where his buttocks meet at the base of his spine. The line dead-ends where his asscrease makes its final curve toward the back of his thighs.

"What?" he asks.

I've stopped chopping. I'm staring.

"Sweat," I say and wipe some of mine from my forehead with the back of my hand.

"Yes," he says. "And don't you wear it nicely?!"

He has a nice smile that shows strong white teeth. His canines are pointy but not vampiric. His upper front teeth overlap slightly, right over left.

Both his cheeks dimple -- dead-center.

Am I the only one who feels the electricity so palatable that I almost see its fiery arch from his crotch to mine? Am I the only one who fantasizes replays, here and now, of other Basiff-Rooge rituals that possibly united black and white men as thoroughly as this harvesting of sugarcane provides, to this day, the covenant that unites Basiff to Rooges, that unites both of our families to the land?

I fear I'm alone in sexual fantasies, in that Caldron becomes increasingly more distant and modest, after each successive workday. He begins to find the least excuse for not showering with me, or of showering at some separate time. Often, he goes so far as to bathe in some distant part of the irrigation system.

Now that I no longer fall exhausted into bed, at the end of each day, he never detours into my room.

Our time at the canefield draws ever nearer its end.

Until the day comes when all of the cane is harvested, most of it crushed and leeched of its juice. Open pans of sap have bubbled, have been skimmed, have crystallized brown sugar, have provided molasses drained into small barrels.

All of our premature harvesting and refining, admittedly crude, has produced far less than the possible maximum yield. However, the results will provide more than enough to divide between the Basiffs and the Rooges for use, over the next year, especially in the making of family-consumed traditional sweets at the holidays.

Suddenly, there's only Caldron, a skeleton work crew, and I who remain for a final clean-up.

No need to replant the cane, in that the next crop will sprout from whatever the stubble that remains from this year, albeit with even less potential yield. So on, and so forth, up until the fifth year, when harvest leftovers will be plowed under, new slips will be placed in newly cultivated rows. I wish we needed to replant this year, in that it would provide me a bit more time with Caldron, even though we've used the time already given us for nothing more than the physical labor that the harvesting and processing has required of us -- not counting, of course, my runaway sexual fantasies.

Then, only Caldron and I remain. Once again I, for maybe the last time within this cottage built on the outskirts of this cane field, am alone with my boner. I throw back the covers and completely bare my stiffy in all its impressive phallic splendor. With one hand, I fist as much of its meaty circumference as I can and commence my now regular night-ly ritual of conjuring my more-obliging-that-the-reality phantom Caldron, for fun and games.

This fateful night, I turn loose of the fantasy, and turn loose of my stiff dick before my cock spits. There is always going to be time for me to indulge make-believe sex with Caldron, but how much time remains wherein I have as ready access to the real thing as I have now?

Except, if he, likewise, wants sexual fun and games, why isn't he here, in my room, with me? I've made my sexual availability obvious, haven't I? Or, have I? Granted, I've never come right on out and said, "Let's fuck and suck, stud." Nonetheless, I've assuredly sent out none-too-subtle non-verbal come-ons. Maybe he just doesn't like white boys, in particular, or doesn't like boys, in general.

I start flogging my dick again. Stop again.

"Christ, Adrian," I say to myself, "what's not to like about you?"

I'm faced with the very good chance of opportunity lost, possibly because I've been biding my time, waiting for Caldron to make the first move, just because Caldron is bigger, just because Caldron is older. When bigger and older don't necessarily mean more aggressive or less confused. Maybe, from the beginning, all that's been needed has been my applying a bit more initiative. Some times, some things don't come to those who wait, no matter the old saying. Some times, some things must be set upon and seized.

I get out of bed, walk my boner as far as the door before I decide to detour for a robe. My blatant display of erect manhood may provide too open an invitation to the increasingly shy and reluctant Caldron. This late in the game, so few opportunities left, it isn't likely wise to risk scar-ing the stud away with desperate overkill aggressiveness.

I belt my robe, confident that my hard dick, covered though it is, still presents enough bulge in the terry cloth to make itself well-known with-out more obvious flaunting.

I open the bedroom door and enter the hallway.

The door to Caldron's bedroom is open. He's not inside, though the mess of his bedsheets retains a rough definition of where his body laid not that long ago.

I stroll other empty rooms.

The front door is ajar. I go through to the outside porch.

Encompassing darkness is balmy with day-heat retained by the ground and only now released to night-air.

There's a light in the processing shed.

Barefoot, I breath faster and cross warm soil.

Caldron, in a robe, stands inside the roofed work area. He stares at something directly opposite. When I follow his gaze, I see nothing but buckets, evaporating pans, pails, and other harvesting gear stacked and/or hung in storage.

I make a noise, so he'll know I'm there.

"Adrian," he says, even before turning. Not that he has all that many choices.

Is that the bulge of his chocolate-cock erection that tents the front of his robe, or am I the victim of wishful thinking?

"I couldn't sleep," I say.

"Neither could I," he says. Can he possibly miss my passion-stiff cock that jerks beneath its flimsy veil?

"I never had a problem with insomnia at the beginning, did I?" I say.

"No sooner hit the sack than you were out like a light," he agrees.

"Never asleep, though, before you managed to slip in and offer a few encouraging words," I say. "You quit doing that. I always wondered why. Still do."

"When you became less and less likely to drop right off to sleep, I became more and more apt to sprout a boner in your company."

Which leaves me pretty much speechless for a count of ten.

"What kind of man gets a hard-on while watching a teenager sleep?" he asks.

"And if the teenager would merely have seen that boner as an opportunity to be advantaged?"

"My even greater fear," he surprises.

"I'm not sure I understand," I say and close most of the distance that remains between us.

"Just think about it," he says. "You have a brother. Your brother has a son. I, on the other hand, am my parents' only child. There have always been Rooges and Basiffs. I can't risk being the one responsible for the end of my bloodline."

"From what I understand, more than one Rooge and Basiff has coped with that particular problem," I remind, unless he's not heard the rumors.

"I have hopes of marrying and treating my wife better than a brood mare."

"There are always women who marry and breed merely for the money. Some women actually prefer it that way."

"Still ...." he says.

"You ever fucked a woman?" I ask; inquiring minds want to know.

Certainly, I have never fucked one. Never have had to, my brother sufficiently heterosexual for the both of us. His wife blessedly fecund. Can/could I fuck a woman? The histories of our families certainly have proved such a thing possible.

"I've fucked a few," he says.

"And how many men have you fucked?"

He shakes his head. "I've been fully aroused by a few, but I've always had enough willpower not to go farther. My plan has always been to go the whole way with a man -- if ever -- only after I've married and had an heir, maybe had a spare. I feel confident I could have done just that waiting, too, if not for a certain white boy I once spotted spying on me in the shower, three years ago this summer. From then on out, it has been me trying to figure how to get naked with that certain white boy when he was of legal age."

"You knew I was watching you?"

"What do you think gave me my hard-on?"

"And your hard-on, now?"

"Caused by one and the same. No less disconcerting for me, how-ever."

"Who do you suppose gives me my stiff dick?" I ask and pull back one flap of my robe so he sees my naked erection in all its balls-drooped-from-its-thick-base splendor.

"Jesus, kid, what if sex with you were to ruin sex for me with women?" he asks, his face made more handsome by shadings of gen-uine concern.

"Fucking women is like riding a bicycle, isn't it?" I say; as if I know jack-shit about the subject. "No subsequent ride possibly as satisfying as the first, but never all that big a deal to get back on again."

If I believe that, it's because I have to believe it, not because it's true, or because I've thoroughly researched the subject. I see the tragedy of Caldron unable to provide a Rooge heir. On the other hand, there's no way I'm prepared to come out of this processing shed without having had sex with him.

I let my robe again conceal my stiff prick. I step in closer to him. I reach for the pint Mason jar of molasses left behind by crewmen who used the contents for sweetening their coffee. I unscrew the lid. I dip a forefinger into the viscous goo. I present my sticky-tip finger for his closer examination.

"You've worked hard and long to get you and me here," I say, flattered he's stuck it out harvesting sugarcane enough extra years so as not to come across to anyone as having preplanned his time now spent with me. "I'm of legal age. We're both pretty much naked."

I put my molasses-dipped finger to his jugular notch. He steps back, only slightly; not so pronounced a withdrawal by him that it prevents me from maintaining finger-to-flesh contact.

"You and I have wasted a helluva lot of time," I say and drag the tip of my finger down the center of his chest, down his belly to his navel. The molasses leaves a glossy trail amid beadings of his sweat so minuscule that I've been, until now, totally unaware of them.

I take hold of the sash that holds his robe. I release its loosely looped knot.

He wears white-cotton, form-fitting, underpants that conceal his stiff dick without really concealing it. Through the fabric, stretched tautly over his upthrust mass of dick, I see ready evidence of the bas-relief veins that lattice the belly of his erection. Where the tip of his dick presses against cotton, his cockmouth leaks a damp spot of preseminal lubricant. I see chocolate-brown bulbous cockhead showing through made-transparent white material.

Increasing my anticipation, my attention veers momentarily from his shorts to his robe. My hands slide into the breach of material that hangs his chest. My palms seductively chafe the tautness of his brown nipples. My fingers slide upward and over the upper curves of his powerful shoulders.

"Sweet ... sweet Jesus, kid," he says but makes no move to stop me.

I push his body-draped terry cloth up and over. It's own weight causes its fall behind his back. He interrupts its tumble by bending each of his arms at an elbow. I think he may shrug the material back on. After a moment, though, he drops both arms to his sides, and the cloth sloughs to a pile at his feet.

"Turn around," I say.

"I didn't bring a rubber," he says.

His concern seeming to be not so much that I'm prepared to fuck him, but that neither of us came prepared.

"It's not my unrubberized cock I've presently in mind for your luscious ass," I promise. "Trust me."

He hesitates but turns to face away from me.

Once again, I handhold the pint jar of molasses.

"Bend your head slightly," I say.

He does, and I lift the open jar and tip it so a thick drool of the jar's contents cascades the lip of the glass and touches down at the nape of his powerful neck. More molasses follows, and its leading edge traces the sexy line of his spine, like back sweat flows the same anatomical terrain during his workdays.

The slow-flowing treacle nears the wasteband of his undershorts, and I put the jar to one side. I hook the elastic waistband of his underwear and pull outward to achieve a full view of his asscrack as the drooling molasses takes advantage of the breach.

With both hands, I pull down just the back of his shorts. I drop to my knees behind him and secure the underpants material beneath the thrust of his butt.

I palm his asscheeks. I manhandle his buns open along the run of their mutually shared crack. The continuing descent of molasses slows more each time it encounters another new crinkly black hair within his sweaty asscrease. Finally, the leading dollop of syrup pinpoints his brown pucker, pauses to pool atop it, and magnifies the target area.

I burrow my face into the widened slice of his ass and lick.

"Oh ... oh ... ohhhhh ...." he says as my tongue kitty-licks his sweet ... sweet ... asshole.

Again, I lick his same anal landscape, free his asspucker of molasses and free his buttcrack of sweat. He tastes of black man in heat, of sweetness, of sweat, of heady aphrodisiacal muskiness. He smells the very same, and I breath full of his essence as I steadily lick upward, along the crease of his butt to the base of his spine, then lick onward to the center of his back, then lick onward to the nape of his neck.

I no longer have a sugary trail to follow along his back, all of the sweetness dissolved by my spit and swallowed away. So, I lick around the side of his neck. He unbends his head and drops it back on his neck to provide me free access to his square jawline.

There's sugary residue in his jugular notch, left their recently by my molasses-dipped finger.

His once minuscule beadings of perspiration, couched within his pectoral cleavage, grow visibly more substantial and more tasty as they burst beneath the pressure exerted by my licking tongue. Whatever his sweat's normally saline flavors, they're overpowered by the sugariness of residue molasses. What meets my tastebuds is sweetness with only a trace of salty aftermath. I savor his body elixir which is aphrodisiac-extraordinaire, as my cock bares witness by its commencement of live-ly pulsations and metronome-swaying, all accompanied by the leakage of clear liquid from my cockmouth to frost the bulbous head of my cir-cumcised erection.

It's rock-hard black-man anatomy that I lick. If ever there were the slightest hint of fat on these premises, it has been rendered nonexistent by Caldron and my shared days of physical labor in the cane field. What tells me, though, that I don't perform my labors over real stone, is how his chocolate skin, sweetened by molasses, salted by sweat, stays oh-so-supple, despite all the hardness of impressive underlying mus-cle.

It's as if Praxiteles has sculpted the epitome of male anatomy not from marble but from a hard block of chocolate whose outer surface melts just enough to exude an exquisite and mysterious sweet salinity.

Less residue molasses has bisected Caldron's chest and belly than has ran his spine, so my exploring tongue works all the harder for what's available up-front. Flavors become decidedly more piquant as my lapping reaches that part of his stomach where molasses has caught and coagulated within his black-fuzz belly hair that begins just above his navel.

Before I lick the accumulated tastes from within his navel, my chin bumps the head of his cock. That touch leaves a dot of preseminal moisture beneath my chin. A shift of my head, my tongue still washing syrupy residue from his belly, edges his stiff dick slightly to one side, and draws a trail of his pre-cum up my left cheek as I retrieve the last sugary vestiges of sweetness from his midsection.

William Maltese

The contents of his belly button provide a final jolt of sweaty sweetness, which I savor until it dissolves to blandness.

My head pulls back and removes whatever leverage it has provided to keep his sizable dick shifted and locked to one side. His cock becomes a giant metronome set into motion in front of me. The back of his cockhead grazes his muscled belly and swingingly caresses his recently licked-clean navel. A windshield-wiper swathe of his chocolate-brown abdomen, that includes his belly button, is provided new flavors via the ongoing leakings of his pre-cum lubricant that continuously overflows the cockmouth-puncture within the blunted end of his dick.

"Give me the molasses," I say. I'm on my knees, and he has far easier access to the pint jar than I do.

When I have the container of treacle again in hand, I wait for his cock to cease its back-and-forth swing, amazed at how a shaft so ponderously large can maintain its standing position without breaking off at its base.

His erection never comes to a complete stop, merely converts its side-to-side into a series of little jerks instigated by his spasming groin muscles.

Undeterred, my fist wraps his prick and momentarily takes control.

"Oh, sweet ... sweet ... sweet," he says, and my fingers clasp as much of his dick's circumference as they can manage. Despite the admitted largeness of my hand, it actually succeeds in securing only a small fraction of his cock's total girth. My fingers can't begin to close completely around his phallic pole which is hot as hell and steely hard against the inside curve of my wrapping fingers.

I can't resist the temptation to advantage my handhold and manhandle his chocolate foreskin in an upward slide that provides a chocolate cowling for the chocolate head of his chocolate dick. I force the cowl into a miniature chocolate-kiss snout.

It's into this again slightly opened end of his foreskin that I pour molasses. His cratered prepuce accepts its capacity of sugary goo and begins to be overflowed by it as my handhold pulls his loose outer cockskin down his solid inner cockshaft. His emerging cockhead is spread with the sticky gloss of molasses that quickly mixes with his pre-cum.

I empty more of the jar and watch viscousness engulf more and more of his erection, like oozed pitch, from prehistoric trees, embed flora and fauna in what may one day become luxurious amber.

When the drool reaches my fist, slid to fondle the last four inches of his boner, I stop the steady pour and remove my cock-fisting hand. Immediately, renewed jerks and throbbings of his dick jiggle already gravity-coaxed drool into an even more complete cover of his cock-shaft. There's even enough residual gravity-coaxed ooze to proceed into the curly black pubic hair that grows his balls. On certain individual strands of his scrotal hair, molasses clings precariously for dear life and refuses to let go.

"Adrian ... Adrian ... sexy, Adrian," Caldron says, his voice low and husky. He knows, as well as I do, what comes next.

I hand the considerably drained jar to him, and he sets it to one side before he turns his full attention to me.

"Caldron ... Caldron ... sexy, Caldron," I say and put a stabilizing hand to each of his hips.

Like a butterfly hovers the head of a flower that's shifted in a hot summer breeze, my face hovers the upthrust head of his dick. I match my movements to that of my landing pad, until synchronization is achieved. Touchdown provides another explosion of sugary sweetness on my tongue.

Caldron's hands drop to my shoulders and give such a forceful squeeze that it seems he needs that support to keep his knees from buckling.

"Oh, yes, suck my big brown dick," he confirms his commitment.

My lips, a mere pucker attached to the unveiled and sugary tip of his massive erection, open wider. I'm a python prepared to swallow an even larger snake that's first been drowned in treacle.

Luckily, I've swallowed big cock before, all in preparation -- since first having spotted Caldron naked in the shower -- for sucking this one. Not that I've ever really expected that wildest of fantasies to become this present reality, but I must have wanted to be sure I was up to the task if and when confronted by the possibility of it.

Despite the popular misconception, all black men no more come with enormous schlongs than do all Orientals come with tiny pricks, but there's no denying Caldron's phallic wonder is very much the tired stereotype.

Having just his cockhead eaten up, and viewing his cockshaft, all of the way down to where it anchors to Caldron's lower belly, I see what appears to be possibly too much of a good thing. Nonetheless, it's so

inviting a challenge, my mere samplings of it having tasted so intense-
ly delicious, I can no more stop myself from eating more of its chocolatey wondrousness than a chocoholic can refuse sudden access to
candy-factory stockpiles.

The top of my head presses more firmly against his belly. My mouth
gapes for an additional downward slide. Multiple ropy veins visibly
entwine, in hybrid caduceus, the unswallowed segment of his cockshaft. My lower lip detects these veinal filigrees as more and more of
them disappear slowly into my face.

"Ohhhhh, good God!" he says. His hips helplessly buck in a reflexive fuck stroke that force-feeds me a good four inches of his addition-
ally stiff dick.

Having anticipated, I'm still not convinced I'll survive it. Much to my
surprise, either because of my sheer decision to succeed, or because
of my many practice sessions on other cocks, I experience only minor
tightening of my throat as his next helpless thrusting of three more inches proves equally harmless.

"Soooooo good," he says. "As I always knew ... knew ... knew ...
Jesus, knew ... I'd be hot, kid. Fucking hot. On-fire hot. Burning-alive
hot Guts-steaming hot. Just for you. Just with you."

In emphasis, his hands lift from my shoulders and lock on to my
head.

Momentarily, I panic at the thought of any sudden and forceful impaling of my face over the still remaining inches of his dick. However, the
impaling, when it comes, is anything but sudden or forceful. Whether
from pure instinct, or by specific design, honed by his having had his
stiff dick sucked by women, he knows how best to get me to the very
bottom of his dick, where he wants me. First, he yanks my face back
up his erection as far as his cockhead. Sweetness plays on my tongue
the whole way. Then, he leaves me poised atop his boner where I
greedily munch on his luscious coronal lollipop. Only then does he
drop me over all of his inches I'd previously claimed, plus a bit more.

Up, down, up, down ... up, down. Each time, my face presses a bit
farther toward the stalwart roots of his dick. That's how I finally achieve
what we both want ... need. My ovaled lips come to rest snugly against
his taut, pubic-hair grown lower belly. His total, sugary cockshaft is
sucked so deeply inside of me that I suspect it stirs the very contents
of my stomach.

His balls hang from my lower lip, along my chin, like enormous chocolate drops. My right hand finds their shifting masses. His hairy scrotum goes even more and more compact. I give a squeeze.

"Hot ... hot ... Jesus ... hot!" he says.

I surrender his nuts and go in search of my stiff dick that's so painfully solid between my thighs. I fish the breached material of my robe, take hold of my swollen erection with all intentions of jacking off in a way that will see me match his spermal explosion. Except, his, "I'm going to come!", suggests my plan for mutual orgasm is doomed to failure.

It'll only take me a few pumps of my cock to achieve my rip-roaring climax, so horny have I become by the mere thrust and taste of his dick in my mouth and throat, but my swallowing of his dick has Caldron poised even closer to the brink of orgasm than I am.

"Sorry, kid ... sorry ... sorry, kid," he chants.

His handholds on my head, and his several successive hip fuck-strokes, coordinate to cock-fuck my face like crazy. My head is pulled as far up his cock as it can go, on each upstroke, then pushed all of the way down to his belly. Up and back, up and back, all accompanied by sexily wet suck-sounds as I take full advantage of the meal he feeds me.

"Jesus fuck, sorry!" he says, grunts, thrusts, jams my head completely over his dick one final time.

I release my cock and clamp both hands to his hips. His flesh is slippery with sweat.

My hands slide to his perspiration-soaked ass, and the tips of my forefingers lead the way to the mouth of his pucker.

As the first pearly slugs of his creamy discharge blast the far back of my throat, I send one unlubricated finger through his sweaty sphincter to bury deeply up his butt.

"Aaagghhh ... aggghhrr ... atthrrungh!" he says, trembles, shakes.

His asshole, like a triggered snare, clamps the length of my submerged finger so securely that to pull my finger free would turn a good four inches of his lower bowel inside-out.

His sweaty belly grinds my face. His fingers knead my sweaty scalp and comb my sweat-drenched hair.

His fully buried cock floods me. I swallow each creamy cannon shot and find it sweet to the taste, as if essence of sugarcane has somehow flavored it by osmosis.

He feeds me so much more sweet eruption that I have doubts I can contain all of it, as well as his cock, in the minimum space my mouth and throat provide. Those doubts minimized by a well-timed series of reflexive swallows that keep his spermal fluid drained as quickly as he blast-feeds it to me.

Finally, I suck and there's no more of his spunk to drink. The resulting vacuum of my come-up-dry siphon stretches his dick to an even more impressive length inside me.

"Oh, sweet Jesus, but no woman ever gave my dick the ride you do," he says from somewhere above me. "Just as I always knew you would. Just as I always knew."

I would savor his lengthy meat a bit longer, but he pulls my head upward. I let his cock come free: my mouth and throat a sea-cave that disgorges slippery moray eel.

When his dick finally pops free, it maintains enough starch, despite its recent blast-off, to stand under its own retained stiffness. Not, mind you, in the same impressive stance it achieved before I'd had at it, but enough so that it's more half-mast than completely hang-dog.

I prepare to stand and join him, but, his knees touch down so close to mine that we touch. On his way down, his dick drooled the last of its residue slime along my chest, along my stomach, and along the belly of my uplifted dick.

He's no sooner down than his hand returns his slightly limp dick to full standing position. With both hands, he securely locks the somewhat softened broad belly of his dick to the admittedly harder belly of mine.

"You sexy, sexy teenage stud!" he says and begins a hearty masturbation of both dicks. He leans his torso slightly back as he does so.

I lean back slightly, too, and put a hand to each of my buttocks for support.

I look down the slant of my tanned white skin to where it merges with his tanned chocolate. We construct a seemingly rock-hard chasm, from whose rugged vee erupts two impressive columns of hands-held meat being whipped like sixty.

Actually, I feel the increased stiffening of Caldron's dick as it's kept pressed tightly against the belly of my cock by Caldron's faster and furious whipping fists. The re-hardening of his prick, within the snug confines provided by his vising grips, increases the sensuous friction that speeds my boner toward eruption.

Already made sexually hyper by having had his cock blast off inside my mouth and throat, I don't hold out much hope -- despite my decided experience in such matters -- of holding off my orgasm long enough to match anything his cock might come up with by way of seconds.

"I'm close," I warn him, in case he has any misconceptions that he's actually going to manage another explosion of his nuts before mine spill their ballooned-to-capacity reservoir.

"Shoot your white-boy gallons!" he commands and commences to beat our dicks all the harder. "Shoot! Blast! Squirt! Baste me and my dick in your fucking white-boy goo!"

I do my damnedest to do just that. Even I'm surprised by the volume of creamy sexual liquid that suddenly gushes from the head of my cock and seemingly keeps right on gushing.

His fists become soupy with wet ribbons of cream. Large globules of quickly coagulating spunk touchdown along our necks, splatter our chests, hang as streamers within the clumps of pubic hair that vee our lower bellies.

It's only after the cataclysm of my orgasm, when my senses function again, that I marvel as to how I haven't been the sole contributor to the mess that paints us. Somehow, Caldron, quick on the heels of his massive spermal ejection up my gullet, has performed an encore performance, his cock locked within its hugging embrace with my exploding erection.

This time, when he releases his dick, we're talking major droop. His dick flops against, and careens off, my less-pronounced softening dick. His cockhead plops against his thigh with a sound that's audibly wet.

After which, for two years, he and I meet regularly for sexual fun and games. We even take the couple of weeks each summer to return to the California sugarcane acreage and cut and process the stalks as we enjoy the sweet benefits of our attending physical and sexual labors.

When I'm in my senior year at UCLA, Caldron marries. He wants heirs. His wife wants money.

Caldron and I don't screw around while he's married. Not because of any high moral standard, arrived at by either of us, because I would have fucked his ass at the drop of his trousers, and vice versa. Rather, Caldron insists he needs every iota of his concentration focused on fucking his paid brood mare to pregnancy. A chore -- for that's what he calls it, after having experienced sex with me -- that produces, in quick succession, an heir and a spare.

The divorce amicable, in that she gets a sizable settlement, and he gets the rugrats.

Caldron buys an exceptionally large house in the Hollywood hills. He moves his two "tricycle motors" into the east wing with their nanny. I move, with Caldron, into the west wing.

Our present situation probably wouldn't work for everyone. However, at least for the moment, and thank-you very much for asking, it certainly works for us.